Meet Me at the Surface

Meet Me at the Surface

JODIE MATTHEWS

4th ESTATE • London

4th Estate
An imprint of HarperCollins*Publishers*
1 London Bridge Street
London SE1 9GF

www.4thestate.co.uk

HarperCollins*Publishers*
Macken House
39/40 Mayor Street Upper,
Dublin 1,
D01 C9W8, Ireland

First published in Great Britain in 2024 by 4th Estate

1

For Lily

'You said I killed you – haunt me, then!'
EMILY BRONTË, *Wuthering Heights*

PART ONE

HIRETHEK
Cornish, *adjective*: lonely, homesick

FOLKLORE

2019. Here's how it starts. A farmer says goodbye to his cows, what remains of them – he's lost two in the past week already – and climbs over the shaky fence that divides his parcel of land from the rest of the moor. His dog lowers her belly to the ground, cat-like, and squeezes below the fence. Then, the farmer calls the dog daft: daft dog.

What he doesn't know is that women understand the moor differently. In his truck, the farmer sees nothing at first, just sketched-out roads leading through the heath. It is only when the dog barks that he sees a blonde head, diving through bracken. The face is thin, body wiry, laden with bags. A tramp, he thinks. He watches as the boy (for he's decided that is what it is) scuttles up the side of the big rock, scarab-like, all arms and legs and joints. The farmer grips the steering wheel. He thinks he can hear the click-clacking of limbs in the distance.

He wishes it were ten years ago, perhaps twenty, when he could pull his air gun from the back of the truck and scare the strangers off the moor. Now the world feels all about sympathy and understanding. He's supposed to consider the feelings of the youths burning blazes on dry gorse, leaving spent barbecues and rusted cans across his fields. He thinks of his daughter, gone now. He thinks of her more often now that she is back in the ground than he ever did when she was alive, but this is not something he would ever admit to himself.

The dog barks: daft dog. The farmer leans over and opens the passenger door, sends the dog a-running to the boy. Of course, the dog sees what the man can't. The stranger atop the rock is not a boy, or even really a stranger. See, women know the moor differently, and the moor knows its women well.

DAY ONAN

i.

As I stepped on the moor for the first time in a little under a year, I told myself that it didn't resent my absence. It wasn't my jilted lover, or a mother left to rot. If it did care about my return, it would have no way of showing me. All its little expressions – the Neolithic huts and stalagmiting granite ruins – were 10,000 years in the making. In any case, I would not be there long enough to hear what the moor had to say.

Stood there once again, everything as it ever was, as it ever would be. I felt as if I could catch sight of every version of myself that had ever moved across this land.

There were few signposts, but I followed my own waymarkers – the angry little dog that screamed from the green gate by the road, a circle of burnt gorse with crisp limbs, the paddock of Shetland ponies, bouncing across the field. The evening hadn't fully fallen yet, instead the moors burnt orange.

Gorse bushes were blooming on the banks, small cups of flowers that uncurled a bright yellow. I picked the petals, sniffed them, crushed them between my fingers. I thought of making tea, imagined being a person who forages and makes the most out of everything. The flowers smelled like coconut, and the scent would linger on my hands for the rest of the evening, but I wouldn't recognise it until later in the night, when I wiped sleep from my eyes and was transported somewhere tropical.

I took a detour on my way to the house, climbing up a bank into towering bracken. Rounding a corner, it loomed over me, just as I remembered. Stood on Pendrift Downs, Jubilee Rock. I had always found it humbling, this thing that was named 200 years ago. Side-stepping the tufts of baby gorse creeping by my feet, I rounded the rock, reaching the carving on its flattest side.

A coat of arms larger than a grown man was etched into it in 1810. The creatures that flanked either side of the shield looked like lions, but there was something off about them. Part way down, they devolved from lion to sea creature. I wanted to see the fault that had been branded on the rock's side. I traced my fingers across the lions' mane, over the whipping tongues and then lower where, instead of hind legs, there were mermaid tails, and ridges that lined the backs of the lions like the fins of seahorses. I had always imagined this carving was an act of rebellion, a young man left to work alone by gaslight, toiling through the night as he committed the image to the rock, deciding to make his own history.

With Jubilee Rock blocking my view of anything apart from the waist-high bracken, I felt like I could stay just there and forget about Trewarnen completely. When night fell, I could shelter by the rock. In the morning, I could drink water from the stream. I would turn my trousers up at the ankles and stand barefoot in the river, catching brown trout with my hands, or maybe even a freshwater eel if I could bear the whistle of its slimy skin against my fingers. I would carry them back to my rock, fingers hooked through gills, eels worn round my wrists like cuffs. I'd find flint in amongst old ruins and start a fire as the fish baked in the afternoon heat on the hot stone. Roast them on a spit. In summer I would pick elderberries. In autumn, blackberries. I would crush furred nettle leaves between hardened fingers and stew them in water over my fire for tea. I could stop, keep clear of the farmhouse altogether; my mum and aunt and all the ghosts could stay locked up there without me. I could miss the memorial, pretend I was still packed away in the city. Avoid the faces of the people I'd left behind. My return would be just another rumour on the wind. I could live off the moor, hidden, another urban legend. The Beast of Bodmin and I, both creatures with too many stories to live up to.

I scrambled to the top of Jubilee, the stone grazing my palms as I dragged my body upwards. Once there, I sat and licked the blood off my hands and looked across at the moors. Above ground and sludge and mulch, where everything should blend into a smudge of earthy paint, I saw something moving between the bracken. The ferns bent over themselves, parting a green sea. I craned my neck and saw the docile horns of a highland cow, but when the cow stopped to graze, the movement carried on ahead of it, disjointed.

Even the gorse seemed to fold, creaking apart as something pushed through. For a moment, I thought I saw a person – *her* – a black coat, a drape of material blurring into the bush. I clambered to my feet, stood high on the rock, feeling ridiculous, but suddenly, fully, desperate. Was it, could it – but no. On the balls of my feet, at the highest point of the rock, the darkness I had seen was just shadow. I couldn't tell what was causing the land to split. Instead, I saw, in the distance, the house. Trewarnen. Twice gabled, fronted with a mouldering porch. It stood low and wide, spreading across the land like a fungus.

I climbed down from the rock and started back along the road, the house in front of me. My phone vibrated in my pocket, I checked who was calling and then ignored it: just Chris. We hadn't spoken properly in months, although he'd tried – messaging me, ringing, at one point he sent a letter – and I still wasn't quite ready.

My aunt must've told him I was coming home. They ran into each other quite often, always moving in the same small circles, the way people who never leave home tend to do. Chris was my only friend left here, my only friend anywhere, and it sounds heartless to say but I had no desire to see him. I knew he'd want to talk to me about Claud. He'd dealt with all the repercussions of what happened without me. He'd been to her funeral whilst I stayed hidden away in the North – I had only left Cornwall two months before the service. I imagine he would've comforted her mother, shaken hands with her father. I know that he answered a lot of questions on my behalf; people were angry. I know, because he sent me an email, a long diatribe about the state of 'backwards village life'. He called it homophobia; said they were just trying to blame me because they thought I was Other.

'You're part of this community, Mer,' he'd written, 'you belong here as much as anyone else. More than most, actually. You know they've always been this way; they did it to your mum too. Don't let them scare you off coming back home.'

In fact, I had pined for the place where I grew up, the open moorland and the quiet sky that I couldn't find in the city. I wasn't frightened of the villagers, no. I was scared of what would greet me as I opened the door to Trewarnen.

ii.

My mother used to make up stories about the moors. All the best ones were about the sea, usually. You had the mermaids of Zennor and the knockers in the coastal mines, selkies dragging themselves ashore and swapping seal-blub for woman-fat. Everyone else had a version of Cornwall – beach Cornwall, magic Cornwall – that seemed sunnier, brighter, richer than ours. We had marshes that drowned sheep and cow shit on the road. Farmers with burst blood vessels and ponies with curled hooves. Other people had surfing lessons and expensive dogs that their mothers took on coastal walks.

My mother would sit me between her legs as she scraped at my scalp with a nit comb and tell me the moor was magical too, with secret treasure and hidden spirits. She'd wrench lice from my hair and squeeze them dead between her thumbnails, their little bodies bursting open – *pop!* – with a gush of my blood. She didn't like to sit still, my mother. Her hands needed to be busy, so story time would come as she combed, her drolls punctuated by the pop, pop, pop of my parasites.

The stories weren't always good. Most of the time they were stops and starts, the beginning of a tale that would turn into a lament about the village, or a boyfriend, or the shopkeeper who always put the change onto the counter, never into Mum's palm, as if she were grubby. Sometimes the stories were about her and Ysella, my aunt, when they were young, my grandmother playing the part of a bastardised Baba Yaga, an old crone with chicken legs putting curses on happy children. Other times, the stories were about me, as a baby, a time that I couldn't remember no matter how tight I squeezed my eyes and wished.

'You were perfect, perfect, perfect. Perfect and wee,' she would say, splitting a section of my hair with the comb and scratching near my scalp with her nails when she found gold. '*Eggssssss,*' she would hiss, stretching out the discovery – and then the story would be gone. My hair is scalp-shorn now, bleached like wet sand. More than a decade since she last took a comb to it, now there's nowhere to hide.

The best stories were about the sea, but there were others, ones that weren't told so often, about rivers and quarries. Mermaids aren't just for salt, she'd tell me, there's freshwater secrets in the lakes you see on this land. The bronzy murk of them might keep it hidden, but right at the bottom of each lake there are eels the length of dragons and oysters with pearls like puffballs. There are fish with legs and frogs with teeth, and all the piskies and spirits that guard them. There are little girls born from the mud and boys made of stone.

'It's a wonderful place to live, little sprig.'

When I was a baby, my mother moved us to a small cottage in the nearest village to Trewarnen, Blisland. She had fallen out with my grandmother, Esolyn, and became the first Tregellas woman to leave Trewarnen. Our time in the cottage wasn't happy. As a child, I believed my mother's discontent bled into the walls themselves, marring my childhood with an uneasiness I couldn't shake. My mother had fled her mother, returning to the family home only once Esolyn was dead, but there was an ill in that cottage that followed us back to Trewarnen.

Only once I left for the city, for Manchester, did I start to feel well, less soul sick. Fleeing mothers proved to be hereditary, though I had run further from mine than my mother did from hers, but mine would still be rooted in Trewarnen when I reached it.

I had been asked to return, not for her, as I had expected, but for Claud's memorial. Her funeral had been rushed, arranged in the days after her body was found, and the impact of her death stuck to the local area. When my aunt rang to invite me to the memorial, I was surprised. I couldn't imagine why Claud's family would want me there, or how my aunt had been told about it. I had spent the last year in the city rotting in my grief. I'd left because I wanted to be away from all of it, from my mother, from Claud, from Trewarnen. I wasn't expecting to have one of those things taken from me forever in return. But time away from the moors had given me a clarity, an ability to look back at the things I had done; that we had done to each other.

iii.

Stood in front of Trewarnen, I was surprised by how stark and small it seemed, squatting in a patch of land. The house looked shorter and thinner than I remembered, rising from the ground like a baby tooth. It seemed to lean in the wind, the dark grey stone a shadow against the fields. When I had left, home had been a moving beast, stretching its foundations out towards me, fingers trying to pull me back before I crossed county lines.

Now, I could see it for what it really was. A humble cell, a faulty seedpod. A place in which my mother and aunt had sat and grown, and would eventually die, without breaking through to the light of real life. I had been trapped here, I realised. Squashed under the weight of its beams and limestone walls, thick to keep the outside world away. And now I had no choice but to enter again.

My mother was fizzing when I arrived. The lights were off in the hall, and I could just make out the outline of our sharp nose, her eyes yellow.

'I've been reading about beetles. Sex something. What was it, Ysella? Ysella? Sex?' she said, as she held me by the shoulders and appraised me, taking in the hoody, the short hair, the trainers. As she held on to me, I faltered at her scent – not the essential oils and cigarettes of my childhood, but something new, something earthen. The taste of it filled my mouth.

'Sexton,' Ysella shouted from inside the kitchen.

'Yes! Sexton beetles! Little gravediggers,' Mum said, walking me towards the dark kitchen. 'Eating dead things, Sprig. Mice, voles.' Only my mother had ever called me Sprig. The childhood nickname made me twitch. 'Bury them underground and then eat them! Like undertakers,' she said.

'Weird,' I replied, feeling around on the wall for the light switch. My hand brushed against something soft and damp before I found it. I recoiled.

Yet, once illuminated, I could see nothing but dry wall.

Away from my mother the smell remained, coating the kitchen. 'Why were you sat in the dark in here?' I asked, pushing a crate of mouldering bulbs and some wellies out of the way so I could put my bag down on a clear patch of floor. I picked up a bulb, a tulip, and held it to my nose – nothing. I scraped the blue fuzz from its base.

Mum sat herself at the table, unaware of the mess and the smell as she talked quickly. She didn't offer me a seat. In front of her was the debris of her nail-biting habit, tiny crescents of white keratin positioned like a swirl.

'The birds are back, you know. All up in the chimney again. Haven't been able to light the fire in nine months, have we, Ysella? Bloody thing's still letting in smeach, mind. Stinks of ash.' She bit at her thumbnail as she spoke.

Not ash. Salt and rot. That was the smell. Clay pulled from an old marsh. It was fertile, the smell of an animal locked out in the rain. A damp sweetness.

Mum flapped her hand at the large stone fireplace behind her. Her eyes were still, set on my head. Ysella was crouched down behind the kitchen counter, searching for something. Her disembodied voice shouted a greeting from out of sight.

'How are you, Ye?' I asked.

'Oh, surely well,' she said. Something clattered onto the stone floor, and she swore. 'Has your mam told you about the birds?'

'I have, aye,' Mum said.

The birds used to come every year. All throughout the winter, my mother and Ysella would make do with rusted radiators, refusing to clear the chimney flue of the twigs, hair, old cigarette packets and horse shit that were loaded in there. They'd say they liked providing a safe place for the birds to nest over winter when the trees had shrugged off their leaves. With the chimney blocked this way, no sound got in, except that of the birds. No traffic noises, no distant moans of the tractors that would normally colour the moors. No whistle of wind. Just a stuffed-up silence, the occasional scratch of talon on stone, and the echo-snap of a wing in a chamber.

I eventually found a seat at the table as my mother watched, resisting the urge to run my hand over my scalp. She wanted to speak on it, I could see, but she wouldn't. It was a rule then that we never discussed my appearance, so different in style from her own. My family were a line of muted, mousey women, often fading into the landscape of the moors in a way that made them appear ghostly, until I arrived. The shadowy mass of my hair had been a point of contention with my grandmother. We became too visible. When I left, I shaved it. Bleached what little was left until my scalp prickled with the burn of ammonia. Now, pale and lost, I looked more like my family than ever before.

The table was almost entirely covered in stacks of papers – letters read and abandoned, shopping lists of items never purchased, ripped from notepads and written on the backs of magazines. The mess made my mouth feel claggy. Perhaps it had been this way before I left too, and it was only now I'd seen another way of living that I'd started to notice. I blinked it away. I caught my mother's eyes, dragging them down from my head, and smiled at her like I had practised, all gums. She smiled back, showing a sliver of bitten nail hooked on her front tooth.

'Tea?' Ysella asked, popping up from behind the counter, waving three mugs.

*

The taxi driver had clocked me immediately at the train station.

I thought I was safe, with my hood up and my voice disappearing the way it had. The edges of my accent were lost somewhere on the train between Plymouth and Birmingham. Over the past year I'd been shedding it like stray hairs. One morning I'd wake up and find violent R's strewn across my pillow. I'd pull Es and Azs and Ens out of the shower drain, trying to fit them into words like puzzle pieces, never quite finding the right shapes again. Somewhere along the way I'd picked up an H, maybe on my first night out in the city. After years of 'ave and 'ope and 'air, I had Have and Hope and Hair. I lay in bed at night, whispering them at the ceiling.

I'd asked the driver to take me to Blisland.

'You sure you don't want the farmhouse? Tregellas, 'int it?' he'd asked, voice all gravel and mud. I looked up from my phone to see his eyes still staring, his expression friendly. So much for anonymity.

'Merryn. Yeah, no, just the village. Please.' I lifted my phone up to signify the conversation was done, but he carried on talking anyway, asking me how the farm was doing nowadays. It was little more than an empty plot of land with the house stood in the middle, and everyone local knew that well enough.

'Moved back to the village, have they?'

'What? No, no, still at the farm.'

He overtook a tractor on a blind corner, almost rear-ending a Jeep. He let out a small grunt when we escaped death, whereas I was white knuckling it in the back seat, my fingernails cutting into the worn leather. There was a split in the seat next to me, silver duct tape pressing the bursting foam back into place. Each time he spoke, I ripped off a little bit more of the tape.

'The village is dead these days, of course,' he said, complaining about ghostly second homes, parish council cuts and emmets – tourists who mine the county like ants. 'Full of strangers. Not you though,' he continued, catching my eye, 'you might sound like one, but you're made of these parts.'

He was saying too much. I didn't want to hear any of it.

'Back for your summer hols then, are you? Sure, your mam'll love that.'

'No, just a few days. Maybe a week.'

'Don't you know how long, maid?' he laughed. I forgot myself then, screwed up my face at his nosiness, and he saw me. I watched his back stiffen against the seat.

'Sorry,' I apologised, shamed by his discomfort. 'I'm a bit distracted. I'm back for a memorial, so.'

'Ah. The Hawkey girl, right. Terrible shame, that. Terrible.'

*

Mum coughed, straight into her cup of tea, and I stared up at the faces hanging from the ceiling. Toby jugs. Hundreds of them, with garish moulded faces. There was a new one, a ginger tomcat, hanging from the beam over Mum's head. It had already taken on the blurred quality of something coated in dust. The others were a mixture of impish and goblin faces, each jowly like a melted wax-work. They gave the impression they were always watching.

Esolyn had referred to them as an inheritance and I overheard enough as a child to know that it was bad luck to throw out anything with a face.

Nothing else looked new, but unlike the moor, the house itself felt changed. Ill-fitting. The jugs, especially. There seemed to be more of them, jostling for space. Looking up felt like standing in a house of mirrors. Too many yellow-tinged eyes staring down from above. Hanging above the fridge, a Toby jug shaped like a mermaid was being slowly choked by a spider's web.

'What time do we need to leave on Saturday to get to Claud's thing?' I asked them both, as I took my cup of tea from Ysella. I was normally a very organised person, but this was the one thing I couldn't bring myself to investigate.

'Claud's thing, dear? Your Claud?' she said, not looking at me as she held out a second cup to Mum, who grabbed it with both hands.

Who else had a Claud? 'The memorial. Mum said it was Saturday, right?'

Ysella went back to the counter for her own tea. At the table, my mother dipped a finger into her mug, winced at the heat and then stuck the finger into her mouth. Neither answered me.

'This Saturday?' I asked again, fishing an island of limescale from my cup, 'Anyone?'

'Your mother knows more than I do,' Ysella said.

'It's been delayed, I'd say,' my mother said, suggesting rather than answering.

'What?' I asked. I turned to my mother, waving a hand to pull her attention from the tea, 'Mum?'

She moved her eyes from the mug slowly. 'Oh, yes. Yes, it's been delayed. There's an issue with the roof, at her dad's. It's leaking. They're rearranging though, no mind.'

I could still have been in the city, on my own. I felt duped, then. Dragged home early for little reason. I looked pointedly at Ysella, but she simply shrugged and turned to Mum, 'You know, Lo, they're named after the sextons who look after church graveyards, your beetles.'

She was right about the sexton beetles: they bury corpses for food.

It's more than that though. They don't just bury them, they breed on them, too. A male and female beetle will meet at the site of a dead animal, and if they're a match, the pair will bond and fight off any other beetles that approach the food. Together, they strip the hair and feathers, plucking the body clean, and then they mould it into a ball, before pushing it deep underground.

They arrive on the moor in April, just in time for the resurrection, and by October they're gone, just below ground. The bones of their meals stay in place forever, breaking down gradually to feed the soil. And so the cycle continues.

Knowing that I shouldn't have returned so soon left me uneasy. I had been home for mere hours, and I was already seeing things

I shouldn't. I missed the city, where I had clean mugs and a descaled kettle and my own space. A place where the air smelled like traffic and takeaways, instead of the rot of this kitchen.

FOLKLORE

The moor knows its women well, but it is men who have tried to carve apart the land many times over. First came the names: Black Down, Kerrow Down, Metherin Down, and the place in which we stand: Pendrift Down.

Step back 200 years. In the cities a revolution was booming, but on our land the same men were stuck arguing the same cases. The Morse code of ownership – dots and dashes signed across pieces of paper – that held before were no longer enough for the land-owning sons.

The sons raised stones and marked their boundaries with their initials, laying claim to land even the ice age had not mastered.

They were wrong to think the land would bow to them. The granite they cut from our crust, the cattle they grazed ate from our bounty; we were the hands that fed.

Now the stones lay broken and wilted, trampled by animals and ignored by the woman who walks past them, limbs long, joints creaking in the wind. She does not look below her feet. She does not crouch by granite, nor does she scrape lichen from old letters to see on whose land she walks. She doesn't need to. She knows in her bones – those click-clacking bones of hers – that this is not a land that belongs to men.

Listen. Place your ear to the ground. Hear the hush first, the cloying earth.

Now, raise your hand, press your bone knuckles down and knock. Quickly now, whilst the birds are silent in their nests and the wind is holding its breath. Knock.

You hear it? You must. An echo, ringing below like a cough. Hollow ground. Hallowed ground. A cavern of roots and stones, and deep beneath:

A womb, a holding place, a growing place. This is where She keeps.

iv.

Later, I drew myself a bath. I cracked the window and rolled myself a cigarette, pinching only the stingiest amount of tobacco into the paper. I was trying to save the little money I had left until I started my summer job in two weeks' time. It wasn't much, but I'd managed to get hired writing technical copy for an import and distribution company. No one's dream, sure, but it was a step closer to being independent and staying in Manchester.

I ran the bath hoping to cover up the smell of smoke, but when I searched, I couldn't find even the most basic of shower gels. I made do with Ysella's homemade bath oil mix and an old jar of dried flower heads I found behind some cinnamon toothpaste.

I held myself still, watching as dried camomile flowers drifted on the water around my ankles. The heat of the bath made my chest mottle, my toes burn. Hard water had drawn green rings around the plug hole and eaten away the top layer from the ceramic, leaving the tub rough against my skin. The floor was limestone, freezing any time of day, and a threadbare towel hung on the iron radiator, collecting flakes of peeling paint. It was a room where time would stop.

I had stayed downstairs with Mum and Ysella beyond the first cup of tea, which grew cold, and well into the second, also untouched.

They'd been talking about Ysella's job. She'd been a history teacher before she retired, and now she spent her time as a volunteer folklorist of sorts, storytelling for tourists and occasionally scouring archives for the ancestry of people's last names.

At one point, Ysella, who'd forgotten her tea, had moved back into the kitchen. She pulled a Pyrex bowl from the fridge then searched the cupboards as she spoke, before coming across a masher. She was telling Mum and me about an old woman she'd interviewed called Mrs Rowe, who'd been frightening some emmets holidaying in the cottages in Halagenna – a little hamlet nearby.

'I don't know if you remember Halagenna, Merryn. Or Rowe, but our mam knew her well. Hers was the grandest house there back in the day, before they started evicting all the locals from the cottages and dolling them up for holiday lets.'

'Mam used to say Trewarnen and Halagenna were two spots of pure Celtic history, didn't she?' Mum said, eyeing Ysella and me over her brew. She was the only one who braved the limescale to drink the tea.

'Aye,' Ysella nodded. She turned to me. 'Your gramma hated Rowe but the two of them practically went back as far as Jubilee.'

'What did she do with the tourists, then?' I asked. Ysella's wrists were washed in pink. As she moved the utensil, little specks of silver glittered all over her hands. The thing in the bowl looked like the raw meat of a cow's tail, or perhaps a limb belonging to a tall baby – long and fleshy and tube-like.

'The emmets? She's been telling their kids that a ghost drowned in the river by Bradford. Saying that the cows drink there, so all their cups of tea and lovely milkshakes are haunted.'

I laughed and glanced at Mum, who was chewing her finger-nails again and looking at the bowl in front of Ysella.

'I hope that's not our dinner, Ye,' I said, as I got up to pour my tea down the sink.

'It's not for eating, maid,' she replied, nodding at my mother, who took her hand from her mouth long enough to say, 'Eel. And lard. For a project.'

A project. I nodded and dropped my mug into the brackish

water of the sink. I assumed she was making something exotic for the chickens.

I asked Ysella why Rowe thought a ghost had drowned at Bradford, mainly to distract myself from the mess in her bowl, and she told me Rowe was just doing what they all were: looking for answers.

'It's just a theory. People have been thinking there's something off on the moors for a long time, just no one can agree exactly what it is. Rowe reckons it's a haunting. The folks over at Jamaica Inn reckon it's the Beast of Bodmin – though of course that helps them sell tickets for that museum of theirs, so they would say that. The farmers think it's something else.'

'Same as our mam,' my mother said.

Ysella cleared her throat. 'All just old superstitions.'

'Why, what did Granny think it was?'

Mum shifted in her seat, as if she wanted to answer me, but a look from Ysella silenced her.

'She didn't think anything much about it, Mer. She just never really trusted the moors all that much. Didn't think it the safest place.'

Ysella tapped her fingers against the side of her bowl and then smiled at me. 'Ain't it time that you go and wash off? You must be exhausted after all that travelling.'

'I don't know why you had to go to a university so far away,' my mother said.

'It's the best thing you ever did, that,' replied Ysella.

Mum scoffed, and I nodded at Ysella, grateful that she was fighting my corner for once. I had applied without telling them, sending my forms in from Claud's flat. I thought they'd never approve of me going, not so far away, not on my own.

At the time, I'd thought Claud and Chris would be coming with me, or at least going somewhere else, but neither of them even tried. Chris said he was going to go to London, but I know he only set himself a big goal so no one would actually expect him to reach it. It meant he could stay at home near his mum and everything he knew without having to feel guilty about not leaving. And Claud, well. Claud was in no state to go anywhere.

My mother hadn't approved, she'd been furious. Ysella, on the other hand, had supported my decision. I was surprised. I'd thought she'd want to keep me closer, not encourage me to broaden my horizons. But she'd told me to get myself off the moor, experience a different way of life.

I was gathering my things from the kitchen so I could go upstairs when Ysella moved past me, carrying her bowl over to the window. The stench of it trailed behind, the same smell as when I arrived: silt and decay and something animal. I picked up my bag and trainers as she scooped the paste out of the bowl and smeared it onto the windowsill and around the frame. It caught in lumps as she spread it across the uneven wood. I could see the meat of it, the shine from the fat. Silvery scales and red and white flashes. Was it the blood that had curdled the butter?

I was about to ask her what she was doing when a movement caught my eye – my mum, stood silently in the doorway. She saw my hesitation and shook her head, bringing her fingers up to her mouth, before disappearing back into the hallway. I took my things and hurried upstairs.

*

I couldn't tell you how I fell asleep in the bath, but I did, and I woke abruptly. There was a crash somewhere behind me, and I jerked upwards involuntarily, causing a tide of cold water to rush over the sides of the bath. Then banging, so loud that it seemed the very foundations of the farmhouse must be moving, dragging themselves out of the ground. My body shivered with fear or cold, or both, and I gripped the sides of the bath to pull myself up, almost slipping as I did so. Clumps of lavender stuck to my body; in the lower light, the dark heads looked like ants swarming my stomach. A hundred little legs and bodies, moving together. I flicked one off and swatted violently at my pickled skin. I knew killing an ant caused the rest to swarm, and I shrank into myself, expecting pain.

Of course, it didn't come. It always took me a minute to place myself when I woke somewhere different – there was a moment where the dream would soak through into reality, and I would wait for it to recede, moving cautiously until I felt real again. I took a moment before I was back in the room.

The clanging in the walls had stopped with a loud whirr: old pipes. In the newly silent bathroom, I remembered: wasps. Wasps swarm, not ants. And certainly not buds of lavender.

My mother let herself into the bathroom as I was picking bits of flower from my hair and wiping them onto the wall. She peered out of the little square window as I wrapped the sandpaper towel around me.

'You left this,' she said, thrusting my phone towards my wet hands before turning on her toes to stare out of the window. 'Did you see anything on the moor? Or hear anything outside?'

I wiped my phone on the towel, trying to dry it off. 'What, just now?' I asked.

'Now. And on your walk up earlier?'

I thought back to the strange parting of bracken, the invisible trail. The moment I thought I saw her, in her coat. For a woman so often away in her mind, my mother occasionally had an uncanny sensibility about her. How did she know to ask? It could've been mother's intuition, but I wasn't going to give her the satisfaction of reading me correctly. 'No, not really. I went to the rock though, Jubilee,' I said.

'Ah, with the Merlions,' she said as she pressed her face against the glass, hands cupped around her eyes.

Of course. The confused lions on Jubilee weren't a mistake after all, or a rebellion by the carver. They were always intended to be beastly. I'd been told that before, but forgotten in the moment, taken in by how stark the moor felt whilst I walked on it alone. How easy it was to make up my own myths when I had been away for so long.

I rubbed the sharp towel against my arms when she wasn't looking, watching the little curls of dead skin that it pulled up. I pressed them against the wall too, next to the lavender buds.

She cracked the window open and pushed her head out into the darkness, staring at the ground below and then turning her face to the sky.

'There's been more talk,' she said, her voice outside, 'of something dark on the moors. It's not just Rowe.'

'Dark how?' I asked, as I turned my back to her and pulled my hoody on over the towel.

'Like Ysella said. Beast, maybe. Something dark and too long to be a fox.'

'That's nothing new,' I said.

''S not the Beast, that's the thing. Too big. Not animal.'

'A person?'

'Mmm. No. Not the type you want to go hunting,' she replied, pulling the window closed.

'Who's hunting?' I asked.

She motioned me to the window, and we both stood, leaning forward. She pointed out into the black night and when I said I couldn't see anything, she told me to wait. And then: blink, blink, blink. One after the other, low roaming gleams appeared outside, near the edge of the field. Torches, sweeping the ground and the skies.

'They're after it,' Mum said, her eyes following the lights of the whole village.

'Surely they're not actually trying to hunt the Beast of Bodmin?' I asked, holding myself completely still – it had been a long time since we'd stood so close to each other. I kept my eyes trained on the lights flickering ahead, unwilling to spook either of us out of this almost-intimacy.

'No matter what it is, they won't find it in here. Ysella's made sure of that.'

'What's Ysella done? She doesn't believe in any big cat; she's said it herself enough times.' I said. I spoke too fast, too dismissively, and she pulled herself back from the window. I was left with a circle of her breath on the glass.

She cleared her throat and then spoke again. 'I told you, it's not the Beast they're hunting, Sprig.'

I turned to look at her and she pantomimed checking her wrist, though she was wearing no watch. 'You ought to get yourself off to bed. And wear something warm, it gets cold in that room of yours.'

When my mother left, I went to Ysella's room and sat on the floor in front of the window. Her bedroom faced out onto the same section of the moors as the bathroom, and I wanted a better look at who was out searching for something at this time of night.

They disappeared from view shortly after I sat down, walking up and over one of the hills. This was the way they'd searched for Claud when she was missing, before they knew she was really gone. A group of them, farmers and fathers and brothers, had all taken themselves out across the moor with torches and walked, scanning the ground for anything unusual. Torches, even though it was midday when they finally clocked that no one had heard from her for two days, and her flat was empty.

My mother and aunt hadn't joined in the search. They'd wanted to, but from what I could gather from Chris after it all – after they'd found her, after she'd been buried – the villagers wouldn't let them help. They said the family, my family, was bad luck. They didn't want to risk it.

We spoke on the phone one night a few weeks after it had happened. I wasn't sure I'd be able to face all of it, so I'd taken to calling Chris late at night from bed. I'd told him that it was bullshit. 'Who would turn down help when their daughter was missing, over some stupid superstition?'

He'd agreed with me, but then he said 'You've forgotten what it's like down here, Merryn. You've gotten out, and you're seeing a different side of the world. But people aren't like that here. Things stick. You've got no dad and no granddad.'

'Hey!'

'I know, I know. I'm not trying to be a prick. I know how fucking horrible all this is. For you, for me, for everyone. I'm just saying what I can see. They don't trust your family. I know it's not fair.'

'No, it's not fair. No one was closer to Claud than me. They're a bunch of bigots, all of them. If they were trying to keep me away, I'd understand, maybe. But my mum? My aunt? Not helping would've killed Ysella, especially with where, you know.'

'With where she was found, I know. I'm not sure it was the gay thing though. It might've been. But that's not what they said.'

'What did they say?'

'They said . . . well, it's stupid. It really is.'

'Tell me.'

'They said your family lose people.'

From Ysella's room, I could hear the performance of end of night tasks downstairs. The scratch of old ash being pulled from the fireplace, the steady procession of locks on the front door being fastened. They'd both been alone for as long as I could remember, my mum and Ysella, and they seemed to cope OK. I had been alone for – well, I wasn't sure how to quantify how long . . . I'd been without Claud for a year. She'd been gone for ten months. And before that? I didn't want to think of all the times Claud had brushed my hair behind my ear, kissed me gently on the forehead, slept next to me in either of our beds.

Now I was home, I would have to find a way to function through the week. I couldn't let myself go to seed the way I did in the city. If Ysella thought I was out of control, she'd never let me leave. A week was all I needed to get through. The memorial, a general catch up with Chris, and then I'd be back on the train in time to start work before second year.

Just then, something caught my eye. As I went to lift myself from the floor, I spotted something in front of me, pushed underneath the chest of drawers by Ysella's window. I pulled my phone from my pocket and shone the torch towards it. It was a notebook, fat and full, hidden away.

I pressed my face against the floorboards and peered beyond the dust to the wedge of leather and paper. I crooked my fingers under the drawers, twisting my knuckles against the wood to reach. An unassuming thing, it was coated in brown leather that peeled at the corners and was held closed with an elastic band. Page after page of cheap off-white paper, easily greased, with thinning grey lines stretching out endlessly.

I stopped about a third of the way in, at a tear, a ripped-out page, with just the straggly hangnails left. I flicked on through a few blank pages before I found more torn paper. Something else had been removed. I picked at the cuticles of paper by the binding as I thought about what I had found. Ysella was not usually a destroyer. An historian, she often crossed the academic bridge into hoarding, and threw nothing away. Everything had its place in her room, with her work neatly filed in her desk.

I tucked my find into the waistband of my joggers and spirited myself out of Ysella's room just as I heard her heavy tread on the stairs. She placed a hand on my shoulder as she passed me, and I held myself still until she was gone, determined she wouldn't see what I'd taken.

When I got to my room, I was too struck by the change in it to look at the book right away. *It's not changed a bit* – that's what you always hear people say when they return home. They go off to uni or run away or they die, and their bedroom remains the same, a shrine coated in polythene. My room had not stayed the same.

Mum's bags and boxes were once confined to the free-standing wardrobe next to the window, but they had escaped and were roaming free. Someone had taken the wardrobe doors off, and her belongings were purged across the floor. I kicked at an old CD player with my foot, picked up a crocheted bear and dropped it on the bed. Tired from my poor attempt at vandalism, I moved a wicker basket full of electrical cables on to the floor so that I could sit on one of the sturdier-looking boxes.

Underneath the basket was a photo frame. I knew the photo, vaguely. Before I came home from the city, Ysella had sent me a picture of her and my mother. I had replied 'Very nice!' without really looking at it.

It was a photo of the two of them, stood side by side in front of Trewarnen. The door to the farmhouse stood behind them, black and imposing. Ysella, wearing grey and white linen, looked like a college art teacher, free and wise, a little spaced out. Mum melted into the door in her all-black outfit, no more than a withered head.

She was still young, though you couldn't tell. We had moved back to Trewarnen when I was eight, hoping that the change would make her better. Life away from Ysella and her mother hadn't treated her well. Leaving the village, returning home: it was supposed to help, and it had done for a while. But now, after more than a decade of living back in the farmhouse, she was pale and bent out of shape, as if the wind had moved the very bones of her, and they had set back together wrong.

I took the photo frame and placed in on the little pine bedside table. I thought of the months before I left for the city, when I spent most of my nights at Claud's. How each time I came home I'd find something else burrowed in my bed. Another coat hanger. A remote beneath my pillow.

One month, all the electronics in the farmhouse found their way into my room. Mum had read that teenagers need constant stimulation to keep their brains active. I sat in bed on a Saturday morning with two TVs, three radios and a landline to play with. Some weeks later, all the electronics were out of my room. My straighteners, my phone charger – even the lightbulb was gone. I'd explained to her that a lightbulb wasn't the same as a television, but it didn't work. She'd read a new study, listened to a new rumour, given herself a new belief. It was electricity; it was bad for your brain when you sleep.

Standing in the centre of the room, I pulled the notebook from my waistband. The torn page told me something had been started over, cleared up. Something writ, then thrown out. I turned my attention to the pages that spread themselves on either side of the tear and held the book towards the window, angling it at the light. I was looking for the residue; the fingerprints left behind in the form of imprinted letters. A forceful biro pressed in urgency always has a ghost. Just when I thought I could make out the shape of letters, ascenders scattered by hand, the cross of a T, the drag of an F here and there, the light shifted again – the house was fighting against me, I swear – and the lines were letters no more, nothing but a hazardous scribble, carved deep into the pulp.

I held the pages between finger and thumb, flicked between them at speed. The *prrft* that followed sounded like some ancient bird call. On the sixth or seventh flick, a shadow of black appeared. I stopped and leafed through again until I saw the hidden text. I couldn't understand how I'd missed it before, holding it up against the lamp on the bedside table as I did.

It was Ysella's handwriting after all, tight and looped, written as if under the duress of a strong left wind. Three tight pages of text, two small, hurried drawings, one of which is on a dissected page – the top torn off. I unfocused my eyes, staring up at the ceiling. Blurred, so I couldn't read the pages. A moment of morality had taken me over – I wasn't sure I wanted to invade my aunt's privacy like that. What if it truly was just a diary? No part of me needed to know my aunt's unspoken secrets.

Being at home sent me back into a childlike state. I had been raised on secrets, so although I wasn't surprised by how quickly I began hiding things from my aunt, I'd hoped I'd have been home longer before the weirdness crept back in.

I couldn't help myself. I told myself I had to check if it was a journal, or work. I turned back to the three pages of text, thinking I would skim read until I had a verdict. I didn't get very far before

I saw two words that made me fling the notebook away from myself. There, in the swirls of Ysella's handwriting, one word I had never before seen: *Pedri*, and one word I knew too well: *Claud*.

vi.

I left Ysella's notebook where it landed after it had hit the wall, slipping between the wardrobe and a nest of bags. I didn't want to read Claud's name in my aunt's book. I wasn't ready to see Claud through anyone's eyes but my own. Already it was too late: just seeing it washed me with grief. I closed my eyes and let the feeling take me, just for a moment. I had been managing my grief as best I could. I allowed myself small portions, focusing on just one part of her at a time, to stop myself drowning in it. I thought of her hands. Just her hands, no further than the wrist. The white half-moons under her nails, the vein on the back of her hand shaped like an H. How her fingers were long and thin, like a painter's, or a pianist's. How, for a while, her hands only smelled like me, and I couldn't brush my teeth in the morning without tasting her, and oh!

I let myself relive her, only for a moment. I felt her loss in every part of my body, my limbs pulling away from me to reach out and find her. The hairs on my arms stood, the pale flesh of the backs of my knees crumpled, my gums ached. It exhausted me, this longing with no end.

Sitting back down, I pinched the sweet skin between my fingers until I felt calm. No, I couldn't read the notebook. Not yet. I would be undone. It didn't make sense that my aunt would have written about her, she never spoke about Claud, she even left it to my mother to ring me and tell me to come home for the memorial. My aunt always seemed to be out whenever Claud came round, and she was never particularly pleased when I left the house to stay with her.

'That girl will hurt you,' she'd said. I hadn't listened hard enough to ask why.

My mother had more of a relationship with Claud, though barely. Growing up in isolation, my aunt and mother had only ever had each other and made no effort to foster relationships outside of the family unit. My desire to create other friendships must've been alien to them. But I think a part of my mother missed the freedom she'd had when she lived away from Trewarnen, in the village. She hadn't been built for the farm, but growing up here had made her the way she was, and now she could never be any-where else.

I didn't want to leave the notebook exposed to the wilds of my old room where I might lose it, so I grabbed it and wedged it under my pillow, unread. Firm, it pressed against the back of my head.

In bed, in the dark, the room was a stranger. The boxes and bags that I had woven through moments before conspired to slug their way towards me once the lights were off. In my memories, the bed is moored in the middle of the room, a safe island, not pressed against the wall, which was how I found it. It was shorter than I remembered too, my outstretched arm dangling in space. It didn't take long for me to remember the way I slept as a child.

Somewhere between rest and waking, I felt something crawl into the bed and curl around me. At first I thought it was the cold creeping through, and I tried to move the covers, but found myself pinned in place, the quilt pushing down on my chest. I moved around until I had shifted myself up onto one shoulder. I was convinced an animal – *a rat?* – had found its way under the quilt and was prowling around me. When I reached out, my hands grasped air.

A dream, then. A miscommunication with my senses in the dark. Frustrated, I pulled the quilt back over my head, cursing myself for waking myself up. I closed my eyes, focusing on my warm breath reflecting back on me from under the quilt, self-soothing like a long-limbed baby.

And then I felt something move against me again. It was cold and almost wet, and it moved up my side and settled on my chest. The weight of the cold thing pressed down on my lungs and after a moment I whispered, unsure, 'Mum?'

It was when I lived in the cottage with my mother that I first started to wake in the night to a figure sat on the end of my bed. I was young, perhaps six, the first time it happened. In the dark, I stapled my eyes shut with my fingers. Each time I woke, the figure moved closer to me. Sometimes it crawled along the bed, brushing against my legs, edging past my arms, and then, when I felt brave enough, I would turn my head to the side and see it properly, finally, crouching there beside my pillow. Its breath was hot against my ear and smelled curdled, as if from a mouth stitched shut. Or maybe that was the smell of a mouth freshly made. A razor taken to a lump of flesh that should never open, the odour the result of contained muscle and fat meeting fresh air.

It didn't feel like a dream; it was real. And in the dark, the thing that crawled across my bed was my mother, I was certain.

The morning after would show me a different woman. A new mother, one made of muslin cloth and soft words. At night, there was a shapeshifter that lived in our cottage. I didn't know whether it stepped into or out of her skin, whether it consumed or erupted. I just knew that it came for me, relentlessly. After my grandmother died and we moved back to the farmhouse, I thought the dreams – or visits – would stop. And at first, they seemed to. I slept peacefully for months in a row, convinced Ysella was keeping it at bay. But it wasn't an ending, only a waning, and eventually, some six months after we'd moved back to Trewarnen, the figure came back to me.

Now, back in my childhood bedroom, I was stiff with uncertainty, too anxious to move. I'd spent the past year in the city, free from this nightmare creature. I hadn't been sleeping well – grief had stripped me of that – but I'd been sleeping alone. The absence of these dreams had allowed me to convince myself that they had simply been that. Dreams. A sort of sleep paralysis that had been unfortunate but was nothing more than bad luck, an active imagination easily influenced by the stories of the land finding their way into my sleep. I was an accordion being folded and squeezed until all the air was gone and I was choking on the lack.

Yet here I was, an arm snaking around my waist, freezing cold, and it didn't feel like a dream anymore. The chill in the bed was real, human. It pulled me closer towards it, and I tried to roll away, but the thing on my chest had squeezed the air out of me and there was nothing left of me to move. There was no face, but it was a thing – someone, pulling me towards them. A hand on my hip, fingers squeezing as I was scraped across the mattress. I couldn't tell what it was saying, could only hear a clicking, clanging noise. Metal on metal. It could have been tin pipes. It sounded like a bag of coins being shaken.

FOLKLORE

There are many stories of many women walking our land, each one born from mud. We begin with the most important.

Up on the land, there is a farmhouse. It lies low and wide, spreading. The house belongs to the great mother, her children, and the girl. On the land of the house, a barn. A barn that is not much now, but once had high walls and a strong, bolted door. From the land, the barn looked right. A rich Cornish hedge made of stone and earth climbed around the perimeter. Dog lichen and wall pennywort communed on its surface as our moss crept over the stone tops. It was a hedge made of querns, cup-stones, loom-weights, quoit-tops, hare-creeps and menhirs. The hedge-maker, the great mother, had gathered every piece of clitter, each boulder and rock she could find, until the hedge that bound her land was one of ancient grace.

A hedge so strong guards more than a house. The hedge held something else: a thing that lived within a cage, sat within a round. The thing stayed within the cage, fed with scraps and hisses. She bided Her time.

We met on the first day of secondary school. I was only just eleven and soon, in under two months, she would be twelve. They felt monumental, the months that separated our births, both of us only just clawing into the same school year. It was not long before we rebranded this coincidence as fate.

Claud. She was the only other child standing alone at the edge of the tennis courts. Claud stood in front of me, blinking. She rolled her eyes at the crowd of students that flushed past us. Her eyes crescent moons. Protractors, orange segments. She stuck her arm out in front of her. Chewed nails, skin covered in blue biro scribbles.

'I'm Claudia. But Claud is better.'

I nodded. I didn't know what to do with my arms. Did I shake her hand, like my grandmother liked to do? Should we hug hello? Or should I wave?

After a summer of isolation, I didn't know how to interact when faced with a real person. I stared at her arm for so long that Claud asked if I was a robot.

I said no as she brought her shoulders up to her ears and swung her elbows back and forth mechanically, dancing. 'A robot!'

I got to know Claud quickly and intensely, the way that you do when you're young and earnest. She was a miracle baby – her term, not mine – born after her mother believed she had become infertile. When she was a toddler, her parents revered her. She was the perfect child that kept the strings of their relationship tied. As she got older, lost her chubby cherub cheeks and became all arms and legs, she seemed less of a miracle to them. Too loud, too stubborn, too dirty – more inclined to be found with a slow worm wrapped around her wrist than any of the jewellery her mother bought her. Her parents wanted her to be their perfect child, the one they wished and sacrificed for, but she couldn't live up to their idea of perfection. I couldn't understand what perfection was, if it wasn't her. To me, Claud remained a miracle. In the beginning, it was her newness that captured me: the smattering of pink pimples across her chin, her bright yellow backpack with the straps hanging low. When I came to know her well, she didn't lose her sheen. I simply felt more in awe that I had found someone so like me, but better.

And then, midway through year seven, her mother left. Gone in the night – *poof* – the disappearing mum, just like a Jacqueline Wilson book. It was a year before her mother called. We bonded over that, in a way. My mother hadn't left, but at times she was gone too. Empty behind the eyes.

That first September of secondary school fell in one of the rare years when the autumn begins in burning heat. The heatwave arrived in July and smothered all life until October.

I spent the last summer of my childhood lying on the stone flags of the farmhouse, dropping ice cubes onto my bare stomach. They pooled in the juts of my hipbones, stinking of forgotten meat and onions – the leftovers that lurked at the back of the freezer. My mother would step over me, heady in her rush to make the most of midsummer before autumn brought back responsibilities – her part-time job, my secondary school. Her linen skirt would brush across the puddle of my stomach as she prodded at my side with her toes, urging me to get up, blossom, celebrate with her. Speckled with grime, I'd plead for things she couldn't give: a bikini, a Mini Milk, a slushie, a swimming pool, air con.

When the sun bore down in early July, I found, for the first time, that I couldn't cope with it. It prickled my skin and made my hairline itch. My farmer's tan was russet brown, my heels cracked after a spring spent barefoot and feral outdoors. I pulled blue-black berries from a sloe bush in the hedgerow, skinning just the edges with my teeth, waiting for the sour dryness to fill my mouth like the punch of a fist. When the juice from the sloe hit the roof of my mouth like sand, the pain shot through my head, above my right eyebrow. I span on my feet, spitting the berry out, accusing the bush first. I thought, poison? Not a sloe but something else? Something deadlier, pokeweed maybe. I pulled at the plant in front of me as my vision blurred, but the leaves were so simple, so easy to identify. Round and pointed, like the first leaf ever drawn.

My mouth felt like it was stuffed with cotton. So – sloe then. I steadied myself against the hedge, twigs poking into my soft edges. I couldn't look up at the sky now, each time I lifted my head – my eyes, even – something weighed me down, pushing my neck into my shoulders, muffling my senses of anything but pain. I remembered Mum and Ysella saying something about the Council the night before. They were killing the hedges, Mum had said, chemicals and poison to kill the jumping jack and fireweed. I ran my tongue across my furry teeth. Not poisoned by nature, but by chemicals. I spat on the floor, but my throat felt dry, and my head was rolling on my neck.

I went back to the farmhouse, shuffling my feet. Mum and Ysella fed me peppermint tea in a Mini Egg mug and rested cold hands on my sweating forehead. Mum asked to see my tongue, and even though I knew my breath smelled stale and peaty, she only blinked and brushed my sticky hair behind my ears. Together they hurried me into the living room, scooped me onto the sofa with a blanket and drew the curtains. 'It's a migraine darling, Granny used to get them too, nothing to worry about.'

I moaned theatrically – now I was out of the sun my head was no longer swimming. When Mum switched the telly on and Ysella handed me a pair of black plastic sunglasses 'for protection', I knew that being poorly-sick had some benefits.

I spent a lot of those summer afternoons, when the sun was a pinprick in the top of the sky, shielding in the living room watching Mary-Kate and Ashley Olsen in *So Little Time* on CBBC. They were Chloe and Riley Carlson: twins living in Malibu. Their bedroom was bigger than the entire top floor of the cottage. They had air con and surfboards and ankle bracelets with pukka shells and streaks of yellow-blonde highlights that curved around their identical apple cheeks.

By the time summer ended, I was eleven years old, and I believed I was world-weary. Something about me felt off. It was to do with the way I spat on my hands to smooth down the wired frizz that stuck out from my ponytail. The way I pulled a hat low over my ears whenever Ysella dragged me to the supermarket with her, hiding myself from the girls who lived in town. The way their hips moved separated them from me, like marionettes with secrets that come from living near the high street.

I saw it in Mum sometimes; I recognised it in the way the men, folded up with cigarettes outside the pub, nodded at her slowly, their fingers black from leather polish.

She would wave one finger at a time, sometimes walking past, sometimes stopping to chat. I'd stand beside her, feeling as prickly as gorse. Bitter. They would shift themselves in their jeans, touch the top of her arm, smudge her skin. Ask her when that sister of hers would babysit the wee maid next.

School came, and it was still so hot. The black plastic sunglasses sat at the bottom of my schoolbag, just in case. The bag was blue and purple with a drawstring top – new from Par Market. Mum took me to the stall with incense and little resin figurines of fairies and dragons. The fairies were in dresses made of flowers, their skin creamy white, hair orange and flowing. I asked for one, but she said it'd make the piskies mad, and the woman behind the stall wearing a wolf T-shirt laughed.

Mum laughed too, winked at the stall holder, said 'Can't anger the locals, aye?'

The market smelled like raw fish, donuts, and the fleshy tang of meat from the butcher's stall. The smells all mixed under the low ceiling; I could taste them.

On the back wall, behind the ashtrays and the diamante skulls, were the clothes. T-shirts with a green leaf and 'addicted' printed in large, rounded letters. Red and black striped legwarmers in clear plastic packaging. Black fishnet arm warmers. Whole rolls of sweatbands: black and white checkerboard, red, green and yellow stripes, childish smiley faces. There were backpacks with stars, with crescent moons and polka dots. Handbags shaped like corsets, pale pink with white lace pushing up invisible breasts. Leather coffin bags, black with red silk lining. I didn't know much, but I knew I didn't want to dress like the lady in the wolf T-shirt. I started school in two days – Mum had left the shopping until the last minute – and I had to get a bag.

'You need to pick one today Sprig or Ye will be mad at me again,' Mum said, turning me towards a pinstripe clutch bag with a skull badge. I wouldn't even be able to fit my pencil case in that. Eventually I saw it, tucked behind two other bags at the top right of the wall: a flash of soft blue fabric. The wolf-woman tutted and tsked when Mum asked her to bring it over, dragging a step ladder out from under the table, unfolding it and climbing ever-so-slowly, as if Mum would change her mind from the inconvenience.

For two full days, the bag was my pride and joy. It was cotton with shiny satin lining and little silver beads stamped with crescent moons at the end of the drawstring. Up close it wasn't only blue, but veined with purple and pink and gold flecks, like the night sky. When I showed Ysella, she said I could carry the whole universe in it.

I realised my mistake when I stepped off the village bus onto the school grounds for the first time. Around me, in amongst the sea of grey shorts and black skirts and red ties, there were bobbing pink plastic fish. All of the girls – the ones with yellow stripes in their hair and silver charm bracelets on their wrists, with black ballet slipper dolly shoes and small mounds under their shirts, the ones who already knew to knot their ties short and loose, the ones that mattered – were moving in groups with hot pink plastic shopping bags swinging on their shoulders.

With their gold-bronze cheeks, they looked like they'd stepped out of Chloe and Riley's Malibu beach house, not the market town estate. I broke my nail as I removed the Cornish pisky keyring from the front pocket of my bag. I buried it at the bottom, next to the too-brown banana I'd forget about until Sunday, when I'd find it smeared into the fabric of my PE shorts.

DAY DEW

i.

In the morning, the quilt was tangled around my ankles. I was damp all over, even though the air still felt chill, and had to peel myself from the sheet. I closed my eyes for a moment and wished I'd not come back to Trewarnen. That I'd stayed out on the moors instead, with the Beast to protect me. Being home was bringing too many memories back and I wasn't sure what to do with them.

Maybe it was the sensation of sleeping in a different bed, or the shock of being home. Maybe the journey, the six hours from city to countryside, had unbalanced me. Or maybe it was the low ceilings, the thick walls that trapped the air inside the house. In my memory, it was large and sprawling. But when I arrived, it felt as if it had shrunk; the ceilings lower than I remembered. During my absence, the house had remade itself into a place where I no longer fit. I hit my head on doorways that I once glided under, stubbed my toe on a fireplace that had spread itself an inch further across the floor.

I felt the farmhouse rejecting my presence, squeezing me out. I didn't know the history of the house, beyond the fact that the women in our family had always lived in it. My mother and Ysella were both born here. We belonged here, as my grandmother used to say. The only ones who'd ever left were Mum and me, and even then, we returned quick enough. There was no reason for the house not to trust me.

Still in bed, I took my phone from under my pillow and googled 'Pedri'. The notebook, also under my pillow, was calling to me. I wanted to look at it desperately, but I knew if I saw what was written inside, I would be changed. It was safer to learn what I could about the word Pedri for now.

When I tried to search for the definition of Pedri on my phone, the worst thing happened: nothing. Every time I refreshed my browser, it came up blank. In the corner of my screen, next to three measly bars of signal, was an 'E'. Which meant there was no 4G, no 3G, no way to connect to the Internet at all. It was going to be a long trip if I had no way to access the outside world. I sent Chris a text, asking him if he wanted to meet me at the pub the next evening, and then I switched my phone off.

I couldn't understand why Ysella had hidden the notebook under her drawers. Usually with any new project, Ysella would want to share any and all findings with me and my mother – the fact that I had never heard her speak the word Pedri was bizarre. If Ysella hadn't told me the story of the Pedri, it meant she didn't want me to know. I knew I should respect that, but I didn't want to – I couldn't understand why it would be a secret. The word stuck to me like a tick, so I decided to use the old computer in the living room to try and look it up. Of course, no amount of hope would get broadband to work in the farmhouse, so I had to ask Ysella for the ethernet cable so that I could dial-in to the Internet. She couldn't understand why I'd possibly want to use the Internet, what questions I could need to ask that she, my mum or the stacks of musty books in her bedroom couldn't answer. I have flashbacks to a childhood spent using an out-of-date set of Encyclopaedia Britannica to write my geography homework on tectonic plates.

I convinced Ysella to relinquish the cable by telling her that if she didn't, work might not have me back at all. I laid it on thick, told her I'd have to move back home for good if I missed something important. Before I could finish, she was dumping the dusty cable into my arms.

It was a pointless lie in the end. The Google search gave me nothing at all, beyond a Spanish footballer called Pedro, who used Pedri as a nickname. Unless she'd really pushed the boat out in retirement, I was certain Ysella had no interest in football, Spanish or otherwise. And even if she did, she'd never refer to anyone by their nickname. She'd never agreed to calling me Sprig, even when Mum insisted on it when I was little.

I googled Claud instead, then. She still had a Facebook page, a memorialised one that her father kept up. I had never written anything on it, but I visited it often, just to scroll through the photos of her from when we were together. If you were to look at her page, there would be no evidence that the two of us existed in the same world as each other, apart from one blurry photo. Me, Chris and Claud, sat on the moors, two tents behind us. Chris is sat on a twelve-pack of Bud, his hand over his eyes, shielding himself from the sun. I'm lying down, propped up on my elbows. My hair is long, wild in the small bit of breeze we had that day. Claud is alongside me, her head in my lap. She's wearing sunglasses. There are freckles on her shoulders. You can't see them in the photo, but I know that they're there. She was so thin then. Already. That day was the last good day, the last pure afternoon before it all went to shit. I think I would give away whatever future I have to be back there again.

Before I switched the computer off, I checked one last thing. *Is it normal to think you see someone after they die* I typed, feeling ridiculous. I scrolled past results about open caskets and landed on a page about visitations. Feeling a ghostly presence, hearing voices, white feathers. It all felt too airy-fairy for me. When Claud died, I saw no signs. There were no visiting birds on my windowsill or final messages in my dreams. I didn't have a sudden sense that she had left, like people so often talk about. I knew that she was gone through text messages and phone calls. Nothing ghostly or unusual happened to me in the city, the only thing that haunted me was grief.

I closed the page I had been reading. I had thought, earlier, that I had seen Claud, her coat, walking through that gorse. But I wasn't seeing a ghost; I was seeing a memory. Back home, on the moor, I was too close to what had happened, and my imagination was in overdrive, that was all. That was all it could be.

I was in Manchester when I found out Claud was gone, and I couldn't face it at first. I couldn't face anything. The city felt too full for my grief – there wasn't room. Each night of that first week after it happened, I would pull a hoody on over my pyjamas, slip out of my shared house in Fallowfield and into the shed in the yard.

The shed was nothing but a dumping ground for the landlady's belongings. Things she left for her underpaid, overcharged tenants to deal with, rather than move to her own five-bedroom house, where everything was owned by her and there were no Ikea utensils in the kitchen. Tins of used paint, the expensive type with existential names like Sulking Room Pink and Borrowed Light, abandoned there after her latest renovation project. Colours too rich to grace the walls of the rented accommodation. The room I had been renting was painted in a dull cream I named *Possibly Damp Magnolia*.

Each night, I tucked myself away in there and smoked, directing my ash onto my landlady's belongings, angry at the £680 I paid in rent for a room with an MDF wardrobe, angry that I couldn't smoke on the doorstep because my housemates didn't like it, angry that Claud was dead and I was 300 miles away.

I wanted to set the shed on fire or scream or smash my head against the old wooden walls with all my might, but I never felt mighty. Part of me, the part that had always self-aggrandised, had hoped I could be the type of person to make a Big Stand. I thought all it would take was something big, and then I would finally stand up and take action. I wanted people to know who we were to each other, what our relationship meant, but now she was gone, and there was no big love story for me to declare. When she died, she still hadn't been ready for people to know that we were in love – or, at least, that I was in love with her – and to tell anyone that would be betraying her trust. Still, I couldn't help but think of how disappointed she'd be that our story had ended this way. Her dead and me hiding in a shed, too fearful to do anything good.

I was there because of the tightness of it, the shed. When I sat myself down in the furthest corner, the boxes towered high on either side of me, and I couldn't stretch my legs without dragging an old side table out the way first. When I squeezed into that gap, forcing myself to fold so my knees were under my chin and my shoulders were hunched by my ears, I felt safe, sheltered.

Later, I went back into the village. Unlike my walk when I arrived, this was a walk of convenience, and therefore dreadful and long. I had been trying to make toast in the kitchen, but the bread was fetid and blue. I'd pulled it right from the back of the bag – the crust tended to stave the mould off for longer – but there was nothing to save.

'Just scrape it off,' Mum said.

I turned the slice over in my hand. It was sticky. 'I'm OK. I'll walk to the shop, I think.'

'Walk? All that way?'

'Unless you want to drive me?'

'Oh no, no I mustn't.'

'Right.' I looked for butter but there was only the lard that Ysella had been using, flecked through with hints of silver from the fish skin. 'I'll grab some butter too.'

Me and Claud would walk this route often as teenagers. She lived just outside of the village with her dad, who rented an annex on the edge of a larger farm after his divorce. Her dad would send her into the village to the shop, and I would meet her to walk the three miles home. She would share her observations, and I would give her whatever gifts I could, little shells or stones, interesting flowers I'd found in the hedges. Claud was a magpie girl, a collector. Before her parents divorced, her mum kept a spotless house, she told me. Empty and devoid of anything apart from Claud. At the time, I thought she was handling the abandonment of her mother well. She used to joke about how much freedom she gained from not being loved, and I would laugh, call her a lucky bitch and tell her all about how my mum had thrown all the cereal out of our house that week because she didn't trust fortified wheat.

Still, I met her whenever she asked. Just so she would know she was loved, after all.

'I saw your aunt yesterday, walking along with used poo bags hanging off her fingers.' Claud said.

'Sounds about right.'

'She doesn't have a dog though, does she?'

'No, but she loves to get involved. She hooks them out of trees.'

'Trees!'

'Yeah, I don't know who decides to go through the whole process of watching their dog shit, picking it up, tying a little knot in the bag, and then decides just to fuck it off up a tree.'

'Tourists or Tories?'

'Hmm. Tories. Waiting for someone else to clear up for them.'

'That's it. What've you got me then?'

'OK, so, the middle of a cinnamon bun—'

'The nipple!'

'—right, the nipple of the cinnamon bun, and one of these stones.' I pulled a stone threaded with leather from my pocket. 'I found it on the moors. I made it a necklace.'

She thanked me and dropped the stone into the murky depths of her coat pocket, along with every other charm I gave her. We didn't speak of it again. Claud would often beg for attention or gifts, but once presented with either, she became shy and noncommittal.

We were never a gifting family. It's not easy without means, and a house like Trewarnen sucks the meat off your bones with its need of fixer-upping and its maintenance costs. On birthdays, my aunt would write me stories, page after page until her hand cramped. And my mother knit me scarves – or rather, one long, loose scarf, that she gifted and retrieved throughout my youth, forever purling away at it.

When it came to showing Claud how I felt, I searched for the little I had to give, saving my coins, and using my hands to catch what I could for her.

*

When I arrived at the post office, there were two women behind the counter. One was local, melded to her stool. I recognised her from years before. Joan. Her hair was grey, cropped close to her skull. The other woman was clearly an emmet, volunteering. She was wearing a Breton top, with a bright scarf tied at a horribly jaunty angle around her neck.

'Don't you look different?' said Breton top, looking me up and down. She'd obviously been around longer than I realised. This was exactly what I'd wanted to avoid.

'She does 'n all.' Joan replied. 'Your hair's all gone,' she turned to the other woman and muttered, not quietly enough, 'mind you, her mum was always a queer one. And her nan.'

'Pardon?' I pushed the bread further across the counter, nudging it closer to the long fingernails of the one closest to the counter.

'Oh, not your type of queer, maid. Odd, s'all.'

'Always a funny bunch up there, but I've never had no trouble with any of your lot, no matter what the others say,' said Breton top.

'Who says what?' I asked.

'All talk, innum,' Joan said, 's'pose, trouble follows this one round, you know. Remember May Day?'

I felt a prickle in the back of my knee. I didn't nod or shake my head; I just pushed my change across the counter.

'Proper mess,' Joan tsked. 'Bread'll be 80p. Butter's £1.50. That boy were a state after. Stayed friends though, didn't you?' She looked at the money I'd put on the counter. 'Eighty pence and £1.50, then.'

Breton top picked up the bread and shoved it into a wrinkled Tesco bag, and then turned the butter over in her hands. 'I'd never eat this fake stuff. Bloody awful.'

I tapped on the glass of the pastry counter. 'I'll take a Chelsea bun too.'

Outside, I dropped my bag on the floor and tried to roll myself a cigarette. I felt like I couldn't breathe. The paper stuck to my fingers, tearing the Rizla the first attempt, and the second. My eyes were welling up in frustration, but I knew I couldn't let myself be seen crying in the village. If anyone saw me, they'd view it as an admission of guilt. I knew I couldn't be held responsible for someone's suicide, but that didn't stop other people from believing I was. And whenever I confronted my own memories of Claud, I couldn't shake the feeling that it had been my fault, somehow.

I was fumbling with my third attempt at a cigarette when Joan appeared beside me, pack of straights in hand.

'After a fag?'

Begrudging, but also pathetically grateful, I took one and thanked her. My hand shook slightly as I lit it. I picked my bag back up and started to walk, but then she called after me.

'You're up at that posh uni, aren't you? Up country, ain't it? Over the bridge?'

I'd been so close to leaving. 'Yeah, by quite a bit.'

'Good for you, to get away. Living up on those moors can send a woman batty.'

'Right.'

'Mind, did your aunt go in for that hunt last night?'

This again. A hunt was no big deal around here – God knows, the people here killed foxes like they had a personal vendetta, regardless of the ban. But that was all pomp and showmanship, horses and red jackets and bloodthirsty braying. It wasn't a group of people on foot in the night. This had to be something else.

'No. No, she was in, why?'

'Funny that. They didn't catch nothing.'

'What were they after?' She looked at me blankly, not responding. I tried again. 'Couldn't be foxes, not at that time of night. Deer?'

She shook her head and continued to shake it with every suggestion I made.

'Badgers? Rabbits? Hares? Escaped circus animals?' I got more ridiculous, reasoning she might snap and tell me what it was if I bombarded her enough, 'the Loch Ness monster? Big cats? The Beast?' She glared at me when I said the Beast.

Joan was one of the locals who swore down she'd spotted the Beast. To the people who lived around here, the Beast of Bodmin was a fact of life, not a piece of folklore. It was one of few things that connected my grandmother to the villagers. Many times, Joan saw it, tucked behind a hedge, our hedge, just outside Trewarnen. She'd been convinced the hedge was protecting it, allowing it to blend in, so no one who meant it harm could catch it. Once, when I was thirteen, we were dragged out of the farmhouse by Joan herself, out of breath and pink-cheeked. She took my aunt by the wrist and pulled her across the yard, 'You've got to see it, Ysella, I think your ma was right, over by the hedge, clear as day.'

Of course, when we got there, there was nothing to be seen, apart from the crumbling Cornish hedging that looped around part of our land. It didn't look like a usual hedge. It was covered, almost haphazardly, with different sized granite stones on either side, like a wall. But the centre was filled with earth, the top covered in scrub and grass, and in between the stones, bits of moss and small flowers that looked like daisies peeked out. When Ysella found no crouching big cat outside, Joan seemed upset. She slumped against the hedge, rubbing her palms against her thighs.

The whole thing had felt like the ramblings of a gullible woman, and I had enough of that in my own family. I didn't want to entertain the superstitions of every person in the village too. It was only now that I began to wonder why Joan's sightings were always on our land. What was it about Trewarnen that shook her up enough to see things? Was it how old it was? Or did the dilapidation and the way it stood alone make her feel uneasy, the way it sometimes made me? Perhaps it was nothing like that, and she was just a lonely woman who knew she'd have an audience in my aunt and grandmother.

Outside the village shop, I suddenly felt cruel for the way I had been taunting her. I softened my tone.

'Will you just tell me? Why did you ask if you weren't going to say?'

'I was curious, maid.'

'Well so am I!' I'd had enough of people avoiding my questions. 'What were they hunting, Joan? What's so important that you'd follow me out here asking about it? The way you're acting it's like a group of you tried to end some emmets last night. Was that it, a bit of people hunting?'

'Course it wasn't.' She sighed.

'Ghosts? Smugglers from Jamaica Inn? Have we gone back a couple hundred years?'

'Something like that.' She looked at her feet, her old leather sandals, her pale toes.

'What?' I waited for her to continue, but all she did was squish the end of her cigarette under her shoe and rub her hands on her jeans.

'I've got to get back to work, girl. I can't gab out here all day. Tell your aunt I'm thinking of her.'

I grabbed hold of the door so she couldn't shut it. I couldn't let her go until I knew something. 'You don't know what a pedri is, do you?'

Joan had one foot in the shop. She didn't let go of the door, and nor did I. I saw her grip change. It faltered.

'What're you asking that for, maid?'

Why was I asking? I couldn't be sure. Something had felt wrong since I'd come down from the city. Trewarnen felt off. Unhomely. I was out of sorts, and it wasn't just grief. There was something else going on. Joan was about ten years older than Ysella, which meant she'd known my grandmother as well as my aunt and mother. It didn't seem like too much of a leap that she'd know something about what Ysella was researching. Once I said it aloud though, I felt anxious. I thought Joan would've laughed at me, accused me of making up words, asked if it was something I'd picked up from 'up North'. But she'd seemed rattled. Suddenly, it didn't feel like a stupid question. It felt like an important one.

I fiddled with my cigarette, ashing it way more aggressively than I needed to. The cherry ripped off the end and floated down to the floor, fizzing out of the ground. Me and Joan both watched it go out before I spoke. I tried to sound nonchalant, but my voice hitched part way through, betraying my nervousness.

'Just curious. Heard the word and wanted to know the meaning.'

Joan shook her head and offered me another cigarette. This time she didn't take one herself. 'I think you'd be best leaving that well alone until you're back up country. Bigger folks than you have been trying to work that one out and not found answers. Shame you can't ask that grandma of yours.'

Had Esolyn known what the Pedri was? It wasn't the reaction I was expecting. I thought she'd tell me it was a stupid ghost story, but she spoke about it like it was a conspiracy. 'What's Esolyn got to do with it?'

'Esolyn, is it? Well, haven't you got some airs and graces now you've been off to the city,' Joan was back to her old self. 'Imagine, calling your own grandma by her first name. That probably comes from your mam, don't it? Couldn't be me. I would've gotten a slap round the head if I called my mam her Christian name. Though that would've done your one some good, by the sounds of it.'

'What?' I'd had enough. There was no way she was going to tell me anything. She'd seemed worried before, when I was asking about the hunt, but now she was defensive, rude. She didn't want me to ask her about the Pedri. The sensation that I was being lied to by omission by those around me strengthened.

'A good slap would've sorted your mam out a long time ago and then nobody would've been in this mess. Walking round asking such stupid questions,' she tuts, 'young ones don't even know they're born.'

'Oh, fuck off, Joan,' I said, walking away before she had a chance to respond. I heard another tut and the slam of the shop door. I'd have to get Ysella to give me a lift into town the next time we needed bread.

FOLKLORE

1970. New owners came. They bought a barn from a man, a man who sells the land on behalf of the great mother, his wife.

A family of strangers, from a city far beyond the boundary. Far enough that they knew nothing of Her, trapped, or the women who walked the land.

Of the ancient hedge, they knew only of what they could take from it. They lit fires in dry months using the thatch and then snatched bluebells for their windows. The stranger children picked bark lice from the hedge, pulling them apart with spongy fingers. The stranger mother collected butterflies, graylings and hedge browns and fritillaries, pinned them to boards, and hung them upon the high walls of the house. And when the stranger mother took the last of the garden orange-tips, deep in the ground, She woke up.

The stranger family takes from the hedge. They take insects and plants and soon enough, they take the clitter too. The stranger father wants a sign for the house, so he unsheathes the quoit-top and carves their initials in it. The stranger mother takes a cup-stone. The stranger children hide stolen sweets and magazines in the hare-creep.

And beneath, She waits.

ii.

Occasionally the birds that roost in the chimney of Trewarnen die from exposure, or bad luck. A runt in the nest can't shriek quite loud enough to be fed its fair share. Or the air is too dry, and the twigs that hold the nest in place begin to shrink. The frame of the nest contracts, balancing in place by a hair. When the nest is too small, the birds collect warmer materials for the chicks. Mud, horseshit, and, if they're lucky, they find human rubbish too. Things that have been fly-tipped on the edge of the moors, thrown out of visiting cars. The foam padding from a sofa cushion. Loft insulation. An offcut of carpet. The odd piece of tent mesh.

All of these things add extra weight to the nest. It slips again, further down the flue now. Too far for the littlest chicks to fly out. Too tight for the larger birds to risk attending the nest; if they drop in, they won't find the lift to rise out again. So the chicks die, trapped there in the cell of the flue. And maybe they're mourning, throwing handfuls of soil on a casket, or maybe they're just burying their shit like cats, but sometimes the parent birds will sit at the top of the chimney, dropping in more fur and twigs and leaves, covering the bodies of their chicks. And then comes the final straw, and the whole nest, rotten bodies and all, will land with a softened 'clunk' into the hearth, usually just as we're eating dinner.

I was back home, part way through my breakfast of Chelsea bun and mould-free toast, when the latest nest collapsed onto the floor of the open fireplace, and a host of bluebottles took to the air.

Ysella ran to open the front door, bypassing the windows, as my mother attempted to herd the swarm away from the table. Eggs which were burrowed in the folds of the chick's wings had birthed into flies in our kitchen, which was full of food scraps and sweating human skin.

I shoved as much toast into my mouth as I could before anything landed on the expensive fake butter and then pointed Ysella to the windows.

'Shouldn't we open those?' I asked as she whipped at flies with a dishrag.

'Don't be ridiculous,' she said.

After they had disposed of the nest, I watched as my mother scraped the mould from the old bread, leaving festering scraps on the bread board. I'd offered her the new loaf, but she said she didn't like waste.

'I saw Joan in the shop. Still a horrible bitch.'

'I'm sure.'

She started to poke at Ysella's lard. I took my butter from the fridge and slid it over to her.

'Use this.'

She nodded but didn't look up. Ysella walked in then, bucket in hand. She saw me hovering and waved to the table, 'Sit down.'

I did. I ran my fingers under the edge of the table, and found a carving of my name, spelled incorrectly: MERAN. I'd done it the day after that summer fete, when Mum and me had come to stay at the farmhouse for a week or so to let the neighbours 'calm down'. I spent most of the time under the table, hiding from my mother and aunt and gran. They would forget I was under there, and I could listen to whole conversations before they realised. An accident, my mum said, again and again, as my grandmother disagreed. I'd sat on the floor and scratched into the wood above my head as the adults had talked around me, each of them just Legs with Voices. I had felt a need to claim the space as my own, a pull to mark that I had been there. I knew how to spell my name, of course, but Meran wasn't in trouble, I was. And if I was Meran, I couldn't be told off.

I decided I'd try and breach the subject of the hunt with Ysella. I took my fingers from my name. 'I saw Joan at the shop.'

'In the village? I could've taken you to town,' she said.

'It was only a twenty-minute walk.'

'That's not the point, you know how they talk about you down there.'

'Thanks for reminding me,' I said. I'd slipped down in my chair as we'd been speaking, slumping like an angry teenager. I pulled myself back upright. I wasn't going to regress. I spoke again. 'She started talking about Esolyn.'

Ysella grimaced. 'That woman needs to keep her beak out of things she doesn't understand.'

Mum looked at me from over her toast, confused. 'You didn't tell me that. How did you get onto the subject of Mam anyway?'

'I'm not sure. I just asked her a question. She spun it round,' I decided to lie then. I took two different parts of the conversation and twisted them together. 'I asked her if she knew anything about when Claud's memorial was—'

'Why would you ask her that? Why would she know?'

'Of course she's going to ask, Lowen,' Ysella said, sharply. She looked at me, 'If no one has a date for this thing, perhaps it's best if you go home and come back when it's all sorted.'

'Oh, no, no need. It'll be sorted soon,' Mum interjected, sitting up straighter suddenly. There was something else Joan had said that was playing on my mind.

'She also asked me about the hunt last night. Well, she called it a hunt.' I turned to my mother, 'Didn't you say they were looking for something? She made it sound a bit more extreme.'

Ysella scoffed. 'What are you doing putting such ideas into the girl's head, Lowen?' She put her bucket into a cupboard and began to wash her hands at the sink, scraping under her nails. 'Ignore them both, dear. Some of Steve's cows got out, over on South Penwint. They were just trying to round them up. A hunt! Honestly.'

I looked at Mum for confirmation, but she'd started to pick the burnt bits from her toast. Ysella tutted. Joan was dramatic. And my mother had always been fanciful, that much was true.

'What are you doing today, Merryn?' Ysella asked. She buttered a slice of toast and placed it in front of me. I couldn't tell if it was the fresh bread I'd bought, or the old stuff.

'Oh, thanks. I've already eaten—'

'Eat.'

'Right.' I tore the bread into little strips as I spoke. I'd throw it out for the chickens later. 'Well, I need to figure out what's going on with the memorial,' I said.

'What you need to do is eat,' Ysella responded.

I dropped the bread back on the plate and turned towards Mum. 'Well?'

She ran her nail against the blackened crust of her toast, scraping away the burn. 'You could do with eating some more vegetables, you look very pale.'

'She needs iron, Lowen. Meat. She's probably anaemic if she's pale.'

'Can we focus please?' I asked, but my mum had already started speaking.

'Lettuce! Leafy greens, that's what you need.'

'No, she needs kale. Brassicas, that's where the iron is. Or meat. Or nuts?'

Mum left her toast and started ferreting around in the drawers, pulling out herbs and condiments, dumping them onto the counters.

'What are you doing?' Ysella asked.

'We've got some iron tablets somewhere,' she said. Ysella mumbled in agreement and joined my mother, crouching in front of cupboards. Neither of them was looking at me.

'When's the memorial?' I asked, directing it to both, either, of them.

'We're a bit busy right now, Mer,' my aunt's voice called from over the counter.

'I'm busy too! I've only got so much time off until I need to start my new job, I can't just hang around down here waiting.'

'Not everything revolves around you, Merryn.'

Just then my mother shook a jar of tablets in the air, 'I've found them!'

I tried to ignore her, to keep talking as Ysella took the jar from her hand. 'Obviously it's not all about me. But I came down now because you guys told me it was this week, and now you're acting like you don't know. Is it this week or not?'

'Tone.' Ysella looked at me until I shrugged, and then said, 'You can't expect everyone to move at your pace.'

'I just want to—'

Ysella turned to my mother as I was speaking. 'These are fish oil, not iron.'

She spun the jar around in her hand, and the two of them stood over the tablets, reading the small print.

I sat in silence, trying to wait out their distraction. It was harder than ever before to get a straight answer out of either of them. I wasn't sure if I was struggling because I'd been away from home for too long, had somehow lost my grasp of the language we shared. Or if something was wrong and they weren't telling me.

Maybe Claud's family really didn't want me there after all. Maybe they'd forbidden it, and my mum had missed the social cues, and Ysella was trying to protect me. I'd kept away from the funeral, just in case, but my mother had convinced me on the phone that all was fine now, that it always had been, that I was paranoid.

'Mum?' I asked, 'Do you know anything?'

Finally seeing me, she stepped away from Ysella and the tablets and came over to the table. Her eyes were heavy, her mouth down-turned, an expression ready to deliver bad news. I sank down in my chair.

'I'm sorry, the tablets say they're good for your heart, but not for iron.'

'Are you serious?'

'It'll all be fine, trust me,' Mum said, 'we'll cook you up something leafy and you'll feel back to normal! And it's lovely to have you back, isn't it Ysella?'

Ysella tutted in my direction, and I glared back at her. Miserable old woman. They were both as bad as each other. I could accept my mother making little sense, but Ysella was the reasonable one. There was no reason for her to be so unhelpful, unless I was right, and Claud's family were trying to keep me away.

I could tell I wasn't going to get a straight answer from either of them, so I turned back to my mother and said 'As long as you're sure it's all fine. I just – I want to be prepared, that's all.'

She smiled, her eyes and attention far away.

It wouldn't surprise me if Claud's father didn't want me there. He had been kind to me when we were younger, but as we turned seventeen and eighteen, he began to see our relationship for what it really was: burning. I knew he didn't like me, but he loved Claud, wholly, and he must have been able to see that in me too. I couldn't imagine him banning me from the memorial, though. Her mother? Maybe.

I had never met Claud's mum. I didn't want to; I'd heard enough stories. At times I wondered if she were more like my mother than Claud let on.

iii.

There was one crossover in our childhoods that particularly stuck out to me: a kind of fairy tale we had both been told by our mothers. I didn't realise that these stories were unusual until we became friends with Chris and learnt that there were other ways of being brought up, childhoods with traditions rather than super-stitions.

We were fifteen, and the three of us were sat in Chris's house on a Saturday. We didn't come here often, although it was our favourite place to be. The living room was small, with purple walls covered in paintings Chris's mum had done of wolves and orcs and dragons. The sofas had velvet brocade throws on them, and the shelves were lined with various goth-adjacent figurines. The house felt like it had been styled by Par Market and a World of Warcraft forum, and we loved it. Whereas my mother, and my home, felt odd and uncomfortable, Chris's mum wore her differences as a lifestyle choice. She would interrupt us only occasionally, coming into the room in a waft of sandalwood, a plate of mini pizzas offered. She would smile, ask us what books we were reading, and then leave again, dyed black hair swinging in a messy plait down her back.

On this Saturday, Claud had been talking about her mother. She had spoken to her the night before for the first time in months and it hadn't gone well. Her mum had been slurring slightly on the phone, growing increasingly frustrated with Claud as she realised how out of touch she was with her daughter's life. Each of us was nursing a coffee, although Chris was the only one who actually liked it. Me and Claud had accepted the offer from his mum so we'd feel sophisticated. I thought it tasted like the water at the bottom of the washing-up bowl, but I sat with my legs crossed and the mug held in front of my lips. I imagined I looked otherworldly, Parisian. Claud did the same, my coat round her shoulders even though we were inside. Each time she took a sip, she scrunched up her nose. She looked beautiful.

'She was asking me about friends I haven't seen since primary school. When I told her I had no idea how Jenny's horse was or where Sarah was going on holiday this summer, she started to accuse me of thinking I was too important to talk to her, it was stupid.'

'Oh man, that sucks,' Chris said. 'I can't imagine my mum saying something like that to me,'

'Your mum's a babe. Of course she wouldn't,' Claud retorted.

'Yeah, Chris. You're the only one here with a normal mum.' I blew on my coffee.

'OK, OK!' He held his hands up in the air in surrender, 'I can't help it if I'm from a functional family. Just means you guys get to grow up and be tortured artists and I'll have to be something shit like an accountant.'

'That's true. Swings and roundabouts, I guess.'

Claud nodded and stretched her legs out in front of her. She had shorts on, and I could see the light blonde hairs around her knees where she'd forgotten to shave. I wanted to stroke them. 'I'll be an actress, and Mermaid will be a writer, and she'll write the most gorgeous parts for me, won't you?'

'Yep. And Chris will do our taxes.'

'Ha ha,' Chris said, deadpan. 'What happened with your mum then Claud? After that?'

'Ugh. She was accusing me of all sorts, saying I've changed when I wouldn't agree with her.' Claud started to scratch at a dry piece of skin on the back of her leg. I tapped her hand and she stopped, smiling at me wryly. 'She was clearly drunk. She started going on about that stupid story she was always obsessed with, the changeling thing. Her and dad were always arguing about it.'

'Oh, for fuck's sake,' I said.

'Right.' She rolled her eyes at me. 'I swear she actually thinks it's real.'

'So does mine.'

'They're so weird,' Claud said, forcing down a swig of coffee. I was inclined to agree.

In the weeks after her mother left, Claud had overheard her dad on the phone to her many times. At first, she couldn't understand why her mum would talk to him, and not her. Until she heard him say, 'You can't be scared of her Mary, she's still only a girl.'

We all sat quietly for a moment, me and Claud lost in our mummy issues, Chris with a puzzled look on his face.

'Changelings?' he finally asked. 'They're like shapeshifters, right? They go from looking human to being a giant bug, or a lion or whatever.'

'What are you on about?' Claud put her mug down, spilling a little. I mopped it up with my finger and then popped it into my mouth. She watched me do it and then raised her eyebrows at me. I shrugged. She leant towards me and whispered, 'You're gross.' I laughed.

We squeezed each other's hands, turned back to Chris. 'Sorry, sorry. What were you saying?' Claud's hand in mine meant I could hardly focus on anything Chris was saying. Right then, he was as important to me as the sofa was – he was there, but I had no use for him.

'Changelings. They can't actually think that's a real thing, can they?'

We both nodded. 'But they aren't shapeshifters. They're like brood parasites. Cuckoos. When a mother gets tricked into raising something else's child,' I said.

'Jesus.' Chris leant back and ran his hand through his floppy hair. He looked genuinely perplexed. It was quite endearing.

'I mean, I've never met your mum Claud, so fair enough, whatever. But I've met Lowen more than once and I know she's a bit, you know, but surely, she's not that . . . much, is she?'

'I don't know, I can never really tell. I mean, she's never said anything about changelings, but that's not because she doesn't believe in them, she just doesn't call them that. When she told me about them, she called them mylings, so it's kind of different, I guess. But yeah, I don't know if she really thinks it's real life. I know that my grandma used to smack her and Ysella if she ever found them out playing by the standing stones when they were kids.'

'Why?'

'Apparently if you pass a baby through the stones, or something like that, then they can change . . .' Claud let go of my hand as I was speaking and drank some more of her coffee. I paused, waiting for her to hold onto me again, but instead she started plaiting a bit of her hair. My hand rested on the carpet alone, unheld and utterly unnecessary. What was the point of my palm if it wasn't pressed against hers? My fingers if they weren't laced with her smaller ones? I squeezed my eyes shut, just quickly. This kind of thinking had been happening more and more lately, and I knew it wasn't healthy. I couldn't tie my whole being to hers, but I also couldn't resist doing exactly that. Chris cleared his throat, and I opened my eyes to find him giving me a look – an 'are-you-OK-or-are-you-losing-it-again' look – so I tried to give him a reassuring smile, and continued speaking

'Right. I know my mum and my aunt both got baptised over at Dozmary. Well, I don't know if you can call it baptism, actually, if there was no priest, or vicar, or whatever, but I know my grandmother took them when they were babies and dunked them into the water. Apparently, that's supposed to protect their souls so they can't get changed.'

'Woah. That sounds like some proper pagan shit,' Chris said, 'that's so cool.'

'Did you get dunked?' Claud asked, 'Is that why your hair looks so wild all the time, because it's full of pond water?' She wrapped one of my curls around her thumb and bounced it. I heard Chris sigh, ever so quietly, but I couldn't look away from Claud, her grin. I felt myself tip my head towards her, so she could carry on playing with my hair.

'Ha. No, it used to really piss my gran off. I think that's part of why she never liked me, because my mum didn't half drown me when I was a baby. It's crazy.'

'Mad.' Claud said. She was still playing with my curls. 'What's the difference with a myling anyway? I'm surprised I haven't heard that one from my mum.'

'So, a changeling's like a swap, right? Or a trade. But a myling is something else. It latches onto a person and it feeds from them and uses them to build its strength so it can eventually go home.'

'Like a cuckoo?' Chris asked. I pulled my eyes from Claud and nodded. He smiled, grateful to be back in the conversation.

'Like Mermaid,' Claud said.

'Yeah, right. I'm a spirit child sent to feed off you all, you got me.'

Claud clapped her hands together, 'Fun!'

'The way my mum tells it, the mylings start off really tiny, and they climb up onto your back. The more they eat, the bigger they get. And the bigger they get, the more human they seem. So, then you start to think that you've got this child on your back, and suddenly you're a parent, and you'll do whatever you can to keep this myling happy. And it gets really big, but the parent doesn't want to let it go, so they do things like tie material around their waist to attach they myling to them,'

'A papoose!'

'Exactly. A papoose. Or chains. Basically, whatever they can do to attach the myling to them. But then when it's big, the myling wants to go home – that's why it's different to a changeling, because a myling takes what it needs and then it has to go back to its own kind – but, of course, the parent won't let go of it at this stage.'

'So, what happens?' Chris asked. Both of them looked at me intently.

'Well. If the myling can't get free, it keeps feeding from the parent, or the host, way beyond what it needs or desires. It gets so large that it towers above the body of the fully grown adult, its stomach spilling over the forehead of whoever carries it. Its weight will cause the new parent's spine to collapse. And its legs will drag on the floor, scorching the earth they touch. The new parents, even though they're suffering, will love the myling too much to do anything about it. Their slow suffocation will feel like a choice, right up until the myling becomes so big that it consumes the new parent entirely, until there's nothing left of the person, but a pool of skin spread across the floor.'

Silence. I felt a blush prickle on the back of my neck. My mother used to tell me the myling story as if it were something funny.

Finally, Chris spoke. 'Holy fuck. Your mum told you that?'

'That's so much better than a changeling,' Claud said.

'It's wild,' Chris agreed.

'Is it true then?' Claud asked.

'How do you mean?'

'Are you going to feast on us until we're all used up?'

iv.

My mother had named me for joy, just as her mother had named her. Perhaps one of the greatest tragedies of my life is the misplaced hope that comes with a name like that.

She had not often been a joyful woman, although I was told that she had always wished for me, and only ever for me. I was the reason for her living, the root of all her happiness, though that came fleetingly. Attempting to keep her happy took up the majority of my days. When we lived alone in the cottage, she was a wisp, and I would not dare move my eyes from her, having convinced myself that if blinked, she would slip through the floorboards, down to where all things nice were kept.

My mother was not like the other adults I knew. There were women in the village who were strong, shoulders square and brows domineering. My aunt was one such woman. Ysella was large. She had arms that could reach into a cow and pull life out, the calf slick and wet against her gloved hand. Hers was a body that could work the land, seemingly uninterested in desire, it was built to harvest and shear and provide.

My mother was made of a different material. Fragile, but not brittle. Her personality was changeable, bendy. She could be worked in your hands and turned into any shape you required.

I was sat in my room trying to read an old book of fairy tales that had belonged to my aunt, when she popped her head around the door.

'Sorry about earlier. It's been a bit . . . stressful here. I wasn't sure now was the best time for you to come down.'

I put the book down. I'd been reading something garish about a woman stuffed and roasted by a group of sprites. 'Why? Has something happened?'

'Oh, a few things. Your mam, for one. I've been trying to help her, but you know what it's like. She gets overstimulated by change; it throws her off. She was so excited for you to come down; she's been all over the shop with her meds.'

'Has she been taking them?'

'Oh, sure, sure. I make sure she does but it's not always at the right time. You know how she gets. Easily distracted, that one.'

I always thought I'd return home to look after my mother. Once I was aware of her illness – if that's what it was – the clock began to tick. I tried to make the most of my teenage years, fitting in as much life as I could, all the while aware that one day I would be called on to care for her.

That was the worry that had been at the back of my mind over the past few years. Each time I took an exam, went to a party, or spent my money on something foolish, I would remind myself that this could not last – there is no freedom in caring.

I have a job that I must do, and whether that job begins at twenty-five, thirty-three or forty-two years old, or even next year, no one can tell me. But I have always known it's coming.

I imagined myself carefully labelling my mother's medication, finding inventive ways to hide it in her food, like a dog, so the taste does not turn her stomach. I could track her moods, encourage her when she dressed herself, bathed herself, ate well.

One day, her mind would be so far gone, her medication so strong that she would hardly recognise me as her daughter. She would be the child and I would be the keeper; we could rebuild. I would work away my sins in that selfless, flattering way that people thought highly of, and then I would once again be free – free, and this time, redeemed.

This is the story I would tell myself, in the city, whenever I thought of home. There were many things I didn't want to revisit in Cornwall, but I had at least thought that any future suffering would come with a level of retribution; a chance to cast off the events of before. I was waiting for the day that I could egg wash over my teen years until they were murky and covered and I could no longer remember them, distracted instead by the crispness of my good deeds.

That afternoon, I watched as Ysella drove a nail through the head of a dead yellow eel, its nervous system bucking at the imposition. She ran a knife just below the nail so she could unsheathe the skin. It was a slow process, using pliers to hook under the first curl of loosened skin, which she then tugged and pulled at, degloving the thing until what was left on the counter looked like little more than an extra-large drowned worm. I went upstairs to read, my mind full of the violence of that body, ballooning on the counter-top, naked. I wanted to know what happened to the tunnel of skin left on the side.

They didn't bin it – I checked the rubbish that evening. None of the meat was eaten, either. It wasn't smoked or frozen or dried. Nor was it salted, oven-baked or stuffed. There was no frying with dill or salt or jellying. After everyone went to bed, I snuck downstairs to the empty kitchen. I searched in every drawer, cupboard and receptacle, every hole and hiding place, and found no trace of skin from the eels that Ysella had stripped and mashed each day.

It could've been festering in a jar somewhere, or pickled in strips, perhaps, but there was no way to follow the smell, because the whole house was full of it – meat and fish and blood and mud in one go. It reminded me of the smell of death on the moors – the stench would fill your lungs – but it was untraceable. You knew that somewhere, a forgotten sheep hung from a piece of barbed wire, but no matter how much you searched, you couldn't find it and end the suffering. You just had to live with the smell until something came to devour it.

I got no clear answer from Ysella that day, on the hunt or the memorial. I had little choice but to accept what she said – Joan was nosey and untrustworthy, and my mother was too unstable to tell the truth. It had only been two days though. I had time. By dinner, my mother seemed calmer. When I told her I would be going to see Chris the next day, she seemed pleased for me.

'Such a lovely boy, that one. I'm so glad you stayed friends, after what happened.'

FOLKLORE

1972. Summer comes once again, and the stranger father flays the hedge. The machine rumbles and struts and strips the hedge of all the life it held within.

He loses the mullein moth, the cardinal beetle, the froghopper nymph, the hoverfly, the short-tailed vole, the pigmy shrew, the yellow-hammers, corn buntings, the finches. He loses the bumblebees, the hedge-browns and the stonechats. He loses the white dead-nettle, the red campion, the bittersweet and the field pansy.

He loses Her. Or rather, loosens . . .

v.

We went to the village fetes every year until we moved back to Trewarnen, whether we were wanted or not.

'I've got it this year, Sprig, just you see!' Mum had said, dragging me out of the house at 9 a.m. on May Day morning. I was seven then, and it was the first time we were involved with the fete rather than being bystanders. This, my mother told me, was the clinching point; being part of it meant you stuck like glue, no one could turn and ignore you then.

The best thing about being involved, to me, was that Mum would be busy all morning. Whilst she helped out at the Sunday school next to the church, serving rock buns and watery cups of tea, I could play on my own. Once Mum's table was set up, she placed a handful of fifty-pence pieces into my palm and off I ran, tight-fisted, to the green.

I bought myself a pork pie from the snack stall set up outside the pub, sitting on a rock to pull it apart. I only ate the pastry, running my thumbnail across the inside to scrape off the jelly so I wasn't poisoned. I waited at the swings for a while, hopping from sandal to sandal, but no one got off. The swings were full of children I'd never seen before being pushed by grey-haired adults I recognised. The grandchildren of the villagers, visiting for the day, getting smiles from the old ladies who chased me out of their gardens spitting when I'd lost my ball.

There was one boy there that day who wanted to play with me – Chris. Chris was from Preston, but he'd moved to the village when he was six. He was an outsider, just like I was. I had grown up apart from the village, out of sight in Trewarnen; Chris had grown up outside of Cornwall altogether. He had been accepted more easily than me though, as his mum was married to a lifer called Ken. The kids in the village claimed Ken himself had lived in the village for 100 years. Chris told me that was the reason, when I asked how come everyone spoke to him really nice when none of the grown-ups wanted to speak to me. His voice had a soft northern burr, so different to the hitching Cornish accent I was used to.

Chris was part of a family. Mum and me were not. He was a sickly kid, frail and slow, his skin always kind of shiny. Even the freckles that scattered across his nose looked like a rash, the sign of some illness spreading. The villagers thought him precious.

That day at the fete, Chris was tired. He'd dragged his feet past the bric-a-brac stalls, ignoring the broken Crazy Daisy sprinkler, the possessed Punch and Judy dolls, the stall full of tiny cat figurines. He barely even glanced at the Beanie Babies I pointed out – Schweetheart the Orangutan, Swirly the Snail, even the deep purple Princess Diana bear – even though I told him we could pool our money together and buy the Teenie Babies – Inch the Wiggly Worm *and* Zip the Black and White Cat – that came free with Happy Meals. The nearest McDonald's to us was twenty miles away, so this was our chance! We could get the good stuff. Chris just rolled his eyes and coughed spittle all over the table.

We watched the dog show next, but Chris's allergies meant he sneezed every time the winner was announced, so I didn't hear who won Best in Show, or Cutest Puppy. Eventually, I decided the only thing for it was a bit of physicality. Whenever I was grumpy, Mum would call me a moody bint and tell me to shake it out. That's what Chris needed to do, shake it out. Without giving him chance to complain, I grabbed his milky shoulders and shook with all my might. His eyes went really wide, and his head snapped back and forth, bobbing like a daffodil in high winds. For a second, I thought he might cry, and I quickly tried to think of an excuse to give the nearest adult. Instead, he grinned, all gums, and asked me if I wanted to race.

We spent the next hour rolling down the bank at the edge of the green. Forward rolls were the best, but they were scary, because we knew we could snap in half if we rolled onto the road. Sausage rolls were less fun but faster. With our arms and legs pointed straight out, we could throw ourselves down the hill over and over, speeding up each time. Our bare skin was stained green from the grass, and I collected a crown of tiny twigs in my hair as we went. We scrambled back up the hill, both of us slightly out of breath. Chris lay down and asked me if I'd give him a push so he could go superfast.

I took a deep breath and shoved him, one hand between his shoulder blades, the other on his lower back. I blew out my cheeks as he tumbled away from me, rolling down the hill like a barrel of rocks. Somewhere in the background, there was a shout and the ring of a bell, followed by the screech of an accordion: the Morris Men were starting their dance. I turned around to see where they were, forgetting about Chris as he rolled down the hill, elbows and knees bouncing. There was another shout then, but all the Morris Men were dancing, spinning in circles with bells on their feet, like they were stamping on broken glass. I turned around and saw Chris, part way down the hill, his leg at a funny angle.

I stood at the top of the hill, torn between the bang-crash song of the Morris Men and the bend of Chris's leg. He was sat up, one leg in front of him, the other out to the side. Something was stuck out of the back of it. He looked at me, looked down at his leg and then threw up. Vomit dribbled down his T-shirt and he started to scream, louder than I'd heard anyone scream. His screams were so loud that I couldn't hear the Morris Men anymore, and I wanted him to shut up because he was ruining the show, and his leg couldn't be that bad. It just needed to snap back.

My mother taught me that screaming is never the answer. She told me that she didn't even scream whilst giving birth, that I was a miracle, that other babies scream and scream, and I never did, because I was good. I wanted Chris to be good, because it was May

Day and I had lots of fifty-pence pieces in my pocket and Mum was selling rock cakes, and we were finally included in something, and that meant we could be included in more things, like birthday parties. And I didn't want Chris to ruin it, just like he ruined the Beanie Baby stall.

I ran over to him as he was screaming and clamped my hand across his jaw, my fingers sliding in the greasy sick around his mouth as I held it shut. His thin little fingers scrambled against my left hand as I used my right to grab his leg and twist it towards me. If I could just straighten it, he would shut up and we could still play. I tried to move it, but I wasn't strong enough, he just twitched underneath my touch like the spiders my mum caught in jars. I moved to the back of his leg, where a branch grew out of the back of his knee. When I touched it, his shorts darkened, piss and blood, and I felt the warm flush of his vomit paint my palm.

I took my hand from his mouth and wiped it on the grass; the next step would take all my strength. I put both hands on the stick and pulled. It snapped in half, and he made a noise like an already dead thing. Before I could get the rest, I was pushed out of the way by a big arm. His dad had seen him on the ground and run over. He scooped him up, like Superman, and ran out into the road, shouting, 'Someone call an ambulance!' The Morris Men stopped dancing then, and everyone turned to look at Chris, curled up in his dad's arms like a dormouse, and me, stood on the bank alone.

I didn't get to take any of the Beanie Babies home that day, but I did keep the tip of the stick, which I hid in my pocket. Years later, when I was old enough to tell the story my way, I gave Claud the stick. She liked to keep little pieces of me that way.

vi.

That night, I was left home alone in Trewarnen. I'd expected them to want to spend as much time in my company as possible, but there had been complaints recently, issues out on the moor, and the locals were meeting in the village to discuss it all, or so Ysella said. Animals were turning up dead; Mrs Rowe was frightening the emmets with her stories of curses.

When they left, I stayed in my room, still leafing through Ysella's weird book of fairy tales. The cold had set in completely. It was the type that needles at the tips of toes and scratches collarbones, and it made me think of Claud.

Her dad's annex was all draughty windows and leaking taps. He moved there after Claud's mother left, taking what he could afford – an offer of pity from an old friend – without considering where Claud would go. When she was young and small enough, she would sleep on a sofa, her father on the single bed, both in the same room. Nothing in the annex ever worked as it should, and as a result Claud walked around with a look of mildew about her, with stonewashed skin and hair that always felt slightly damp to the touch. Once she was old enough to need her own room, her dad pulled various strings until a rotting two-berth caravan appeared on the patch of scrub outside the annex, and Claud moved in.

With her dad kept at a distance by the fibreglass shell, me and Claud spent as much time as possible falling into each other in that caravan. We would sit on her bed, which she never put away, warmed on cheap beers and amber leaf. She would cup her hands around her mouth and blow on the parts of my skin that couldn't get warm – the back of my arm, an ankle, my shoulder. A massage made of warm air, tangy with smoke.

I brought the inside of my elbow up to my mouth now and blew, the hot air passing from my skin to my lips and back, until my arm was sticky. I tried to pull myself out of the painful memory – to focus instead on the details. Mouth. I spoke it out loud. Mouth. Her mouth. Snaggle tooth, chapped lip, menthol cigarettes with a Juicy Fruit chaser. Staying open when she slept. Smelling like kitten milk in the mornings. The time she accidentally spat on my school shirt when she was laughing. The time I bit her and her lip tasted like a two-pence piece.

This was not how I had pictured grief. In the early days of mourning, I often felt like I had been turned inside out by Claud's death. Inhabiting a body felt wrong. I couldn't sit, I couldn't dress, I couldn't eat – all of these things felt like the actions of someone protected by skin, someone who wasn't raw, as I was. Existence belonged to those who were fully cooked. Even the breeze felt painful, invasive. As the weeks went on and I missed her funeral, ignored Chris's calls, and spent hours at a time scrolling through her memorialised Facebook account, my hypersensitivity dulled. The pain that I had felt at everything became a simple numbing. I was no longer inside out; instead I was wrapped in layer after layer of gauze, seeing nothing, reaching no one.

No part of me wanted to live without Claud, but I was never sure if she had expected me to follow. I'd always followed her lead. No matter how often she pulled away, she knew I would be waiting, a battered bouquet of Asda carnations in one hand. She pushed me, sometimes. Tried to see how far over the edge she could take me before I'd give up. I never did. I still feel sick to the soles of my feet when I think of how hungry I had been for her.

Her memorial would give me the chance to apologise to her for the fact that I let her go alone. I wasn't there when she first tried, I wasn't there when it was all over, and I didn't follow her into the breach. She had left me, and although I was waiting, I knew she couldn't come back. Each time the memorial was delayed, I knew I was being pushed further from Claud. She would've wanted to see me cry. She would've needed me to be ruined by her death. And I was, I was. The sickness in my feet moved to my ribs when I realised, she'd never see that now. I couldn't show her anything again, sat in my room at Trewarnen.

In the silence of the empty house, without my mother wittering or the steady thud of Ysella's hammer and nail preparing the eels, I could once again feel the notebook calling me. I tried to keep my mind busy, but whenever it cleared, thoughts of the notebook rose. It was becoming harder to resist.

A cold wind found its way in, even though the curtains were drawn and the windows closed in my room. I lit a few stubby candles and placed them beside the bed, hoping their tiny flames would get notions and warm me like a proper fire.

The pages that Ysella had written were unreadable, her hand-writing hurried. Whole letters were missing from words, worn away by smudging fingers. The ink changed throughout: some sections written in a biro so old that the words had faded on the page like names on gravestones. I found more torn pages, some ripped.

And then there were three pages of text, starting with the one where she had written *Claud* and *Pedri* in the margin. Looking at it again, I could see that Ysella had written out a story entitled 'The Baker and the Bread'. A ripped page showed the bottom half of a crudely drawn illustration: bare feet, vertical as if the owner of the feet was lying down, and nearby, a child, holding a loaf of bread. The bread was the most detailed part of the drawing, with deep scores across the top of it. Tiny dots of crumbs surrounded the baby and the disembodied feet on the page like a trail of insects, hungry.

The drawing was the only introduction the story had.

The Baker and the Bread

Undated – possibly 1840s, recorded much later

In the earliest hours of the morning, a small parcel of dough is placed upon the front step of the local bakery. The shop is closed, the lights and ovens are off, the bakers themselves are mostly still asleep. Except for one: the young man who wakes early each day to place a loaf on the step.

In the last hours of the night, a young woman paces the rooms of her house, child in arms. She takes the baby to her breast, tries to feed, nothing comes. The child's hunger is only matched by her own, an empty stomach that leads to dried-out milk. When she cannot feed the baby, she leaves home and walks. In the streets, she dodges the jellied limbs of drunks, skirts around stained alleyways. She walks until she finds it – the heel of bread, the misshapen roll. There is always something waiting for her, a small kindness, an honest gift. She's grateful, but it is never enough.

The baker tries. He has seen the woman; the dry-suckling. You cannot feed on empty. He wants to line his apron pockets with plump risen scones, thick-crusted baguettes, bronze-fluffed loaves. He wants to fill the woman with yeast and flour and pumpkin seeds. To make her strong and hearty and bursting. To let her overflow.

The baker can only steal the things that people don't want. He can only offer the burnt ends, the hollowed buns, the hardened cakes. The woman eats what she is given with gratitude, feeds her baby with what she gains, but like the baker, she longs for the golden loaves.

In the earliest hours of the morning, the baker and the woman are watched. Each morning, for weeks, they are watched.

The woman is walking home, child swaddled to her chest, gnawing on her piece of burnt bread, when an arm extends from an alleyway.

Clothed in black, a figure with an offer: a way to stop the baby's hunger. The woman accepts, pulls the last of her coins from her pockets quickly and hands them to the figure. And so, the Pedri makes a trade.

There it was. Pedri, with a capital P. A name then. A creature, or a person, rather than an object. But this was just a story. An old scrap of nothing, a tale of hunger and bread. How was any of this relevant to today? Joan had responded so angrily when I asked her about it, I'd thought it meant something important, or that it could be a code. Ysella's notes stopped abruptly at the tear. The next page nothing but a series of dates, all crossed out. I turned back over the pages again, skim reading as I went, until I found a page photocopied from another book that Ysella had glued in.

Here, the story continued. The Pedri took the coins, and the next morning the woman awoke to a baby that still couldn't feed, but no longer cried with hunger. Presuming the child to be happy and full, she stopped walking the streets at night, no longer picking up the baker's scraps. Desperate for her to return to the bakery, the young baker became reckless, stealing better and better loaves and leaving his plumpest offerings out each night. But the woman stayed inside, smitten with her quiet baby, unaware that she herself was now starving. This went on, until the baker was punished for stealing, ending up homeless and destitute. At the end of the story, the woman died, having forgotten to feed herself now that her body wasn't required to keep her child alive. I ran my eyes across the text once more, trying to pull some meaning together and coming up blind. Was it about gratitude? Should the woman have been happy with what she was offered by the baker, and not accepted more? Was the baker too selfish in his apparent selflessness? Should he have just accepted she was gone, and not tried to tempt her back? Or was the moral to put yourself first, rather than sacrifice for others? I couldn't tell if it was a story about temptation, desperation, or both.

I felt hungry, the same way I did whenever I read true crime or caught news of a brutal event happening nearby – peeling the curtains back to see which of the neighbours are being rushed to hospital, slowing by a car crash to see if limbs have lost bodies. Since Claud's death, I had felt a pull towards this kind of information, graphic detail, feeding a need to be horrified. Staying up late in the city to watch documentaries about women without names who were beheaded, their bodies packed in suitcases, murdered by husbands and boyfriends and strangers. I had sought out stories of people who had suffered worse than her, an attempt to shock myself into feeling better about what had happened.

There was nothing scary in 'The Baker and the Bread', not really. It was too far-fetched to feel real, too close to a fable to ring true. But the mention of the Pedri, that was real. That was the thing that sparked the hunger in me.

The churn in my stomach was a drum of guilt and desire. I wanted to know more, and why. Part of me wanted to look away and forget, pretend I knew nothing of the Pedri, but I also wanted to eat it up. Rip out those pages and swallow them down so I could know what they knew.

FOLKLORE

On the moors, something moves outside of a farmhouse. In the shadows of evening, even the birds resting on the dry stone wall do not notice the black shroud that scrapes across the gravel.

She raises a hand to the peeling paint of the front door.

I was still in my bedroom when I heard a loud crash across the hall.

It's funny how instinctual and immediate fear can be when you're alone. Had I been in a house full of people in the city, I would've paid it no mind, or made a joke about someone trying to join the party through the window. In Trewarnen, my first thought was that someone had come to get me.

If Claud were alive, it's the type of thing she would do – sneak around to make me jump, anything to prove that I was more frightened than I let on. She could be stood out there on the drive, throwing rocks at the window, come to tell me I was depraved for wanting to read stories about rape and murder, waiting for me to pull her in from the dark night.

She had been softer than me, for a while at least. When we were together, she easily scared in the dark and was often in need of comforting. I would try my best, but when I wasn't there, my words weren't enough for her. I could feed for days on the memory of our time, but she was a much more tactile person than me. She wanted something from me, always. I think she had wanted to claim me, right from the beginning.

I first noticed when we were fifteen. It was lunchtime, and me and Claud were in our usual spot at the bottom of the field at school. In summer, everyone would sit out here during breaks, rolling their trousers up to their knees and taking off their ties, trying to sunbathe or flirt. There was a spot right at the bottom, where the slope of the field dipped suddenly, and no teachers could see you. We came down here to smoke, more for effect than anything else. I had just taken a drag from the cigarette we were sharing when Claud said, 'Someone told me today that you were bi.'

I coughed up smoke, Claud's words catching me on the inhale. It wasn't my classmates' assumption that got me, but the fact that Claud had believed them – she must've thought it was true, to bring it up. 'Why? Who?' I asked.

She decided to only answer one of the questions. 'You were staring at Sarah in art class.'

'You're not in my art class.' I passed her the cigarette.

'I know, someone else told me.'

'Oh.' It was all I could say. I wasn't going to deny it. What I'd meant to say was yes, I was staring at Sarah. I was staring at Sarah because you weren't there, Claud. Sarah was lovely. She had two long braids that she never took out, and she smiled whenever she saw me. She was always carting around these big fantasy books, brightly coloured with gold writing on the front, the pages dog-eared. They sounded awful – elves and swords and chosen ones – but the fact that she liked them made me feel hopeful. Hopeful that she liked things that were a little bit strange. Sometimes I thought she could have been my girlfriend if it wasn't for Claud.

'OK. So? Sarah's nice'

She rolled her eyes. 'Ugh. I can't think of anything worse than someone calling me nice.'

'What's wrong with nice?'

'Nice equals boring. You know that, Mermaid.'

'It does?' I didn't mind the sound of boring. 'Am I nice?' I asked.

'Ha. No.'

I watched her as she played with the cigarette. She'd bring it up to her lips, not inhaling, just holding it there. Posing, almost. I wondered who she thought was watching, or whether it was for me. Her curly hair was pulled up into a pineapple on the top of her head, and her jumper was tied around her waist. She'd recently started wearing makeup, thick black eyeliner and clumps of mascara, the same makeup she'd keep for the rest of the time I knew her. Something about the way she was stood – so casually – made her look like she knew everything. Beside her, with the sleeves of my jumper pulled down over my fingertips, my hair tucked behind my ears, I felt like a child. And, like a child, I was tense, unsure as to whether she was about to tell me off, disturbed by this new revelation about my sexuality. I decided to be brave.

'I don't think you're nice either,' I said.

'You don't?'

'No. I think you're something better than nice.' My voice wavered.

'What's that then?'

I took a deep breath. 'Fascinating. I think you're fascinating.'

A moment of silence, then:

She dropped the half-smoked cigarette on the floor without offering it back to me and, before I could react, reached over and took my hand. Something cracked inside of me. I looked at our hands, the way our fingers were linked together, the chipped nail varnish on her thumb. I didn't dare look at her face, not until she was stood in front of me. With her free hand, she lifted my chin up so I was facing her. I squeezed my eyes closed. I didn't want to break the spell. And then she kissed me. It was a hummingbird kiss, quick, flighty, insistent. I stayed completely still. I couldn't scare her away. And then, then, the best moment of my life – she laughed. A sound that was so full of joy, so self-confident that I could do nothing but cup my hands around her cheeks and kiss her deeply.

After that, nothing would stop her from grabbing me. We needed to be close to each other. The Christmas after our first kiss, I gave her a coat, a massive one that once belonged to my mother but had been draped over me whenever I fell asleep on the sofa since I was little. I told Claud it had kept me warm when the heating ran out, and she wrapped it around her body like it was fire.

It was black, long and silky, like a shroud, tightened at her waist with a belt. She had the bones to carry a coat like that, with her rounded cheeks and frightened animal eyes. Even though it had been mine, once Claud put the coat on, I no longer believed it was mine to touch. Sometimes I felt so sharp next to her, in that swaddling coat, that I was sure it would rip. No one at school knew that it had belonged to me, but each day that she wore it, I felt a sense of pride. She hadn't told anyone we were together, but by wearing it every day, I felt like she was telling me that I was hers, and she was mine.

Even when everything changed for us after that night on the moors, Claud kept the coat on. It became an extension of her too-small body. She was always losing things in the pockets, hung low like saddlebags, the lining old and rotten enough that it was full of holes. Every time she picked the coat up it jangled, lighters and coins and chewed-up biros tinkling against each other. When she was upset with me, I stitched a heart into the inside of her sleeve as an apology. She cut a piece of fabric from my favourite shirt and looped it through the buttonhole. I wrote her name in the collar and gave her every piece of treasure I found.

If Claud were alive, she would want to be the hero. She would assume my fear before I admitted it, saving me from the embarrassing admission that alone in Trewarnen, I was scared.

Throughout this trip home, I had been proving myself to be easily defeated. The women in my family had lived in this house for generations, and never had the land or the locals driven them out. Why should I be the first to feel unwelcome?

I scurried through the dark hallway into Ysella's room, feet never leaving the floor. Her window faced out onto the drive, and the moors beyond, so whatever had made the crash must've been outside after all. I flattened myself against the wall as best I could, cringing as one of my nails scratched against the scuzz of damp, careful not to let whoever was outside see I was home.

When I reached the window, prepared to recoil, I found nothing – I was on the second floor, after all – what had I expected, a creeping, crawling monster scaling the side of the building? When I pressed my forehead against the glass, I saw what must've caused the noise: a blackbird, prostrate on the ground below the window.

Death was frequent on the moors. Often, the creatures I would see were already well on the other side of life, old shadows of themselves – sheep skulls bleached by the sun, an adder spread across tarmac by a wheel. The acidity of the peat slows the decomposition, so you can walk past the same belly of bones season after season without change. The blackbird might have a similar fate. When Ysella came home and found it, she would scoop it up and throw it over the hedge, back onto the land, to feed the peat. Or she would drop it in the bin and leave it for the council to deal with.

I used my moment alone in Ysella's room to search the top of her desk. I had the thought that I might find something else relating to Claud, and the Pedri. The drawers were all locked, the top of the desk scattered with receipts and letters from the bank. I leafed through them idly until I found an envelope marked with my name in my mother's handwriting, bulging. Peering out the window once more to make sure I was truly alone, I ripped it open and greedily clawed at the contents.

What I found didn't make sense. I pulled it from the envelope and walked into the moonlight coming through the window, rubbed it between my finger and thumb, and held it against my cheek. I even bit down on it, placing the end between my teeth, prodding it with my tongue. There was a saltiness to it that I remembered as being a reaction to the bleach, a taste that wasn't there before, when it was virgin. From the envelope I had pulled strands of hair – my hair.

Before I shaved my head, my hair had been my one noticeable feature – long and frizzed. I left a trail of it everywhere I went. Shortly after I found out about Claud, I buzzed it all off. I didn't want to remember how she used to collect the hairs I shed, picking them from her pillow, leaving them piled on her desk so she could tell me how much of a mess I'd made.

One day we sat still for hours, Claud reading passages from *American Psycho* out loud to me as I plaited our hair together. Black and yellow spirals like the ropes we drew in art class. When I was done, we were conjoined, our hair lazily knotted at the end. We couldn't pull our heads apart, and I started to panic, until Claud reached out for the nail clippers on her bedside table, brandishing them like a weapon. I cringed and closed my eyes as she hacked at our hair, expecting her to be angry, but it took so long because the clippers were so small and she just kept calling me a fucking idiot, so soon enough we were both in hysterics.

Afterwards, our little knot of hair sat on the bed between us like a furball and Claud grabbed it, announcing that she was getting full custody of the fur baby. I pretended to gag, but I let her keep it, secretly glad that she wanted all parts of me, even the gross bits.

Although I knew there was nothing there, I couldn't help but run my fingers all over my scalp. I imagined strands plucked from me one by one by a ghostly hand, months or years ago, collected as they fell from my head onto the bathroom floor, caught on jumpers and scarves, or plucked from the nest of my hairbrush.

I held the hair, the last known piece of my hair, in my palm and watched as it kinked in and out of shape. I saw how it still held onto its curl, even after so long away from the root.

FOLKLORE

Her hunger began as revenge. A vindication for the time She was trapped, muzzled. That first winter, it coated the moor and all that moved on it until little was left.

We are used to the hunger now – the same starving neglect we have seen in animals. They are turned out to pasture upon us, only for our reserves to wither, choked by frost, hardened by the biting cold, called down by Her.

The creatures scratch at us, at the ground, mourning until they can no longer stand, until they fall. When the hunger has left them legless, She allows the thaw. We soften, squeeze moisture from the dankest reaches to provide them the relief of water, and a warm place to rest. We aid as we can, until the flesh gives way to bone.

We become one. We bring it down into our bosom, into that hole beneath the ground, the ones that echoes. She uses the husk to feed the other animals who are starving, so that more may last throughout the winter.

We do not feed often. We cannot spread and scourge like the ones we watch; the ones that live from us. The animals and the people, spreading their seeds fast and desperate. The pieces we leave above are our kindness. We let them succeed as we wait. So fleeting, their lives, so in need of joy. They know not what She brings.

We know their hunger. We have felt the slow melt of muscle as it rots down into our soil. We have grown, gently, strand by strand over crisp shards of bone, holding them close until those above can see them no more. We have swallowed skulls whole, deep into our wettest parts. Kept them shiny white with our peat. Pointless though, this nursing in marshes and river silt. In time the sun will parch us, the river will recede, and our treasures will be back upon the surface again.

DAY TRI

i.

When I woke the next morning, it was to voices, two I knew – one hoarse, one wispy – and then that of a stranger. Low, a voice that drags along the ground.

I pressed a palm to the wall closest to my bed, following with my ear, expecting the voice to be lurking under the drywall. Like a child waking in the night on Christmas eve, I thought I had caught the adults in the process of something magic.

An ear against the wall only blanketed the sound, and I moved away from it slowly, unsure but still unwilling to be caught out.

I moved back under the covers then, pointing the blanket above my head. Breathing sweet-stale against the sheet, I resisted the urge to pull away from the scent of myself. I heard a loud burr, as the low voice came again, this time answered by the familiar voices. Again, and again, this sequence came, a call and repeat.

Whilst the voices reverberated in the walls, I checked the envelope I had found the previous night again. I hoped that I had been confused, that it wasn't hair in the envelope after all, or that, if it was hair, it was from when I was a baby. But when I looked in the light of morning, I saw that it was adult hair, and that it was mine. It sat stiff and brittle in the envelope. My hair was natural up until the summer before I moved away, which means this hair, this stolen chunk, had been taken from me a year ago.

I knew some mothers kept mementos of their children: baby teeth, a shorn-off ponytail, the faded lace from a christening dress.

I had no such things left over from my early years – my mother had always seemed to relish my ageing, encouraging time to pass quicker so I could grow up, become her companion rather than her dependent. No matter how much I asked – and I did, often, when I was young – she would not dwell on the time I was a baby. The story she told me was simple: I came as a surprise and together we moved to the village, away from the scorn of her own mother.

There were things I understood: my grandmother, though never religious, was pious in her own beliefs, and particular about how children should be raised. Her husband, my grandfather, was little more than a shadow in my mother and aunt's childhood. When they were old enough to notice his absence, he left for good. There were rumours of other women in other villages, younger, more domesticated than Esolyn with her weather-beaten hands, less strict.

It seemed to me that men did not do well in the farmhouse. My own father was an unknown, though I suspect he may've been from upcountry. My grandmother had a saying: 'No good comes from over the Tamar.' She thought of it as rootless land, the people floating on the wind like seeds, dispersing themselves wherever they want. Esolyn said anyone born upcountry had no respect for heritage, she believed in the dissolution of the British rule over Cornish waters. The religion, the trade, the rules, everything the Cornish had inherited from the English tainted the wilderness she grew up in. Her favourite work by Daphne du Maurier was not *Jamaica Inn*, or *Rebecca*, or *Frenchman's Creek* – fiction was too frivolous for my grandmother. Instead, it was an article Du Maurier had written, calling for Cornish independence. Esolyn wanted them to hurry up and start blowing up bridges.

For my mother to hook up with a man from out of town, someone who wasn't Cornish, would've brought a great shame upon my grandmother. When they fell out after my birth, Esolyn must've felt vindicated in her opinions. My mother, unstable and flighty, was not the kind of woman you saw in a long-term relationship.

I understood why she would want to forget an absent father, a move from home, a splinter within the family. I knew that time must've caused her pain, but I never expected she would want to erase those early years of my life.

Around the time I became curious about my father, I started to search the house for baby photos, assuming that if I had been captured, then my father would have too. I had looked in the dust under my mother's bed, between the pages of her books, in the pockets of her thick woollen coats. When I found nothing, I asked my aunt. She told me there were no photos, although they'd tried. Ysella had taken plenty in the first few weeks of my life, but in the carnage of her falling out with Esolyn over my lack of baptism and uncertain heritage, my mother had never gotten the film developed.

'Lowen didn't want you studied by a stranger,' my aunt had said after I pushed for more of an explanation. She could never tell me why they had kept none of my baby teeth, or clothes, or curls. At those questions, she would simply shrug. Why would my mother decide to take a keepsake from me – in secret – when I was eighteen? And why would that keepsake end up in an envelope in my aunt's desk?

The rise and fall of voices continued. It sounded like a man. Trewarnen rarely suffered guests gladly. I knew my mother and aunt didn't often have visitors – people don't happen upon Trewarnen like they may houses in the village, and it usually wasn't worth anyone making the journey. I could only think that something must've happened when they were out last night, and now someone had come to the farmhouse to follow up or make arrangements to meet again. I needed to go and see who it was.

I attempted to secure the threads of sound that climbed the stairs, shuffling my feet along the floorboards in a way that would cause Ysella to clip my shoulder if she saw. Whatever the conversation downstairs was, it continued to evade me, until I was tricked by the house once again. I lifted my foot to step down onto the first step of the stairs, only to find it was gone. Instead of meeting the worn fabric runner that sat upon the first step, my foot hit the wooden floorboards of the hallway, sounding a quick percussion that announced my presence. Outed, I rushed downwards, chasing my own sound, eyes wide for any fleeting changes in the house's topography. Blissfully, the remaining stairs were as I remembered them, but as I rode my heels from the bottom step into the kitchen, I caught only the ending of the conversation before Ysella closed the front door.

'Who was here?' I asked, looking to Ysella and then my mother, who sat at the kitchen table, painfully upright.

'No one,' Ysella said.

I knew the shape of the house; I knew it well. I knew the number of steps it took to cross the hallway. I knew which stairs to avoid when sneaking out. I knew the height of the fireplace, the windowsills, the arches around the doors, my growing height marked next to each. I also knew my family. I knew how much it discomfited my mother to have guests in the home, how formal she would become, straight-backed and near silent, as if she were a child about to be told off in company. I knew Ysella. I knew that she did not lie, not unless she thought doing so would serve a greater good.

'I heard someone,' I tried again.

Ysella looked at my mother and rolled her eyes. 'You're probably just used to all those noises in the city.'

'What?'

'You've forgotten how quiet it is down here, and now you're hearing things.' Ysella said. Mum was nodding, but I could tell she was as lost as I was. Was Ysella trying to say what I'd heard was all in my head?

'There was a man at the door, I don't understand why that'd need to be a secret—'

'Get you! No one's keeping secrets from you Merryn, we've got better things to do with our time.' She paused, and then visibly softened. 'It's an old house, sound carries. You probably just heard me talking to the chickens.'

For the first time since I was a child, Trewarnen was starting to feel too big, unknowable. I was lost in it. It had felt like home to me once, but now it felt wrong. The rooms were rambling, out of control. Nothing fit as it should.

Ysella tasked me with helping to prepare a Sunday dinner, and then said she was off to buy some milk. I was suspicious that she was going to find the man who'd been here, but as I prepped the food, slowly washing the grains of soil from the vegetables, removing the dirt until they shined, I started to think she'd been right – I had been hearing things. Just last night I'd run into her room after hearing that bang, convincing myself in a moment of madness that the creature from my nightmares had untethered itself from my dreams and was roaming the house, only to find a bird, stunned from slamming into a window. The easiest explanation was likely the right one, and I wasn't sure why she'd be lying to me.

I started with beetroot, raw and pulled from the ground. I peeled first with a knife, then later with the sharp edges of my nails, pushing them into the flesh and watching how it burst up through the skin, moist and bruising. It didn't take long for the kitchen to be cloaked in the pressure of scent: roasted vegetables, the soil still dusting the countertops, and the sweet scent of lavender, bunches hung above each doorway, overpowering all else when the wind blew through the open front door. As I worked, I watched my mother with the same intensity I had as a child. Ysella might not have been lying about the voice I thought I heard this morning, but my mother was definitely hiding something – she had an envelope of my hair. It was weird, even for her.

I was stood with my hands in the sink, scraping dirt from some borage, thin white roots snapping under the force of the tap water, when I said, 'I found something last night'.

She spoke at the same time. 'Ysella and I argued this morning.'

I paused, waiting for her to go on, but she said nothing else.

'Is that the conversation I heard earlier? Was that the two of you?' I asked. She looked down at the table and shook her head. I pressed my thumbnail into the leaf of the borage, felt it tear clean through.

'We argued because I said we should go out to Dozmary, the three of us, but she didn't think that was a good idea.'

She hadn't answered my question, but I was too distracted by what she had said to focus on what she hadn't. 'Ysella hates Dozmary, she always told me not to go. Why would you want us to go there?'

She paused again, picking at her nail with a concerned look.

'Mum?' She didn't react. She clawed at her cuticle for another minute.

Eventually, she said, 'Sometimes things need returning.'

I turned back to the sink, tired. She clearly wasn't with it. I doubted her and Ysella had had a conversation at all; this was just the way she was when she got lost in her own head. Speaking in riddles.

'I'd like to return to the city,' I said, harsher than I needed to be. She didn't respond, clearly didn't care – or notice – and I continued to scrub at the borage until it was wilted and bruised. Ysella could go and buy a bag of romaine for all I cared. If she wanted greens, she could pick them up in a plastic wrap like everyone else did.

'I thought Dozmary would be best,' Mum said, her voice quiet and slow, 'because of today. We weren't sure if you remembered, you see.'

I felt her eyes on me as I turned the tap off, my hands shaking lightly. I'd forgotten. I'd come all this way and I'd forgotten. I pulled my phone out of my pocket, hands still wet, and struggled to unlock it. When I saw the date, I began to feel sick. She was right; I had forgotten the date. Saturday 8th.

Claud's birthday.

My head felt heavy with the sea foam of churning memories. My breath grasping, lungs corrupted. I struggled to catch up as air escaped me, the way it does whenever I am reminded of what happened next.

I see her, stood on the coast path. Opening her lungs to the biting North Atlantic wind.

The loping waves turn violent, rearing, spitting across the beach until they rip the dunes apart, pulling up the roots of the wild grass that grows there, revealing decades of abandoned rubbish beneath the sand.

She crouches down, puts out an arm to steady herself as she almost loses her balance – but it doesn't happen, not yet, not then.

She steadies herself, and then has a cigarette, just one, just quickly, before slowly untying her shoes. She places them on the bank, carefully tucking the laces beneath the tongues. Lining them up so they face out to sea. She unzips her jacket next, folds it neatly and drops her jeans on top in a pile. It's early, too early for the sun to be risen fully; the sky hangs low with the weight of the day. She stands in her underwear, chest concave, flesh stippled in the cold.

That was not the final time, but it was the first. The first time Claud gestured to the world and said, 'I'm finished'. She took herself off that ledge silently, but she was seen by two students, who called for help. Walking past her on the coast path, with their hiking bags piled high, she seemed no more unusual to them at first than the tomb stoners or surfers or wild swimmers they saw each day on their walk. A part of the landscape. They saw her begin to scale down the cliff face, lowering herself over the basalt onto a ledge. But when they called out to her – just a friendly hello – she didn't respond, just moved faster, before stepping off the edge, without checking to see where she'd land. She was lucky, then. Though to her it must've been something other than luck, to be pulled back when you've already departed. She shattered her ankle on impact with the water, but the rest of her stayed intact. When the coastguard grabbed her, she immediately told them that she was a wild swimmer. She did this often, always alone, and that day she had misjudged her landing. That was all.

Everyone believed her, for a while anyway. Until it was finally done, and there was no way to interpret it otherwise.

My mother's hand on my elbow, guiding me out into the back garden. The grass brittle beneath my feet. I started to come back to myself. I felt sun on my shoulders, and somewhere from the gables of the farmhouse, a mourning dove called out, low and pitiful. As my mother drummed her fingers against my arm, silent but present, the sea in my mind started to recede.

My GP diagnosed panic attacks: a symptom of an acute anxiety disorder brought on by delayed grieving. They only happened when I began to forget. And it was always the sea, always the first time she tried that haunted me. The ending had felt inevitable, but the beginning, the cry for help, was something I could've noticed.

I knew I lost my breath when she did. Her ghost was buried somewhere deep within my chest, gulping my air down to remind me. My words the stones stitched into the lining of her coat. The sharp little accusations holding her down. It was my fault that she was gone. My self-importance. My self-indulgent suffering. The time I had spent in my head convincing myself that I was a victim, that I deserved more than the happiness I had. My selfish need, my desire to be someone openly loved.

FOLKLORE

She was never particularly benevolent, though it was useful for other people to think Her so. A game of whispers, the stories about Her changed with each telling, until Her trades seemed kind and Her punishments just.

She had just one aim: life. Life, and a little bit of force when things did not go Her way.

It was man who changed the narrative, assigned morality to Her actions, made Her a figure to be bargained with.

She is simpler than that, older than that, harsher than that. She gives only so that She can take back.

iii.

That first time Claud tried, I was in the city, in a club.

I had left Cornwall behind, and had begun to feel the distance keenly. Manchester is a city of brick and height. The office blocks hide the horizon, and I missed the uninterrupted views of the moor. At first, I thought Manchester was a city without lungs – the student houses around me seemed anaemic, all paved yards with only the odd tree. Oftentimes, I took myself for walks into the city on the nights when I was lonely, hungry for the touch of land. I found myself drawn to a park dotted with trees, sturdier than the ones that struggled to grow on the estate. I went to the park with headphones on, blocking out the reality of the city. My intention was always to walk, simply that. And yet each time I took myself to the park, I found myself sat in a copse of trees. It was only when I had dirt in my hands that I started to feel at home. Soon, I began to take a scoop away with me each time I left the park, a pinch in a pocket here, a thimble dropped in my bag. Back in my room, I piled it in the drawer of my bedside table. During the long hours of the afternoon where I had nothing to do, I would sit by the window and watch cranes building – always, more building – as I rolled the dirt in my palms.

For all that I felt the pull of Cornwall, Manchester had given me the key to something else – a community I hadn't had before. I had had enough of hiding behind Claud's discomfort, her secretiveness. I wanted to be seen. The silent nods, from women in boots like mine, with cropped hair like mine. The fleeting looks of recognition from the girls who danced down the street arm in arm, matching blonde hair and dresses, pretending like they're sisters. The women saw me.

The club was small, barely more than one room. All dancefloor, sniffing and touch. In the dark, I felt sure of myself in a new way. I was in uniform: heavy black Doc Martens, purple trousers. My top was vintage leather and cropped, bought off the cute girl with the eyebrow piercing and blue hair in the market. My cheekbones were cut with glitter. That night, I left my breasts behind. Wrapped in a binder that smoothed, the slick lines of my hip bones showing, my breasts bound. When no one was looking, I pulled an ice cube from my glass, rushed it across my stomach like I did that first heatwave.

In the bar, soft hands with long fingers, artist's fingers, slipped around my waist. They belong to strong arms and a hushed voice that whispered, 'You make such a pretty boy'.

All around me pretty boys danced and touched each other. If they touched me, I could see how easy it would be to remove myself and step into them. A pretty boy. But I wasn't that. Not a pretty boy, and not Claud's secret girlfriend either. I felt like a creature.

At the bar, a woman – older, almost my mother's age – used her eyes to take in each part of me, and I stopped twirling. I moved slower, for an audience that appreciated it. The hands of the pretty boys swayed me, and I watched the woman watching me, and I knew that if I tried to speak no sound would come out. My voice had been stolen, my mouth parched. Just like the sloe berry from my childhood, the woman had drunk me down and I was nothing but thirst.

In the bathroom, tinny speakers played Meatloaf, and I locked myself into the unisex cubicle, ignoring the four feet in the next stall. I didn't cut lines on top of the stained toilet cistern; I couldn't bring myself to put my face so close to it. Instead, I pressed my back against the door and reached into the pocket of my trousers, where a small pile of dirt sat. I scooped a bump with my fingernail and held it in front of my face. I took a moment, counted my blessings, before bringing it to my nose – God bless God bless God bless – then I breathed in and let it drip down my throat.

The rusty fizz dripped down, and I fought the urge to spit it out. As a child, my mother would spoon feed me raw eggs for infections. She would crack them in her fist, and say 'Just keep it down, Sprig, it'll be worth it'.

I thought of my mother's words and clamped my jaw shut.

It was hours after, back in my shared house, when the comedown began to drain the serotonin from my body, that I heard about Claud. My aunt texted me: Claud has had an accident, she's injured, but she's fine. At that time, I knew no details, but I knew Claud. I knew what that would mean.

I unbuttoned the closures on my duvet cover and climbed inside before buttoning it back up. Outside of the duvet, the sky was brightening. I thought of Claud, injured but fine.

I thought of the first time she had told me she loved me. I was sixteen, she was seventeen. We'd been to a party where I knew no one and Claud knew everyone, which was the balance of power we often danced across. I knew I was only in the room because of her, and so I did whatever she asked of me, and took whatever she told me to. Everything tasted like salt and our throats burnt with the need for something non-alcoholic.

The morning after, we hid under the covers in the caravan, me kicking my legs in the air to pitch them as a tent, her counting the freckles on my stomach. She kept losing count, starting again, and laughing to herself as I shimmied beneath her fingers. There were only five, but we were in the stage where everything about the other was insurmountable – there was an impossible glory in being together, slightly high yet still so fresh. She said she loved me then, her breath clouding in the cold air. I opened my mouth and caught it, swallowing it down whole. The morning light was streaming in through the window, turning the off-white bed cover into an orange cloud above our heads.

And then I let myself think, yes, this is what I deserve.

Claud tried to end everything on the same evening that I was out, enjoying my freedom away from her, looking at other women. I had felt like a conduit for a tragedy once before then. At Trewarnen, when my grandmother was still alive, and I was living with my mother in the village.

My grandmother hadn't liked a lot of things. I was one of them. Generally, Esolyn was of the opinion that children were both too short and too stupid to be of use, and whenever me and my mother visited the family home, she would want me out of sight.

Trewarnen had been a working farm once. Back then, there were horses and cattle in the stables, just a handful of each, enough to provide milk to some houses in the next village over. The cattle all died after an outbreak of mad cow disease when I was too young to understand, and when my grandmother was old enough to know better. She thought it was my fault, although I was only seven. She didn't see me again after that, claiming I was bad luck. She died a year later.

It was infected bone meal in their feed. They should've been on a strict herbivore diet for years, ever since the earlier outbreak in the Eighties, but they were Esolyn's cows, and much like with her daughters, she followed her own rules when it came to their treatment. She only found out what it was after one died and was tested, and then she was ordered to slaughter the rest. They were taken to the quarry in Liskeard and burned. They had been dairy cows, and as a child I thought of them as muscled, strange, over-grown puppies, who knocked their heads against my shoulder for food.

They ran out of luck on a June day that lasted far too long. We were visiting Trewarnen for the day, and I'd already exhausted all areas of entertainment available within the farmhouse. I was sat beneath the kitchen table, using my claws to peel back layers of wood from the leg. All around me were knees and feet, and if I craned my neck upwards, the sky was only wood. I was a tiger in a wooden cage from an old-timey circus.

I had decided that I would scratch and roar until the ringmaster let me out, and then I would jump through hoops – maybe even hoops on fire – like all the best circus tigers.

Above my head, beyond my circus cage, I could hear my grandmother criticising my mother. The child was dirty; the child was slow. The child looked as though it could have lice. Her own children had never had lice. The child was disrespectful. The child was too loud. The child was too lazy. The child didn't look like a Tregellas. The child needed to learn its heritage. I continued to scratch at the table, wondering who the child was and if we would ever meet.

'Be careful or the tiger will eat you Mummy,' I said, playing both the tiger and the warner, because even though tigers were ferocious, some people didn't deserve to be eaten. Grandmother might deserve to be eaten, but luckily she had not stuck her head in the cage yet.

My mother gave me one of her special twinkly smiles, the kind that had become rarer than four-leaf clovers, reserved for special occasions.

'I need you to go find me treasure, Sprig. Something real rare,' she said.

I gave her back my own best twinkly smile then, all teeth. Even though one of them was missing, I knew it was still a good tiger smile, because my mother bopped me on the nose before she disappeared back above the cage.

It was late afternoon, that hazy light that makes everything look better than it is, and I went collecting treasures and dodging the wind. I tried to carry on being a tiger at first, but there were no rabbits for me to chase. I ran quickly towards a pigeon and roared, but the pigeon flew off much faster than I ran.

It wasn't much fun being a tiger without a circus, with no elephants or ringmasters or twisty gymnastic people, so I was a frontier woman. A pioneer. A farmhand from the seventeenth century. I practised my curtesy, tying my cardigan around my head as if it were a bonnet. I pulled the corners of my mouth down as far as they could go, perfecting my starving expression, walking hunched over with one hand on my lower back – a hungry Edwardian farmhand, desperate for her next meal. I decided I would go back to the house in character, beg for porridge – or maybe toast and peanut butter.

I heard the sickly sound when I was on my way back. At first, I thought it was the wind, calling to me through the cracks in the dry-stone wall, and I was all poised to run away from it, until I realised the sound was coming from the barn.

It sounded animal, but it wasn't like any noise I'd ever heard on the farm. I thought maybe it really was a tiger. As I got closer, it sounded garbled, desperate, which is not the kind of sound a tiger makes.

I edged my way to the stables quietly, convinced some great beast was hiding in there. A crouching giant maybe, its shoulders touching the ceiling, or a changeling baby, crying out for its pisky parents to take it home, its teeth a thousand sharpened nails in its mouth. When I peered over the stable door, sickle raised in defence, there was no magic waiting inside. No circus either.

The cow's eyes were pulled back, the whites showing as they flicked about nervously. Her coat was covered in sweat, but worst were her legs, which had crumbled beneath her. She was trying to pull herself up, but her hind legs stayed folded, dragging across the floor behind her. It looked like someone had taken the cow apart and reattached her wrong, her front half desperate to move and her back half completely dead. The other cows had huddled in the corner, giving her space as she pulled herself forward, nostrils flaring in fear.

I didn't dare go into the barn, so instead I stayed on guard for what felt like years and years. I stayed there by the stables until my mother came to find me, her steps light. She smiled, and for a moment I imagined everything was fine, that I would take my mother's hand and run with her to the field with the longest grass and show her how we could be jungle explorers or bushwhackers, or even tigers once again.

But before any of that could happen, the smile fell right off her face, and then she ran to the house and came back out with Ysella, who was running as well, and my grandmother, who was shouting for someone to ring a vet, even though she held the phone in her hand.

Me and my mother went straight home, and we didn't talk about the cow, or how my grandmother was crying. She didn't ask me why I didn't call for help.

We didn't talk about how my mother had grabbed my wrist so hard that it made my skin go pink and hurt. We didn't talk about how my grandmother's hair had whipped around her head in the wind, leaving her looking like Medusa.

The next time we visited the farmhouse, we only saw Ysella. We had to wash our shoes in a bucket of disinfectant before we crossed the threshold, and my mother washed my hands so much they cracked. I wasn't allowed to splash in the disinfectant even though I really wanted to. The barn was empty and had been cordoned off, but we didn't speak about that either. I wasn't sent out to hunt for treasures on my own that day, I wasn't allowed out at all. We left before my grandmother came back.

V.

When I had calmed down enough from my panic attack, my mother left me in the garden. She didn't speak, she just kissed me on the forehead and walked back inside. I stayed sat on the floor for a while. My hand reached for the only patch of colour on the ground, and pulled at a dandelion, the yellow flower radiating against my beetroot palm. I squeezed the flower, digging my nails into the flesh of it as I made a fist. The white milk and wetness from the burst petals coated my palm. I licked the sap from my hand, letting the acid sting of it burn against my gums as I turned my face to the sun. Once I felt appropriately bleached, I ducked back into the house, grabbed Ysella's notebook, and then walked over to the orchard.

There was no great inheritance or grand gesture left to my mother or aunt when Esolyn died, no money to keep the farm they were left with going. The one thing they inherited was a small orchard. Tucked in one of the back fields were thirty apple trees, planted haphazardly. Each year my aunt would harvest the apples and make crumbles, pies, tarts and jams, travelling to the towns nearby and selling them to the cafés. The apples had spirited names, like Egremont Russet, Pixie and Bramley's Seedling, none of which seemed real to me.

In spring, the trees fizz with white blossom, but by summer the branches will droop with the weight of the fruit, and Ysella will be crawling on her hands and knees, plucking the fallen fruit from the ground before the crows reach it.

She once told me all the things that can go wrong with apples. Brown rot, bitter pit, sawfly, apple scab. All these diseases and pests that rot the fruit from the inside out, devouring a harvest like a sweet-toothed plague. Brown rot is the worst – a disease where white pustules of fungus burst out of the skin, infecting the fruit on all the trees in one wash. It's the disease she was most terrified of, and she would check obsessively for blossom wilt each spring, a sign that the rot is waiting within the tree. She would circle the branches like a hawk, holding white flowers between her fingers, removing any that look even a little odd.

Whenever I found a rotten apple growing on one of Ysella's trees, I would take it and bury it at the far edge of the field, far enough away that she wouldn't smell the sweet turn of the fruit, and deep enough that it wouldn't be dug up by any animals.

I didn't want the whole tree to be cursed, but I always felt sorry for the fungus, the thing that invaded and tore everything down. After all, it was only trying to live, to reproduce. How was it supposed to know what it wrought?

I sat beneath one of the trees with Ysella's notebook. I still hadn't asked my mother about the hair. She had already seemed off, and I knew that my panic attack had drained her energy further. There was no way I would get a sensical answer from her that day. Besides, I was seeing Chris that evening, and I needed to try and calm myself down before then. I decided it was time to read the rest of Ysella's notebook.

'The Baker and the Bread' had told me nothing. There was no connection to Claud, beyond death, which was hardly a connection. Death was coming to all of us. There were only a few more pages in Ysella's book with any writing on, and they seemed to be part of some convoluted poem.

The Cunning Woman and You

You, purveyor of lost hope and long regrets, willing to fold yourself into the arms of any man to pull through a lonely night 'til morning.

You, seed between your legs, womb wrought and tender. A sprouting inside you, a tree that swells, a branch that grows up your throat, your mouth wide with fruit.

You, upon the streets, stomach stretched, birth cobbled, screaming.

You, a babi in your arms, hefty as a tree trunk, a smile full of pips.

You, lost and alone in the furze of your child.

You, shaken awake by a stranger bound in black cloth, who says: Have you any need? Are you alone with child?

You, not used to being asked. Wanting help, you make up a tale about the father, make him a thief and a liar, wanting to punish him for the shame you felt when he left.

You, giving two gold coins at the promise of help, payment for a trade you didn't know you'd made.

You, later, with a babi that has changed. The smile of pips gone rotten, peach fuzz burning to touch.

You, travelling to the next town over to look for the babi's father, meeting a cunning woman instead.

You, hearing the story second-hand; his neck wrung like poultry. Punishment for a crime, a thief and fraud.

You, no time to mourn, the babi is hungry and won't drink your milk, won't take your finger or the teat of the goat.

You, with the cunning woman, laying the babi out at night, alone in the scrub, the only way to fix it.

I stopped reading before I reached the end. There was more, but I felt uneasy. I didn't like the second-person tone, as if it was speaking directly to me. Once again, Ysella had dated it – 1843, Penzance – so I knew she was simply copying the words from some other source. It was dated at a similar time to 'The Baker and the Bread'. There was more, too, more links between them. I turned back through the notebook until I found 'The Baker and the Bread' again. There it was – at the end of the first page, a sentence underlined: *The Pedri makes a trade.* I flicked back to 'The Cunning Woman'. Halfway through the poem, similar language: *Payment for a trade you didn't know you'd made.*

Both women, both mothers, in the stories traded with the figure in black. Coins to stop the baby from being hungry, coins to pay for 'help'. Both women unhappy with what they had before the trade – one, hungry for more than burnt bread, the other, bitter and lying about her child's father.

After each trade the baby itself changed, was replaced. A changeling, like Claud's mother used to say. And the Pedri seemed to be there in both of these stories, swooping in just when the mothers were at their most vulnerable. Appearing to be helpful at first, but each time the trade seemed to be a trick. Make a trade with the Pedri, whatever it was, and suffer from it. Not just you, the person who makes the trade, but the people around you too. The father, the baker, and the children. All of them sacrificed, changed, by the actions of the Pedri – and the mother.

I didn't want to read any more. The images of the starving woman and the baby with a mouth full of pips were looping in my mind. I shut the book and tried to centre myself, pulling out of the world of stories and back to the present, peeling a piece of bark from the tree and placing it on my tongue.

Some trees are easy to peel. Silver birch flakes off in your hands without resistance, but with the apple trees you need to dig your nails in and tear. The flesh under the bark is wet and polished, like the inside of a coconut. People know trees for their sap, the glue they use to hold themselves together, but more often than you might imagine they drip with a thin cloudy-white milk, like the first drop from the cow before you really begin.

Ysella and my grandmother would talk of trees as houses.

Not for birds or creatures that we know to be real, but for the piskies. There were no rope swings or treehouses as I grew up – even climbing the trees would have to be done in a secretive manner, to avoid awakening the imagination of my aunt and Esolyn.

There was something sacred in the trees for them. When a tree is old, its roots lift themselves from the ground, hungry for fresh soil further away, ready to feed the tree in its old age. As the roots stretch, they become crooked, arching above the ground like fingers grappling at soil. The roots create holes, and that's where the piskies get in, in the spaces we don't notice. They slip into the cracks.

On equinoxes they would leave offerings to the fairies. In spring it was always the first brave flowers, cowslips and spring squill, picked and placed in tiny bouquets at the base of the trees, for a bountiful season and calm seas.

For the winter solstice, supplies would be left, things of use: tufts of animal fur, feathers, matches and coal for fires. Anything to keep them warm and happy over winter so in spring they will rise again in good spirits. My fingers would fit into the arches beneath proud roots, and I would pull and pull and pull until their bounty became mine, my cheeks soon full of the offerings my aunt had left.

When I was young, my mother would speak of darker spirits, local ones that lurked in stone circles on the moorland and caves by the sea. Things that would creep along roofs and break into houses through holes in the stone walls.

Ysella would shush her, holding a hand up and throwing her eyes towards me, claiming she didn't want me frightened of Tre-warnen, preferring to tell me stories of pretty creatures in petal dresses and flower garlands, anything to make me feel safe in this land.

My mother has a selective memory when it comes to her parenting. If I asked now, she would deny having ever taught me of anything malevolent. She would claim that they were all just standard fairy stories. But I could see my mother's beliefs clearly, in the way she left saucers of milk on the porch. Or how, in winter, she and Ysella would set tiny fires in the moorland around the farmhouse. How they both walked out each night to light lanterns in the fields and along the driveway, as if they were leading something home, how holy words would find their way under my pillow on quiet nights.

The story of the cunning woman read like something my mother would believe, but my aunt was more logical than that. Her connection to the past, to the Cornwall of before, was strictly historical, cultural. I had always believed that Ysella carried out these acts – the lanterns, the eels – as a form of remembrance, not because she thought they were actually doing something. This is what confused me. If the notebook had belonged to my mother, I would've brushed it off as another one of her fancies. Ysella's behaviour since I had been home pointed to her believing her own stories. And if she went the same way as my mother, I didn't know where I'd be.

vi.

Chris was more my friend than Claud's, which was partially why I hadn't seen him in so long. Although I had known him as a child, we moved in different circles for years.

Eventually, in year nine, he joined our friendship, a latecomer to our island. Me and Claud were already cemented in our duality, after two years of a very singular friendship. Our identities – mine, at least – were formed around the relationship we had with each other. Without Claud, I didn't know what I was. Chris came to us unbidden. After the leg incident, as it had come to be known, he went to a different primary school, and I didn't see him again until secondary. The time away had left him more outcast than ever. He returned to school having missed the years in which friendships are made, when bonds are forged. There was no space for him in the groups, the pairs, the trios. He had been by himself during his recovery, and that made people suspicious, scared of the person who'd spent most of his time alone. He didn't understand the jokes, the unspoken rules, didn't know exactly what to wear, or which teachers it was OK to respect, or which girls he was allowed to fancy. Worst of all, he didn't see himself the way everyone else did – he couldn't acknowledge that he was odd, the kid with the bone sticking out of his leg and the hysterical mother. He wasn't in on the joke, he wasn't humbled by his social standing. Instead, he was just nice.

One day, when Claud was off school sick, he sat next to me in History. Seeing that I was alone too, he started talking as if he had always been there, as if we were already part way through a conversation. The incident sat between us, but it was never discussed. It didn't need to be – it was the one connection Chris had to someone in school, and it knotted us together. And even though I had never given much attention to anyone other than Claud, I suppose I saw something in Chris too, because for the first time, I tried. I opened myself up to him, one question at a time. From then on, Chris was always around. Perhaps he knew I owed him. When Claud returned to school, he gave her the same treatment, greeting her like an old friend he'd spoken to every day for years. We didn't ask for his company, nor did we particularly cherish it at first. One day there was no Chris, then the next there was. Through no choice of our own, somehow Chris became one of us. At points, Chris became a sort of boyfriend to me. One I would revisit whenever Claud chose someone new.

At first, I thought it was shame that made her do this. She was unwilling to tell anyone we were together, and I thought it was because she was worried about how her family would react if she was with a girl. As we grew older, I began to realise that Claud wasn't ashamed of her sexuality – which was a beautiful, flowing thing, much like mine – she was ashamed of being happy. There had been other girls when we were in college. Girls she would grab and kiss at parties, performing for the chants of the boys. Girls I would bump into leaving her bedsit early on a Saturday morning, hair dishevelled, when I arrived to check she had something in her fridge for the weekend. I would spend the night at hers and find women's rings on the bedside table. She wasn't afraid to let people know what she was doing with women, but couldn't let anyone see her happy in a relationship. She wouldn't dare to be caught in love.

Chris was the boy who would stay home forever. The rest of us always knew it, but nobody ever brought it up. Each week he'd have a new big idea, a new place he would go to, a new way he would travel the world, and I'd smile wryly back at him because his eyes would be so eager, so pleading that I knew he needed to believe it more than he needed to do it. So, I'd say, 'Sure, you will.'

Of course, you'll study in London, of course you'll live in Berlin. Of course, you'll get into spoken word and open mic nights, and of course what you've got to say will resonate with people. Of course, when you take me to the station we'll keep in touch.

He drove me to the train station when I left. I went on the sleeper train, with a rolling suitcase and a backpack, and he stood on the platform, one hand in his pocket, the other in a wave.

I'd switched my phone on earlier that day to find a reply from Chris. 'See you at eight.'

I sat in the pub, mildly pissed off at the scenes of drunk joy that were unfolding around me. Bodies were pressed against each other to get to the bar, and I had to fold into myself just to squeeze past them without being touched when I arrived. Chris had chosen a corner table near the back, in a little alcove from which we could watch everyone else. He was pleased with our perch, but I longed to be out of the way, facing a wall so that no one would recognise me.

I needed an evening to be a different Merryn to the one in the farmhouse. I wanted to ask Chris about Claud as soon as he waved me over, but I didn't dare. I saw in his face that he wanted to ask me about Claud, but he didn't dare either.

Instead, we settled on a brief hug – him holding tighter than me – and quickly sat down. The jumper he was wearing smelled of cigarette smoke. I suppose I did too, but I like to think it was less obvious on me. He ripped apart a bar mat with dirty fingernails as he spoke.

'Feels like it's been forever, Mermaid.'

'You think? It's only been a year.'

'A year without calling, or texting, sure.'

'C'mon man, you know it's not been easy. Are we really going to go through this?'

'No, yeah, you're right. You're here!' he said, dragging his hand over his face and then smiling, properly this time. 'Let me get us a drink, beer? Beer. And then we can properly catch up. It's good to see you, seriously.'

He stood up, motioning to the bar, and squeezed his way around the bodies packed by our table. I felt my cheeks flush as people turned to look at me, all of them wondering why Chris was so happy to see some girl with her hair chopped to her temples. I pulled my hood over my head and leant back against the panelled wall. I certainly didn't look like their usual crowd, but I'd rather they thought I was weird than recognised me as a Tregellas.

Chris came back with two pint glasses held high, streams of beer running down his thumbs and wrists.

'Still haven't got the hang of that,' he said, putting one down in front of me and spilling it further. 'Jittery hands.'

I dabbed the puddle with my sleeve. 'Thanks.'

'How's it going with your mam and old aunt? I saw Ye buying milk earlier. She looked furious, like she had a personal vendetta against Big Dairy.'

'She does.'

Chris laughed, but then stopped. 'You all right?'

I looked up at him. I'd been staring at the fizzing bubbles of my pint, distracted by the mention of Ysella, thinking back to the strange scene in the kitchen this morning, 'Huh?'

'Are you back in the room?' He smiled, 'Your sleeve is soaked.'

I hadn't noticed how much beer I had soaked up. I lifted my arm and wrung out my sleeve with my other hand. 'Ah, had an argument this morning, you know how it is,' I said, screwing up my face. He nodded, though I knew he did not know how it was at all. Chris's mum was nothing but gentle. She doted on her only child and let him do whatever he wanted, which luckily for her, was never a lot.

'Speaking of mams, Selena says hi.'

'Ugh, don't call her Selena. It makes us sound old. Still her good gothic self?'

'Yup, she made me go to Stonehenge for her birthday in March.

Freezed my bollocks off whilst she shook a tambourine with some crusties who were protesting.'

'God, I think I'd rather be friends with your mother than you.'

'As if you'd give a shit about some old rocks.'

'Touché.'

'So,' Chris took a swig of his pint, 'are you going to tell me how you are?'

'I'm fine, Chris.'

'No, I mean seriously. When you didn't come down for the funeral, I was really worried—'

'Can we not?'

'Really? We're just going to act like—'

'Yeah, I think so.' I said. He looked hurt. 'I'm sorry, I just, I could really do with a normal evening. Obviously it completely ruined me, you know that.'

'Of course, it did,' he reached out and squeezed my wrist.

'How could it not? I wasn't sure I'd be able to come back at all. But I'm here now, aren't I? And I'm going to go to the memorial.'

'What memorial?'

'The memorial. Cl— her mum's arranging it. Didn't you know?' Chris was shaking his head, 'Shit. They must've . . . no, maybe they just didn't send invites out? I guess it's not the sort of thing you send in the post, is it? I'm sure you're invited.'

'I haven't heard anything about it.'

'Mum rang me up and told me. It must be a word-of-mouth thing. It'll just be a mistake if you've not heard yet. You've got to come; I don't think I'd be able to do it without you.'

'It wasn't exactly a party going to the funeral without you.' Chris said. The words felt like a knife, but his face looked so sad, I knew he didn't mean them cruelly. Sometimes I forgot how close Chris was to the two of us. It might've felt like me and Claud were in a bubble, but that just wasn't true.

He carried on; his tone softer. 'Sometimes I think I see her, you know, out on the moors.'

'You do?' I asked, thinking back to my walk when I first arrived, the long black coat I thought I saw in the distance.

'Yeah,' he said, fiddling with the beer mat in front of him, 'Selena said it's normal, to get visitations or whatever. You're supposed to feel like they're watching over you. She said it's a blessing, to feel so connected.'

'That sounds . . . nice' I suggested, feeling unsure as to whether it was at all.

'I'm not sure, it's . . .' Chris trailed off, sighed. I'd only seen him look so uncomfortable once before, on the day he drove me to the train station. 'It's not nice. It's not like Selena says. I'll be walking home, and it'll be out of the corner of my eye, and I'll think she's there, in that creepy coat – but it won't feel good. It doesn't feel like a blessing, it freaks me out. And I don't even know if it's her. But it has to be her, right?'

It took me a moment to recollect myself to respond to him. This wasn't like Chris at all, he didn't buy into anything even remotely spiritual. 'Why?' I asked.

'Because if it's not her, then who is it?'

The question unbalanced me; I had no answer for Chris. He was opening up to me, but I wasn't ready to do the same.

'I don't know.' I needed to get things back on track, 'Come on. Let's not do this right now.' I reached over and ruffled his hair. He laughed, but it didn't reach his eyes. I'd disappointed him, but he was too kind to show it.

'Your hair's grown,' I said.

'I know. D'you like it? Yours is basically all gone.'

'Yep. Love it. You look like Heathcliff. Or some other moody moorland man.'

'Moody Moorland Man. I'll take that. I like yours shaved, by the way.' He smiled, more genuinely this time. 'How's things at home? Completely unhinged, as normal?'

'You know it.'

'Are they being all right with you?'

'Yeah. I mean, they're being a bit standoffish with the memorial stuff. And there's something else kind of strange too . . .' I had been planning to use this evening as an escape from all the weirdness that had been going on, but the conversation kept toeing the same line. Seeing Chris again, seeing the way he furrowed his brow with such sincerity, even after I'd brushed him off, it made me want to confide in him. He was sat quietly waiting for me to go on.

'Right, so. It's probably nothing, but it still seems a bit odd. I found this notebook that belongs to Ysella, and I've been looking through it.'

'You've been reading her diary?' He pretended to gasp, hand to chest. 'I'm scandalised, Mermaid. Is there anything saucy in there? Any toy boys? You know I've been trying to ride that train for years.' He had a talent for lightening the mood.

'Ha. No, not a diary. It's more like research. There're all these stories in there, some that have been printed out and stapled in, and others that she's written out herself.'

'So, she's got this notebook full of stories. What kind of stories?'

'They're not that wild. They're pretty dark, but no worse than what Mum used to tell me.'

'Lowen always did have an interesting definition of a bedtime story.'

'Mmm,' I nodded and then took a sip of my pint. I needed to tell him the rest, to see if it was as odd as it felt, but I wasn't sure if I was ready. He raised his eyebrows at me, his face open, waiting for me to carry on speaking. I decided to trust him.

'But the worst bit is her name is written in there.'

'Whose? Your aunt's?'

'No. Claud's.'

'What the fuck?'

I shrugged. His reaction proved that it was as weird as I'd thought. It also showed that he was kinder than I, willing to accept my story face-on, not avoiding it like I had with his.

'Hold on, before we dive into this anymore, we need brain fuel,'

Chris said. He reached into the pockets of the battered aviator jacket he'd thrown over the back of his chair. He pulled out packets of Bacon Fries and pork scratchings, splitting both bags down the middle before pushing them between us.

'What?' he said, inspecting a long curling hair protruding from a pork scratching. 'Look, I'm not cheap, but I'm not paying pub prices. A pound a fucking bag in here. Do you know what the worst of it is?'

I shook my head.

'The scotch eggs they sell, £1.50, right? I was speaking to Cal who used to work here the other day – they get them from the big Asda! Four pack for a quid, stick some fucking cellophane round them, selling them for £1.50 each.'

'That's grim. I don't like scotch eggs. I don't understand them.'

'Abnormal. Want a scratching?' he asked, pushing the bag towards me. I tried to choose one without hairs, but once it was in my hand, I could feel the sharp spikes of stubble.

Chris carried on talking as I scraped at the scratching with my nail. 'OK, so, what do we know? We know you found a notebook that belongs to your aunt, it's got some spooky stories in it, and Claud's name's in there?'

'Right.'

'OK, well, that's not actually a lot, is it?'

'There's something else.'

'Oh yeah?'

'Ysella's been smearing this stuff – it's like chopped up eel and butter – all over the window frames, and they're both acting like it's normal. And there was another word next to Claud's name. Pedri. I thought your mum might know something about it. Has she ever mentioned a Pedri? Or "The Pedri"?'

'Because she's weird?'

'Don't be mean. Because she's, you know. Because she owns a tambourine.'

'And a didgeridoo. And a focusing crystal. Sure. Don't worry,

I'll tell her you think she's a freak.' He grinned at me and started swiping at his phone. 'I've got this app – like a translator, but for dead languages, old Celtic stuff. It's all community led. The name Pedri rings a bell. That's an old Cornish word though, isn't it? Definitely doesn't sound English.'

I nodded and popped a bacon fry in my mouth, letting it melt slowly until it was mush. I hadn't thought about the origin of the name before, but Cornish made as much sense as anything.

'How weird,' Chris said. 'I've found it. But it's not a proper noun; it's a verb. It says it means rot. What did you say earlier? It's a story? Or a myth? About rotting?'

To rot. It didn't fit. I shrugged. 'I mean, I don't know. I thought it was a name.'

'Weird name. There's some more here, corrupt or spoil. That's dark.' Chris finished his drink. 'Want another one?' he asked.

'Thanks.'

I was searching through the pork scratching bag for a crispy, non-hairy one when an individual bottle of rosé and a wine glass that still smelled like dishwasher were placed in front of me. Not looking up, I said, 'Ah man, I can't stand wine'.

Someone cleared their throat, and then I heard Chris say, 'You all right mate? You don't usually drink in here.'

Chris was stood, holding two more pints, and next to him was Paul, Claud's dad. Paul was bald and tall. He wore his Fred Perry shirt buttoned tight around his neck.

'Thought I'd bring a drink by for your missus,' he said to Chris, 'but she don't seem best pleased.'

Chris laughed, put a pint down in front of me. I wanted to shrink down into my hoody until only my eyes were on show.

'I haven't got a missus, mate. It's Merryn! And she doesn't like wine. What brings you out this way?'

Paul stared at me, his eyes narrowing only slightly before he pulled a smile from his back pocket. I tried to smile back. He was wearing the black Swatch watch Claud bought him for his birthday when we were fifteen. We shovelled snow from at least eight driveways so she could save up for that thing. I poured the wine into the glass so I could avoid looking at him.

'So it is. You'm all right Merryn, maid?' He nods at me once before turning to Chris. 'Been spending more time up this way recently. Summit weird on the moor. We've been out looking for it.'

The hunt, again. He'd been one of them.

'Merryn's mam lives out on the moor,' Chris said, looking to me. I kept my mouth shut. 'Has she said anything to you about something weird, Mer?'

I tried to say no, but my voice was shuttered. I swallowed a gulp of wine and tried again. 'No.' I had seen the way Paul had tensed when Chris called me Mer, the same as Claud used to.

'All due respect to Merryn, mate,' Paul said, visibly tightening his grip on his ale 'but it's her lot that are the problem.'

Oh no.

'Her lot? What are you on about?' Chris asked, looking from Paul to me and back again.

'If her sort—'

'What's that supposed to mean?' Chris interrupted. He positioned himself between Paul and the table, blocking me from view. Paul downed half his pint, clearly drunker than either of us had realised.

'That batty mam of hers has done something—'

'Don't talk about Lowen like that, Paul.'

'I'll talk about who I want, how I want,' Paul said. He sidestepped Chris and pointed his finger at me, 'especially when it's her batshit mam that started this. No wonder she's turned into a dyke, with a mam like that.'

I closed my eyes and pressed my hand against my mouth to ground myself. When I opened them, Chris looked furious and I could see, rather than hear, that he was telling Paul to get the fuck out in a low voice.

'Your daughter didn't seem to mind me being a dyke,' I said.

'Disgusting.' He spluttered, his face purple. 'Don't talk about Claudia like that.'

'Claud.'

He looked at Chris. 'This is exactly why Mary didn't want her at the funeral. Or any of her lot.'

'Now that's not fair, Paul . . .' Chris started.

'The only person who shouldn't've been at that funeral was Mary. That woman ruined Claud's life. She fucked her up completely. My mum might be batshit, but Mary's fucking cruel. Leaving without saying goodbye? Saying she was scared of her? Cruel.'

'You don't understand anything,' Paul said.

'I understand enough to know that Claud wouldn't be gone if she thought she was allowed to be loved.'

His whole face turned then, as he lunged across the table, knocking the wine onto the floor. I closed my eyes once more, waiting for it, for the repentance, for some smattering of pain that felt like closure, but it didn't come.

When I opened them, Paul was being swallowed back by the crowd as the barman shouted at him to get out. Chris was being calmed down by a man in a flat cap but shrugged him off when he saw I was shaking.

'Shit, Merryn. Are you OK? What an absolute dickhead. I'm sorry mate, I should've got rid of him sooner, I wasn't expecting that. Are you all right?' He put his arm around my shoulders and squeezed. 'Do you wanna go? We can go. In fact, Tony looks pretty mad, we might have to go.'

The barman was making his way to our table.

'I just want another drink,' I said, pulling at my sleeves. My chest was rattling. Chris smiled, just a little, and then saluted me.

'Yessir. Let me sort Tony out, you stay there,' he said, jumping up and intercepting Tony swiftly.

Tony averted; we kept drinking. I was already tipsy when I spoke to Paul, and what I said about Claud had filled me with such a strong sense of embarrassment that I began drinking quicker than Chris. I was drunk within the hour, and not the good kind of drunk, but the drunk that curdles your stomach, where you're trying to crush something down, but it just brings it back up.

Another hour, another two. I couldn't peel back my nails so I pushed them deep into the velvet of the barstool and thought about all the years of dust collected in that cushion, how when I first sat down, the particles would have floated up and gotten stuck in the fibres of my jumper and the roots of my eyelashes. I scraped my nails into the fabric, so all that dust got under them too – thick layers of other people's skin trapped by mine.

I carried it with me, until later when we popped out for a fag, and I complained I was cold. Chris put my fingers in his mouth and sucked to warm them up, before kissing me. And then all that dust, all those people were in his mouth, and his throat, and his gut. All the people that had been in that pub and sat on that seat, leaving tiny traces of themselves behind.

I pushed him up against the limestone wall, moving so his knee pressed between my legs, and I couldn't stop thinking about the dust and the people. How many of them had been stuck here, like Chris? How many of them had been frightened of themselves?

Drunk on cheap pink wine and beer, me and Chris made it back to his and tumbled into each other on his bed.

When I touched his skin, all I could think of was raw meat, the slime of him, jellied eels. His tongue sat heavy in my mouth, but I didn't mind. Told myself I didn't mind anyway, which was practically the same. I kept my arm braced across my chest, my T-shirt still on.

I pressed my face into his shoulder and opened my mouth, nipped at him with little teeth. That part felt delicious. When I opened my eyes, I saw he had new hair now, growing from his back and across his chest. A single sprout had seeded above his Adam's apple. I wanted to flick it, but I wasn't sure if laughter was allowed during sex – or in this case, just before sex.

We had been in this position – this 'almost there but not quite' brand of intimacy – before. He was above me and only slightly inside me when I told him to stop. And he did. He pulled himself back and wiped the want from his face and sat up in bed bedside me.

'Still?' he asked, not unkindly.

'Still.'

He nodded quickly, reaching for a packet of cigarettes. He offered me one, and I accepted as he pulled the duvet back over us, covering up our bare skin. It had been three years since the camping trip, and I thought I would've been OK by now. But I wasn't. I still couldn't have anyone but Claud touch me like that.

Now the illusion of sexual tension had gone, I felt more sober, and I could look at him without picking fault with the way he breathed or the earnest noises he made. He tapped ash onto his duvet and I watched as a burning cherry fell, eating through the fabric drowsily. Just as it seemed like it could ignite, he swatted it away, and I sighed in a way that made him laugh.

'You can stay, you know. There's no point walking back now. Selena won't mind, she likes you,' he said.

'Sure, but I've gotta get back.' Part of me wanted to stay, for the ease of it, the company. But I knew it would be awkward in the morning, navigating that not-quite-platonic space in the light of day, whilst both of us were still dealing with our grief.

'I'll walk with you then.'

'No.'

I leant my head against his sharp shoulder. How different would it all have been if I had met Chris before Claud? Chosen him over her? I could picture it. I would've left the farmhouse and moved into the little terrace with him and his mum. We'd sleep on a mattress on the floor and spend our evenings watching documentaries about fracking and reruns of *A Place in the Sun*, smoking cigarettes and arguing over whether we'd take the apartment in Madrid. His mum would paint me a picture of the moon for my birthday, and we'd hang it above the bed, and every time we had sex (which we would, regularly and gently, but not too often), I would make eye contact with the wolf, and I'd feel safe.

If I had chosen Chris, Claud would've just been a friend, eventually. And all the things that had made me the person I was – the person climbing out of Chris's bed, pulling my clothes back on – would never have happened, and we would probably be happy.

I couldn't find my socks, so I stuck my bare feet into my trainers, ignoring the look of worry on Chris's face. I knew he wanted me to stay, to try out what we could've had before. But it was too late, and I needed to go home. I couldn't change it all.

'Don't worry, I'll be fine. I walk myself home in the city all the time. Besides, you know how me and Claud would walk home from parties together at this time.'

He bristled slightly at the mention of Claud's name, but instead of speaking, he blinked quickly, three times, like she was an eyelash squatting in his view, 'If you're sure,' he said.

He walked me to the door and gave me a hug. As he pressed me against his chest, I spoke into his T-shirt, 'I think I've seen her too'.

When he let me go, I wasn't sure if he'd heard me. He looked as if he wanted to speak, but instead he gave me a cigarette and a spare lighter for the road. He ruffled my hair as I ducked out into the night.

vii.

People in these parts held their stones and granite stacks – menhirs – in high regard. There are Druids and Pagans and Christians all with their own explanations for the stone circles. Like America's crop circles, but these haven't been made by combine harvesters. Esolyn thought the stone circles were true passageways; Mum and Ysella thought they were bad luck.

It gets passed on, that kind of fear. The only time my mother ever hit me, and it wasn't even a real hit, was when I went to cut straight through the middle of the Hurlers Stone Circle. She'd been telling me stories of a piper who played beautiful music, and the young women dancing with them, but the women didn't realise they were dancing on fae land and they were turned to stone. She said the number of hurling stones was forever changing, and I was a sensible child, back then. I wanted to count the stones so that on our next walk, I could see if it was true, see if they multiplied and shifted in the night, but as I went towards them, I was whipped back by her hand.

I tried to tell her that the stones couldn't mean two things at once. I might've been young, but I knew the differences between fact and fiction, I'd done well in school, and I knew there was only one right answer to most things. There was no way pisky traps and fairy punishments were real. It couldn't make sense. I told her so then and she dragged me further away, spitting at the foot of the stones before we left.

It might've been the drink, or it could've been the dark, but either way I couldn't make sense of where I was going after I left Chris's that night. I had been walking for a while, long enough for me to be nearly home, but I still didn't recognise any of the land around me. Where there should've been landmarks, there was nothing of note, just moorland and hedges, which in the night gave the appearance of a hundred hunched beasts lining each side of the horizon. I found myself stood at a turning, the road ahead of me unending, the road behind me gone. I turned around, trying to find my way back to Chris's house.

Our near-miss in bed had me remembering the night three years before, when a group of us went camping. When I think of that night, I never know if I did enough – or if I did too much, if I invited it. Remembering leaves my chest tight, a phrase I never understood before, but I could explain now: it feels as if the centre of me has been hollowed out and someone is slowly churning my lungs until the air is all gone, and it can't be caught. And that, that is how I feel whenever I remember the

pink face
brown hair
wet lips
sharp fingernails.
A jumble of parts, collapsing in on me.

FOLKLORE

Watch. Watch the girl as she runs across our lands. After all this time, the girl is running once again across the moors. Where is her mother now? See this wet blanket of night!

We do not like to see her suffer, but suffer she insists, following whims and wisps – she follows the wisp now, turning off course and running towards that blinking light.

She tremors in the cold, her flesh rising like bumps of our ground. Her gait is looping, her legs weary. She follows a light that is not of our own making, no longer heeds the stories her mother once told her. We press our own light down, scattered as it is above her, old and weary as the stars are now – we knew of this long ago, sent homing whispers across the sky, but as they reach her, they falter, no more than a smudge above, easily missed.

Reach, we must reach her now. She stumbles forth, blind to all but the wisp but we feel it in her gait, her steps push down on us imbalanced, she staggers, and we push back in return: we strain and swell, pull water from deep beyond and rush it to the surface. We ache to meet her at the surface, to cushion the blow. But we turn slowly over millennia. Parts of us, above and coursing through, will peel back our edges with currents of wind and water to create new valleys where once we were only plains.

No, we have only small touches within our reach. A slow peeling back, like stretching out our farthest reaches, and the curl of a fern will unfurl. She stumbles and we focus now, we stand to attention as she wanes, stretch out with bracken fingers to grasp her legs. To pull back, to change course.

She slaps us away with a drunken hand, wipes us off like we are the pest. On she rages, following the blinding light, until, oh!

viii.

Memories of the camping trip rose unbidden in my mind, now suddenly aware of all the bad things that could happen to me here, outside, alone. Every time I stopped, I felt myself back there, in the tent. The dark sky was closing in on me. I cursed myself for my shaved head, wishing I had long hair that I could wrap around my face and throat to keep the chill of the night air out. If I could run forever, I could stop being a girl. I could become a beast. Prowling the moor at night, living as a symbiote on its land. A bird cleaning the teeth of a crocodile. I would be lichen if I could.

Up ahead there was a light, not the steady light of a house or the flashing light of a beacon – this light was stuttering, dipping, and rising in the darkness, swinging. Being carried. It must be the hunt, out again, searching. Out on the moors this late, the only thing they would find was me. I ran towards the light, confident in the raw belief that the moors would keep me safe, that those on the hunt would be inclined to help me, just this once.

As I got closer to the fray of light, it seemed to be coming from a torch. It swung away from me and I saw a figure, one I recognised. Chris's words from earlier that evening rang in my mind. Could it be Claud, like he said? Was she here for me, to help me get home? The possibility drove me forward and I ran faster, wanting to collect my blessing. Wanting a chance to see her, up close, one last time. I tripped forward, my toes sinking into the edge of a peat bog. I jumped back and bent over, hands on knees, letting my heart rate drop back to something survivable.

When I looked up, the light was gone.

I wanted to scream until the rest of my organs joined in, because my heart and my lungs were ready to – they didn't need convincing, and my legs were filled with acid, burning with cramp. Scream. It was so dark without that light, and the peat bog was gone, and my feet were rooted to the ground, not wanting to make the same mistake twice. Claud wouldn't turn the light off on me. It couldn't be her, could it?

The moon was in on it, covered by a cloud, but the stars were still out. They were so far gone that their light couldn't lead anyone home. It was only an echo.

I remembered a poem my mother used to recite to me, from a story her mother told her. I hummed it as I tried to find my way back.

> Jack o' the lantern, Joan the wad!
> Who tickled the maid, and made her mad,
> Light me home, the weather's bad.

The story was about the Pobel Vean, the little people, hiding behind every bank, sleeping under every rock. Joan o' the Wad and Jack o' the Lantern were a pair of belligerent piskies who would show themselves to lost walkers as leading lights on dark nights. If you were good, you'd have safe passage home. If you were bad, they would trick you into thinking their lights were guiding you home, only to lead you until your feet bled, leaving you mazed, in a neverland with no hope of returning.

I was about to give up, just lie down and take it, when I saw the light fizz on – further away now, up and to the right. It wasn't blinking anymore. This time it was steady and proud. I told myself it had to be a torch, had to be the hunt. Unless I had been right before and it really was Claud. I could still see her shape behind the torch. I walked towards her slowly, chin tilted up, eyes locked on the torch. I couldn't let her disappear on me again. As I got closer, the shape behind the torch started to change. It stretched higher, taller than Claud ever was, taller than a grown woman. What I had thought was Claud's coat flowed down and out, spreading across the ground. My vision blurred, fireworks of orange and yellow flares bursting in front of my eyes as I got too close to the light. Chris's question came to me again: if it wasn't Claud, then who was it? Or, what was it?

I could just about touch it, the light that seemed to sit in mid-air, grab it from whatever it rested upon. Turn the light onto the thing that stood behind it, see the imitation for myself. I wet my cracked lips, ready to reach out, prepared to snatch the truth for myself.

Then it blinked, and it was gone. I heard the rattle of something metallic, all jangling together. The rattling of a bag of coins. It took my eyes a minute to adjust to the sudden darkness, the orange glow still settling. For a moment I thought I must've gone blind, or that the carrier of the light had pulled something over my head, ready to kidnap me.

Then shapes came back into focus. The moon shifted ever so slightly from the clouds, pitying me, and I saw where I was. The air felt lighter, my breath short.

I was standing in the middle of a clearing, the ground below me completely bare of anything but the lightest dusting of grass. Around me were figures, as high as my waist, stood like soldiers a foot apart. Stones, stood. I turned, looking for the thing that had held the light. I spun faster, stumbling as I did so, rolling my ankle with a sharp tear of pain. The light-holder was nowhere, the stone figures behind me, everywhere, and I knew I couldn't get past them. Not in the dark, not alone. I had missed my chance.

I slipped to the ground, squeezing my throbbing ankle with my hand, trying to apply some sort of pressure to stop the pain. I stared down at it, not wanting to look at the figures, but even on the ground I felt their presence. There was no movement, no wisp of wind or rustle of gorse. Even the animals were kept away from where I, or we, were.

The clouds had drifted away from the moon by then, and I could see more clearly where I was. For a moment I believed all of it – the shaded moon, the blinking light, even the missing turn in the road – was part of a ploy to get me to this spot. I wanted to stand, knew I needed to move, to get away from that place where nothing felt right, but then—

FOLKLORE

We are warring, here.

We are multitudes, but one. All of us driven by the same desire, to bring her in, to fold her up. Folding her body with a crack of bone, a pop of joint, the squelch – have you heard it? The squelch when a foot slips into mud, when it's pulled back again? Of her damp insides forced together, until we can pull her down. We, the most, are ready for her now. We, the most, do not mind how she falls, how she comes. We are ready.

But I—

No.

We have a dissenter. One who is no longer one but is part of We, who is fighting against the common desire. Who wishes—

What things are wishes now?

—for the girl to fall differently. Who knows how she comes. Who wants more. Who aches to meet her at the surface, and now we all ache too. We all ache too.

And so, the girl. We put her to sleep. We raise 1000 fists until the ground above bursts upwards, and a tussock is raised, and the girl trips, without ever knowing why. And the air up there, oh. It is cold, isn't it? Much colder than what we know. How easy it is for us to forget that. Cold enough to send the girl to sleep quickly. And when she sleeps, we can keep her safe, keep her nursed.

Silly of her to believe in such things, rhymes and poems to hum for protection. Silly of her to believe lights will guide her to any-

thing but ruin. As if an ancient thing could be starved, starved by a couplet.

The only protection from Her is us, Her children. We who know Mother so well.

DAY PESWAR

i.

—morning.

Everywhere was grey, the moor two-dimensional, too early still for the sun to fight its way through. My eyes were heavy with dew and my bones ached from where I'd slept against the hard ground. My hangover was real, of that I was certain. I pushed myself up shakily, trying to keep my stomach contents from spilling out. The hurling stones stood around me, my jailers from the night before now looking a lot less organic. My fear was gone, replaced with a headache and a shakiness of foot, but the air still didn't feel right. Beyond the stones I could see the rustling of gorse and tree branches moving in the wind, but where I sat, there was no breeze. Even the grass just beyond the stone circle – close enough that I could stretch out my fingers and almost touch it – danced.

And just beside that grass, a mound of earth. Freshly dug, the warmth of the ground beneath the surface leaving it steaming. I moved towards it. A hole. It was small, no wider or deeper than a grave you'd dig for a cat. The walls sloped inwards, the hole getting narrower the deeper it went. I reached out with a hand to feel the surface, to check it was stable. As I did so, I noticed my nails, lined with dirt.

Could I have? No.

I pulled my hand away from the hole and spat into my palm, using my T-shirt to scrub the dirt away. It looked like I'd been digging in the night. But sleepwalking wasn't my problem; my night terrors usually left me paralysed, not scrabbling around on the floor.

Once my hands were clean, I checked the rest of my body, a low thrum of fear in my stomach. Maybe it was the work of an animal. I moved closer to the hole again. Warmth seemed to be radiating from the base, pulling me towards it.

I felt compelled – I lifted my foot and stepped into the hole. I could just about fit both feet in it, with one balanced upon the other, but that was all. I stood there for a minute or so, up to my calves in the moor, and let myself be warmed by the ground.

Stepping carefully out, I orientated myself and set off towards Trewarnen. What seemed like a good idea the night before felt like a torturous pilgrimage in the morning. My ankle no longer hurt, but I was convinced the cold had taken my toes in the night, untied my laces, and swiped each one with frost. When I walked it felt like they had been replaced with folded squares of cardboard, the entire roll of them corrugated in my trainers. All I could think of was how it would feel to lower myself into a boiling bath. How my toes, surely white like lychees, would swell pink and hiss with steam when they hit the hot water.

I tried to rationalise what I had seen the night before. It could have been drink-induced fear, or *folie à deux* – a shared madness. My mother's stories of stone circles creeping from memory to consciousness, stealing away my sanity for the night. Or Chris's stories of Claud, confusing me, persuading me in his grief that such things as ghosts could walk the moors.

As I walked down the path to Trewarnen, I thought again of Ysella's notebook in my bag, the words tucked at the back. I wondered if 'The Baker and the Bread' was like the stories my mother had told me when I was younger: passed down through generations of storytelling. Had Ysella's story found its way to her through the lifeblood of her mother, too? Was it something that was bundled up and passed down, fat-trimmed and spit-shined for a new audience? Or was it something without familiar roots, from a different place altogether?

I believed in logic and reason, not fantasy, although sometimes they could be just as scary. If the answer to all the strange occurrences in the farmhouse could be found in reason, then surely that reason had to be that each of us in Trewarnen was unhinged. And I, for one, could not afford to lose my mind; I couldn't afford a loose tongue that spilled secrets where they were not wanted. I needed to keep a handle on myself.

That handle had been slipping away from me. I still couldn't leave the Pedri alone, the chance of a connection to Claud.

ii.

It's 2016 and I'm seventeen. Me, Claud and Chris are at a small camping party on the moors, not far from Chris's house.

Our beers are cooling in the river, tabbed in place with rocks. Someone is sitting on a picnic blanket, but most of us lounge on marshy ground. I coax the spike of a thistle from my heel when no one is watching, using my nails to cut into the skin and pull it out. I'm bored and uneasy, my heel stinging. There's a crescent of blood under my fingernail. Some boys from our year have come, people I don't know well, so I'm drinking quicker than I'm used to. I lose track of the conversation quickly as I try to stave off nausea.

As I pick the label from my bottle, I watch Claud with a brown-haired boy, Rob. He looks bland, a nothing personality, and I am bitter, judging him for the way she is angling herself towards him. She laughs too loudly at something he says, and snorts, and as he recoils from her, removing his arm from her knee, his face flat, I feel the heat of her embarrassment as if it were mine. Claud keeps looking at me as she tries to flirt with Rob. There's nothing sneaky about it; instead, her bare face bores into mine. I drink just enough beer to stop myself from reacting.

The camping party, though a tradition, is ill thought out. There are six of us and only two tents and little food. We have blankets instead of sleeping bags. As the night gets colder, our hunger drives us to the tents earlier than it usually would. Claud is still quiet, but as the only two girls, we automatically gravitate towards the same tent. Chris is lost behind a gorse bush – having broken the seal half an hour ago, he keeps needing to piss – so Rob ends up in our tent.

In spite of her earlier show, Claud lies down at the opposite end of the tent, scooting as far from Rob as she can get. Over the past few days, Claud has been avoiding me. When I text, she doesn't answer. When I call and ask why she's not responding, she says she's out of credit. This evening has been the first time I've seen her outside of college for over a week, and she's clearly still angry about what happened the last time I saw her.

We had been in her caravan. I'd gone round, ostensibly for 'dinner'. There was a routine to these evenings that never faltered. In the kitchen area, Claud would be cooking and swearing. It should've been simple: she was making macaroni cheese. Both of us knew she wouldn't eat it. It would sit on the hob until it was squelching, the cheese sweating, and then the whole pan would be placed on the side. There would be no tin foil placed on the top, and it would sit out for days, until I visited again and scraped it all, in one claggy mass, into a bin bag.

There would be some exceptions to this. Occasionally, one quarter would be carved out with precision, placed into an orange-stained Tupperware and pushed towards me whilst it was still hot. The edges would then be picked at by Claud herself, the pieces of pasta that had gone hard as they sat out, flew too close to the sun, and cracked when you bit into them. She couldn't bear the just-cooked pasta, the soft bits, the slime. Tiny slugs on her tongue. I'd suggest she eats sharper food, rather than nothing at all, if her preference is to be scratched all way the down. Toast turned charcoal under the grill. Dry noodles. She'd say no, I'd plead, then beg, then argue, and the plastic tub of pasta on my lap would eventually go cold as we fought back and forth. Rinse and repeat, twice a week, every week.

The whole time that Claud was stirring the macaroni, I was preparing to tell her that I'd applied to university in Manchester, to study English, and that I would be leaving at the end of the summer.

When Claud turned around with the Tupperware – 'Dinner's served, Mermaid,' – I spoke before I lost my nerve.

'I'm leaving. Well, no, I'm not leaving. Wrong word. Not yet.

But I got in – I applied to Manchester, for English, and I got in, and I'm going to go. In September. I know you weren't sure if you wanted to go or not, but I thought it would be good, to get out of Cornwall for a bit, see a city for once, you know?'

As I spoke, Claud sat herself on the sofa, right in the corner. The pasta was in her lap, and she stared at it, as if it was the thing talking. When she eventually looked up, 'You're leaving me, then?'

'No, I shouldn't have said that. That was stupid. I got a place at uni.'

'Why are you telling me this?'

Her voice had set, lower than it usually was. She didn't look me in the eye, instead she focused on my neck. I knew she was mad at me whenever this happened. Anger was her preference over sadness, it always had been. If she were to look me in the eye, she'd get upset, and she wouldn't have that. I stumbled over my response quickly, trying to direct myself so she had to look at me. As I spoke, her eyes roved around the room.

'There's still loads of time, I checked, and they're still accepting late applicants, if you wanted to do that. But also, I've been thinking, and I thought maybe you could just come with me? Even if you didn't want to study, we could share a room and you could get a job or do whatever you want—'

'Whatever I want?'

'Yeah, I mean, there're so many choices—'

'Whatever I want. You don't have any idea what I want. Why would I want to move to the north with you? To do what?' She started to scratch at her arm as she spoke, sharp, fast little scratches, like an animal burrowing into her old skin.

'There's loads of things—' I tried to move her nails from her arm, she snatched them back.

'To hang out in your student accommodation all day whilst you read books with a load of English students?'

'No, no, you're misunderstanding me. You wouldn't have to wait around for me, but we could save on rent, and—'

'And I could be your girlfriend? Is that it? You want to go to uni and tell everyone you've got a girlfriend? You want me to clean your room and read your shit essays and finger you on Friday nights after you've been for drinks with your uni mates?' Her arm is beetroot, the already irritated eczema encouraged and inflamed so much it's practically bubbling. Her eyes are wide, but she still isn't crying. There's a desperation there. And me? I've moved beyond desperation, beyond the conversation. This is damage control – I need to pull her back from the edge.

'Claud,' I put my hand out on the sofa between us. An offering to break the touch barrier. She sneers at it.

'Piss off, Merryn. I'm not giving up my life to make yours better,'

'I'm not asking you to give anything up. I'm sorry. I promise. I just, I think it would be good for us.'

'There isn't an us. You're leaving me, and I never wanted you here anyway.' And it's done. The conversation never comes back from this point. Anything more that is said I will just absorb, take in through my skin and hold there. It's all I can do.

'That's not true.'

'It is. You latched onto me from the beginning, and I was always too bored to brush you off properly.'

The pasta sits on the sofa between us. Claud rubs at her eyes, smudging mascara across her cheekbones. She's still scratching her arm, up and down, up and down. Her eczema has started to glitter with blood. I can't try to stop her.

'I know you don't mean that.'

'Maybe I don't. But that's not the point. You've ruined it, and you're making me sick, and you're too hard, this is too hard, and I don't want it, not anymore, not like this.'

'I'm making you sick?'

'You wouldn't understand. You can't see it, not like I can.'

She kicked me out then, and I knew it wasn't Claud talking. These accusations rose from her like a purge every now and then. I saw them for what they were: fear. The same fear that reared up every few months and made itself known through anger at me, or herself. As much as I felt physically ill when she got angry at me like that, I preferred it when she took it out on me. When she kept it in, it was eating her, literally. I was stronger; I could take it.

I thought camping could be my chance to talk to Claud again, once she'd finished sulking and flirting with Rob. Maybe she would've changed her mind about Manchester, or at least realised that I wasn't trying to abandon her, or trap her, or whatever else she had assumed.

Instead, I'm a bit drunk, and Claud is still ignoring me, and there's a guy I hardly know in between us.

I am surprised when, a little after Claud's breath hitches with sleep, he moves his body closer to mine, his hand on my hip. I hadn't considered him before that moment, but I was feeling splintered from Claud. Unrejected, Rob shifts so his weight is above me, his elbow by my head, resting on my hair. In the darkness he kisses me, his breath cigarette smoke and Frosty Jack cider. His lips are wetter than Claud's were, the kiss sloppy. As he moves, the weight of his elbow pulls my hair. Claud's soft breathing feels too loud, the tent too small. It's a pop-up, single skin so the condensation from three bodies will catch on the walls, run down and slick us wet in the night. I move myself away, whisper goodnight to Rob, placing my hand gently on the cave of his chest. He rolls off me; I close my eyes.

His hand snakes under my blanket, slithers across my hip, tries to burrow below my waistband. I move his hand away – I'm tired and the game is boring. I'm also bleeding. As I twist my hips away from him, I can feel my pad shifting in my underwear.

Rob did not know this though, so he moves his hand back to my waistband, pulling up the elastic of my pants. I wrap my fingers around his wrist – so thick compared to Claud's – and shake my head. He pulls his hand free and moves towards me again. I start to say, I can't tonight, but I am barely speaking because Claud is asleep, and I don't need her to know I've kissed Rob. He can't hear me, so he shifts closer, turning on his side. He is propped up by his elbow, one hand just above my head as he leans in to hear me say:

'I'm on, I can't.'

A kiss, wet again, sloppy but no longer soft. His loose mouth covers mine so completely, I think he will steal all my air. I lift my hand up to his chest, ready to push him back, but he grips the crown of my hair with his fist, pulls it. My chin jerks to attention, pressing me further against him. His other hand moves. It moves. It moves. It moves. It moves. I say nothing. There is the rustle of plastic. Synthetic like a nappy. The sounds of a foot slipping into a marsh. There is a burning crop circle of pain on my scalp where he pulls my hair back, tightening me in place. It moves.

Claud has stopped snoring. I make no sound and neither does she. Afterwards, there is only Rob's panting breath. I lay still, the bumps of raw ground beneath me bruising my back. I turn my face towards Claud, and I see her, eyes open, staring at the back of Rob's head.

The rumour spread around college on Monday.

Merryn likes getting fingered on the rag, dirty bitch.

I spent most of my day in the music block. During first break, I saw Claud with some girls we knew. As I reached them, she was waving her hand in the air, wrist sticking out the draping sleeve of my coat, fingertips covered in red felt tip. Her face coloured when she saw me, but not enough.

I finally got Claud on her own at the end of lunch, when she appeared at the bottom of the field, in our secret smoking spot. She rolled her eyes when she saw me.

'You couldn't do it, could you?' she said, pulling a ridiculously long Richmond menthol super king cigarette out of a packet in her pocket. She'd never smoked them before. It stuck out from her lip like a lick of straw. Next to my tiny roll-up, it looked obscene.

'Do what?'

'Let me have something – actually, anything – that wasn't you.'

'What are you talking about, Claud?'

'Rob was into me, and you wanted him for yourself.'

No no no no no no no, the chant tumbled from me as soon as she said his name and I couldn't stop it. All I could see was the loom of his face and the whites of her eyes in the dark.

Claud coughed, brashly. 'Jesus, Merryn, you sound properly mental, you know that? Look, just because you want it to be you and me forever that doesn't mean it can be. I told you this the other day. I thought you'd be cool with us chilling things out a bit.'

Chilling out was not what she'd suggested; she'd wanted me to leave and never come back, hadn't she? I suddenly couldn't remember what she'd said when she'd kicked me out.

'I thought you'd get it,' she carried on, 'I can't believe you'd pretend to be into him just to hurt me.'

'Hurt you? When did I? I'd never want to hurt you,'

'Well, clearly you did, because you hooked up with Rob, even though you knew he liked me, and that's really fucking mean actually.'

I didn't understand what was happening.

'I'd never do that to you intentionally,' I started.

'Oh, I know.' Claud ashed her cigarette, accidentally flicking it all over my trainer, 'Sometimes you're just really thoughtless.'

'I'm sorry.'

'Mmm. Thank you. It's going to take me a while to trust you again, you know?'

I nodded. I felt Rob's hand pushing against my thigh. I nodded again.

'Anyway. Bye.' Claud said. She dropped her cigarette to the floor and flashed a wave at me before walking off. The tips of her fingers were still crimson.

Chris came and got me at the end of the day. I'm not sure how he found me, or how he knew, but the next day, he was suspended for a week for breaking Rob's nose.

FOLKLORE

She gave a gift to the women of Trewarnen, long ago. Twenty-one years. A gift they have forgotten, a gift that went unrewarded.

When She saw that the women of Trewarnen did not appreciate Her gift, She was angry, She would not forgive easily. She vowed to punish them differently. She would not kill or feast or starve. She did not take back what was Hers, snatch it from ungrateful hands. Instead, She gave the women a punishment, one drawn over years, built from a hundred little horrors. First, She broke them apart. She made their lives hard. She gave them struggle. She let Her gift separate the women of Trewarnen, let Her presence sully their bond, until the women scattered.

The one who held the gift She punished the most. She followed the woman wherever she went. When the woman left the farmhouse for a cottage, She trapped her. She made the neighbours distant and turned the woman cruel. She found a way to reach into the woman and curdled her inside out.

Eventually, She stopped. She let the woman leave; She went to sleep. When She gave the gift, She was already old. By then, Her bones were weary. She was too tired.

She could live with one gift not adequately repaid.

And then the woman asked for another.

iii.

Once again, the shame of the night before followed me home, and I found myself resolute in the opinion that no one need know. I had no reason for getting lost on a walk I knew so well, or for seeing strange lights, and I didn't want to hear any explanation they'd offer.

Instead of going into the house, I sat in the garden, squeezing myself between a hydrangea and some raspberry canes. As the berries burst in my mouth, I realised I hadn't eaten properly since the toast on the day I walked to the village. More so, I wasn't hungry. My desire for a warm bath was gone too. I no longer felt like I needed to scrub myself clean.

I remembered the garden as a child, when my mother was away with doctors or for appointments, and my aunt would deposit me back here, away from my grandmother's pinching fingers. I would take a glass jar and a piece of cardboard with me and squat to the ground, moving like that, hoping to catch burrowers or fairies in amongst the weeds. Ysella was always too busy – keeping the peace between Esolyn and my mother – to make the garden pretty. Whatever seeded back here stayed, even the invasive plants. So, she let Himalayan balsam bloom, allowing the wind to disperse its seed across the moors into the village, sprouting small saplings of worry like spreading rumours. She let bird seed germinate in the cracks of the path, until strange tufts of grass filled the gaps. Ysella always left last year's bulbs in the ground, refusing to swap them out for newer, better ones, and the second-year tulip and hyacinth rose from the soil like the dead, vaguely reminiscent of their past selves. The tulips were sprawling, yellow-bellied and leggy with weak blooms that would peek out under excessive foliage. The hyacinths naturalised. Instead of sturdy cones full of flowers they spindled upwards in search of light, five or six flowers on each pencil-thin stem.

I could never resist the hyacinths when I was a child, their star-shaped flowers gleaming like sweets. The smell of motherly love that leaked from them dragged bees helplessly towards their flowers and I followed. My obsession was driven by the way the bulbs irritated my skin. I had helped my mother plant them two years before, and after handling the papery bulbs my arms had risen with itchy pink spots, a Rorschach test of allergy. I sat in the kitchen and scratched my skin until the pink spots turned red and bled. When Mum found me afterwards, I told her I never wanted to see a hyacinth again. She laughed and then rubbed honey onto my raw skin and told me to wait until next spring. You're allergic only to the beginning, she said.

By the next spring, all was forgotten, forgiven. Ysella dropped me in the garden, and I brought the petals to my mouth, surprised by how rubbery they were, lightheaded with their scent. I spread the flower open, using two fingers on one hand to part it, marvelling at the cobweb that had settled in the middle. Is it shelter or a trick? I bit down on the hyacinth petal, feeling the small gush as the liquid burst forth on my tongue. I wanted to spit it out but instead held it there, forcing myself to see it through. I was expecting them to taste sweet, like sugar, but they tasted of nothing at all, nothing but wet.

From then on, I thought of flowers as liquid, dripping through your fingers. Leaves were different. Leaves tasted of earth, mud and gravel, wet grass. Real things. It was only flowers that disappeared on the tongue.

I heard a squawk, followed by a crash and the shouting voice of my mother.

A jackdaw, the first I had seen, was perched on the roof, stepping from side to side as it peered down the chimney. The chitter chatter of the babies was gone. Through the window, I could see my mother pulling on her gardening gloves, flinging open the front door. Another nest fallen.

I rose to help, but my mother caught my eye through the sealed window and motioned for me to sit back down. I did as she said.

I pulled Ysella's notebook from my bag and turned to the page I'd stopped at the day before.

The Cunning Woman and You

You, back with the cunning woman, sat at her table. Picking her food from your teeth with hands unwashed, agreeing to kill your only chicken to fix the babi, to feed the babi.

You, your hands steeped in blood, feathers in your hair, the meat grey and tough.

You, removing the plate from the babi, throwing the thighs, breasts and legs in the bin, uneaten. The babi, watching you with its mouth folded shut. Never eating, growing bigger.

You, sleeping on the cunning woman's floor. Your own room gone for coin, your goat tied up outside, coughing.

You, blade in hand, the handle heavy. Your body still sore from the last man you took, your head aching from the babi, the babi that screams and grows, screams and grows, larger than a babi ever should be.

You, come of age and are returned.

You, what's left of your goat at your feet, one last chance for the babi. The goat, unlike most, worth more to you alive than dead, but gone now anyway. The babi, beating its head from side to side, grabbing your legs so hard it leaves splinters.

You, unfocused as the cunning woman says she's out of ideas. The babi, unfixable. Surely dying or surely wrong.

You, thinking of the trader bound in cloth.

Not a changeling, like I'd first thought, but a myling, 'larger than a babi ever should be . . . surely wrong.' If this poem was family lore, it would be mine, not Claud's. The baby, taking and taking as the desperate mother empties herself out. The trader bound in cloth, the one that made the trade and collected the coins, had to be the Pedri, that much was clear. And another sentence had been underlined by Ysella: *You, come of age and are returned.* No matter how I read it, I couldn't make sense of that one. It didn't fit with the rest of the lines, though it was written in the same way. I flicked back to the first half of the poem. The piece that was underlined there was just part of a sentence: *a babi that has changed.* It seemed unrelated, but even so, I wrote both lines in the back of the notebook, along with the line from 'The Baker and the Bread': *the Pedri makes a trade.*

Ysella returned home to find me still sat in the garden, raspberry juice across my T-shirt. She frowned at the mess I had made, but before she could scold me, I asked her if I could borrow her old bike. Need to cycle off this hangover, I told her. She disappeared for a moment and returned with the bicycle. It was old – red, cream and rusty – with two thin tyres and dodgy brakes. It was exactly what I needed.

I took myself out on the moors, heading towards Dozmary pool.

When I moved to Manchester, I'd learnt the city by bike, a habit I'd picked up from home, where no cars and no buses gave me no choice. My city bike was old, with a basket on the front for cigarettes and bottles of water. I'd get up early, at the same time as the birds, and ride right from my front door. My bike took me to work, the shops, to parties. It took the top layer of skin from between my thighs and gave me stories, toned calves and a constant spattering of mud. The bike was buttercup yellow, bought with my student loan money in an ode to my mother.

My mother had a thing about buttercups when I was growing up. Poisonous yellow suns. Their roots creep under the ground like teeth, erupting with golden flowers where you least expect it. A string of them around the neck was supposed to be a cure for madness. Now, children hold one under the chin to see if they're in love. Whenever I find them, I wear mine tightly round my neck.

My room in the city was on the top of a concrete hill, overlooking many more hills and many more rooms, and at the very bottom – the canal. I cycled along the towpath as often as I could, before the creatures would crawl out from under bridges, pushing their way through reeds and rubbish. If I cycled far enough, I found I could change my own landscape, find miniature fields and manicured gardens. I would only stop the bike when I saw something interesting – a heron calling murder, a dead fish, its guts spread open like wings. It was in the city that I built my first nest, wrapping myself up in student bars and greasy spoons, beer gardens and charity shops. I tried on old fur coats and Barbour jackets, bleached my hair, and pierced my nose. I couldn't be further from the city now.

Dozmary Pool was where it ended, for Claud. Out of sight, hidden from the road, scrubbed from the horizon by a sea of bracken and bramble. To get close enough to see it, I abandoned the bike behind some gorse near the road and pulled myself over the locked gate, bouncing on my toes as I landed. I was never allowed to come here when I was a child. When I first found out I hadn't been baptised in the pool like the other women in my family, I had assumed my mother's flakiness was the cause. It was only through talking to Ysella when I was older – around twelve – during one of my mum's episodes, that I found out why my mother hated Dozmary so much.

Their childhood had not been a peaceful one under Esolyn's reign, something I found hard to grasp when I was young, because they had both seemed so very sad when she died. Now that I was older, and my own mother was becoming stranger, I began to understand how you could both need and resist someone at the same time. Where other mothers may've punished their children with extra prayers before bed or a switch on the back of the legs, Esolyn would taunt hers with superstitions. The water itself wasn't the punishment – Esolyn didn't believe that dunking would achieve anything, though she did think of her daughters as terrible little witches: snaggle-toothed and poorly dressed.

She took them there because of Jan Tregeagle. When Esolyn took her children to Dozmary, she would repeat the tale of Jan, although it's not a story you'd need telling twice. At the lake she would tell her daughters to kneel, and they would plunge their small hands into the cold, inky water, and scoop. Tregeagle was a magistrate in the seventeenth century, who was known to harbour a particular type of cruelty. He was corrupt, living a life of luxury as he stole from the poor. When it was discovered that he had swindled a young orphan girl out of her inheritance, his punishment was emptying the bottomless pool of Dozmary with nothing but a limpet shell full of holes. Picture: Sisyphus by the lake.

Esolyn took my mother and the aunt to Dozmary to remind them that going against her word was pointless.

As I walked, the crisp copper of the dying bracken pulled against my legs, I thought of the line Ysella would repeat, whenever she spoke to me about Dozmary, and her mother:

Bos war, beware the waters of Dozmare, for Tregeagle is always there.

To my right, the hill climbed upwards, blanketed with life. To my left, it dropped into the valley, stretching out. I stood at a ninety-degree angle to the land around me as I followed the path to the lake.

Under my feet the ground was made of grasses and thatch, sedge squeezing around the edges of my trainers. If I were to drop and part the grass with my fingers or push back the ferns, I would find an entire ecosystem in miniature.

Insects battling tufts of grass, dodging oil-slick dragonflies on their way to the lake. March fritillary butterflies, their wings stained-church-glass orange beating around me, lazy in the heat.

I walked on my toes, imagining tiny houses hidden in the thatch, tables and chairs and bowls of porridge, all waiting to be eaten within this invisible forest. Above, massive granite sculptures, slabs upon slabs higher than my head. I would climb those rocks as a teenager, rolling my T-shirt up to my ribcage, milk-skin turned to the sun.

The pool was a stretch of still water sunken into the middle of the moor. Rotted wooden fence posts gaped across the centre of the lake, like cragged teeth.

I dunked my hands in the water, splashing my face. It had been a year, and I was still not OK with water. I could bathe, but I couldn't swim. In the city, I was landlocked.

Back home, it was different. Out on the moors like that, I was sure I could see her in the still water.

Drowning is a silent death. On Claud's first attempt, she was so high up that her entry into the sea would've been silent. A clink against a bowl. There was no shouting, but even if there was, the wind and the waves would've eaten that up.

When children fall into the sea, they have a diving reflex. Maybe it's a call back to the womb, or the thought that safety lurks somewhere underneath. Either way, their instinct from birth is to hold their breath and sink when the surface of the water covers them. An adult might make a sound, at first, if they realise what's happening to them before cold-water shock sets in. If they haven't already swallowed half a pint of sea water.

The second time Claud tried to drown, there was no sea, just still water. Her inner child was present that day. She took over, held her in her arms and together they sank down, heart beating so fast the inside of her ribcage was probably bruised.

My bones were bruised too. I needed to shake these memories out of my mind. I cupped a hand into the pool, swirled the water around in my mouth. Salt and sediment.

My mother never told me the story of Jan Tregeagle; she left that one to my aunt. To me, all she said of Dozmary was that I should never to swim where horses drink – and horses would graze by Dozmary all year round. The hair that dropped into the water from their tails would turn to eels, eels big enough to wrap up and around your limbs, strong enough to drown you. They eat corpses, the big eels, whatever starts to decay, just like the sexton beetles do.

FOLKLORE

2019. She knows the girl as she looks now. Of course She does. She knows all the women in that house, has followed them from farm to cottage to city to farm again. The great mother, the daughter, the girl. She has known their ancestors and their mothers, and their mothers' mothers. Like the women in the house, She knows little of their fathers, but the moor has always known the women best, and She is no exception.

She knows what is coming. She knows what has happened and what will be. Humans are familiar to her now.

This is what they wanted.

iv.

I arrived back from my bike ride as it was getting dark and found my mother and Ysella in another argument. I stood outside the kitchen door and listened to Ysella's heavy steps as she walked around the room, my mother silent, no doubt sitting at the table, avoiding eye contact.

'You can't make this decision on your own,' Ysella said. I recognised the tone – it was the one she reserved for the nights she took me from the cottage as a child, my mother keening on the doorstep, Ysella telling her sister all the reasons she couldn't be trusted with her own child.

I couldn't hear my mother's reply. After a bout of silence, Ysella spoke again.

'There isn't anything we need to discuss, Lo. She's here. You got what you wanted,' Ysella said. I pictured her spitting the words out, them falling on the floor.

My mother's response was feeble, disappointing. The same four words she always believed qualified her as a parent: 'She is my daughter.'

'You can hardly say that now,' Ysella said, 'this behaviour—'

'You're not her mother!'

'Well, neither are you.'

I felt Ysella's words as if I were my mother – thrown straight at her chest. They would burrow there. They would stay there under the surface of her skin, feeding on capillaries and motherly instincts until autumn comes and then they would burst out, locusts ready to feast on every bond that joins us together. I hadn't heard my aunt say something so harsh to my mother in many years, and the sudden onslaught made me feel nervous. I knew where I stood with a mother that was emotional and unpredictable, but my aunt was strong. She wasn't supposed to break easily.

It had been an unbearably hot day. There had been no rain since I'd arrived, and none for two weeks before that. Practically unheard of in this part of the country. I had suffered. The sweat made my skin break out, a group of pimples scattered across my chin, and without my hair, my scalp burnt. Everyone in the farmhouse had been feeling the same cloistered stress, tired of stagnating in each other's company.

I sat myself on the front step and listened to the nothingness in the air around me. I used to find it calming, this lack of noise out on the moors, but after last night, it felt heavy, like the air was folding in on me. I felt anxious in a way I couldn't place. As if I had drunk far too much caffeine. My skin was rippling.

It was nearing dinnertime, but my appetite wasn't there, even though my stomach was so empty I felt weightless. The time had passed me by.

This wasn't a new phenomenon. I first lost my appetite when me and my mother lived in the village. Everyone assumed it was my mother's doing. I would overhear them talking about me when she sent me to the shop.

'The girl doesn't eat,' they'd tut, 'her mam's too busy thinking about herself to feed the wee maid.'

The social would've come round if there was one, but that wasn't the way things worked in the village. Instead, it would be people cornering Mum when we were out. Questioning her. Ysella did the same. She would arrive at the cottage door, every few weeks, and take me from my mother, saying 'the child needs food, Lowen'.

Ysella's large hand would clasp my mother's, which would be clinging onto mine, the three of us in a tryst. In those moments she was towering, bigger than us, bigger than our cottage, bigger than the whole village put together. Ysella the Giant, the protector. My mother, the witch.

Of course, me and my mother knew the truth. We knew that each night, my mother would serve me food – egg mayonnaise sandwiches cut into triangles, spaghetti and meatballs, fish and chips – which I would refuse, and each night, she would try again, offering me cereal, pancakes, biscuits, even, and still, I would say no. Eventually, my mother would give in. She would disappear out of the cottage and come back fifteen minutes later, hands clasping dandelions, roots and all. Each time she stepped over the threshold, she looked like the saddest bride. Still, I would take them from her, greedily swallowing before I'd properly chewed, picking dirt out of my teeth afterwards.

The first time she caught me in the garden, she assumed I'd gotten it wrong. I was crouched in the corner, pushing the yellow flowers into my mouth. When she asked what I was doing, I told her they tasted like the sun.

'They are edible, Sprig, but you've got to wash them first, and then we can cook with them,' she said, plucking the root from between my lips. She led me back inside and sat me at the table, where I swung my legs impatiently as she washed and salted, boiled and sautéed the greens she'd stolen off me moments before. When she placed the cooked greens in front of me, I put one slither on my tongue, tasted the flavours – the butter and the garlic – and spat it out.

After that, she didn't try to cook them for me again. Instead, she would pick as much as she could, leaving leaves and weeds and roots for me to forage through.

On the nights that Ysella took me away from my mother, I would eat. She would sit me at the table in Trewarnen and fill me with stew until my blood was stock and my skin potato peelings.

I'm not sure why I ate with my aunt and not my mother. I never wanted to. The stew she made and the milk she served would turn my stomach. I felt the oily broth line my throat and the dumplings sat heavy and swollen inside me. But I forced them down with a pathetic smile, playing the part of a neglected child, all the while thinking of the patch of montbretia in my mother's front garden, how the waxy orange and red flowers would be waiting for me when I got home. I would put four or five in my mouth at once, hold them on my tongue until they started to break down. They turned my smile into a sunset.

The nights at Ysella's were food and baths and mugs of warm, whole milk, the skin curling at the edges, creeping away from the glass. I'd be in bed, exhausted, by 8 p.m.

'Your age plus one,' she'd say. Washed, laundered and full. Full of everything – joy, mainly. She'd read to me then, from a book only she could see.

'A secret story from a secret book,' she'd say quietly, and I'd kick the covers up to check underneath, throw myself over the edge of the bed, looking at the world underneath upside down, trying to find the secret book of secret stories, before all the blood rushed to my head. Then a big hand, gentle, giant, would scoop me up from my underground upside-down secret mission and plop me back in the bed.

'Story time now, little one,' she'd say, 'what do you want tonight?'

I would luxuriate in my aunt's attention, playing the part of the golden child. After she put me to bed, I would hear her and Esolyn, who kept away from me on those nights, talking about my mother. About how unfit she was, how unhealthy I looked. My grandmother would always repeat the same line, 'I told her so,' and my aunt would shush her.

In the mornings my mother would come to pick me up, and Ysella would leave me in my bedroom, instructing me to stay out of sight until she called for me. I would sit leaning against the door, picking red and blue fibres from the rug at my feet, smoothing them out in my palm as they argued downstairs, Mum babbling at speed, incoherent. At times, she would be pushing to take me home, back to the village. On other days, she would tell Ysella to keep me for longer, *there are things I need to do*, she would say.

'Whose child is this?' Ysella would ask, growing more frustrated as she repeated herself, 'Is she mine? Is she yours? Where is the responsibility, Lowen?'

I had thought they were arguing over love, that they each wanted to claim me. As a child, there had been something entertaining about the way my mother and aunt fought for my affection. They were so different from each other, but from a young age I could see how they were bound together, their shared histories lacing them tight. The family had been a trio – them and my grandmother – for so long, I felt like an outlier. The only way I could fit in was to divide and conquer. There was always so much I wasn't allowed to know. So many conversations I was pushed out of rooms for, so many times I was told to go and play whilst the grown-ups talked. They were each always withholding something from me. At first, my desire to break up their party of three was like the urge to pick at a scab. Irresistible.

Now, hearing them argue again, all these years later, I wondered if it had always been me that caused the problems between them, if my existence caused irrevocable damage. Had I been easier, more malleable, less contrary. If I had not left, or not come back. If I had eaten, or listened, or not lied, perhaps we would not have ended up where we are now. Maybe it was never about who loved me more, but who wanted me less.

The door opened then, and my mother looked down at me and scrunched up her face in an approximation of a smile.

'Can I sit with you?' she asked.

'I was about to go in,' I lied, pulling myself up from the step. All I wanted was to take myself away. I didn't want to be out on the moors again, not now it was getting dark, but I couldn't bear to be in the house either. Mum bit at her nails. Put them between her teeth and filleted them slowly. I saw myself in the way she plucked at them, holding those foreign objects on her tongue.

'Have you got to shoot off?' she said, pulling a fingernail from her teeth.

'S'all right, I wasn't going anywhere,' I dropped back down onto the step and pulled my tobacco out of my pocket. A cigarette in her company wouldn't do either of us any harm. Mum and Ysella argued often, the way two people who lived in each other's pockets did – an inconsequential cycle of differences of opinion. Whether the potatoes should be parboiled, if fruit that came from the big shop needed to be washed before eating, if 9 p.m. was an appropriate time to go to bed, how long was too long to spend in the bath. The bickering of everyday life was long and laborious and they went in circles, as if the day was a stage for harmless disagreements.

This felt different. There was no sport to it, no element of fun. There was desperation in their words, an urgency, as if they were, finally, pushed for time. I had no sisters, no frame of reference for how that relationship should be – I could only imagine it was similar to the way I felt whenever me and Claud fell out, like there was an irrevocable wrong in the world.

Mum smiled at me and then turned to face the field. There was something lopsided in her smile, something skewed. She wasn't OK, but I wasn't sure how. When we lived in the cottage I could read her moods well, but time away – time in which I'd left her to her sister – had created a chasm in how much I cared. Her hands were in her lap, fiddling with the hem of her jumper, and she stretched her legs out in front of her, pushing her bare feet against the dirt. I thought she was preparing to talk to me about Ysella, but instead she said, 'Did you have a nice time last night?'

'It was OK. I don't feel great now.'

'Are you sick?'

'Nah. It's just a hangover. Long night.'

'I'll get you some turmeric, later. Don't let me forget. What did you do today?'

'I went to Dozmary, it was all right.'

She scrunched her toes up. 'Alone?'

'I borrowed Ysella's bike and I just ended up there.'

'Did you feel anything?'

I took a drag of my cigarette and turned to her. She sat fidgeting, her face curious. I remembered this mood. My mother, the child. I tried to rearrange myself into a person with patience.

'Like what? I went there because the memorial—'

'Ha!' she interrupted, still facing the fields.

'What?'

'The memorial! I'm bored of it!' She paused. 'Ysella's upset I dragged you back here for it.'

'Upset? Why?'

She starts to shake her head. 'I told her. I said, I said, it'll all be fine, Merryn will want to be here. She'll want to be with us. Ye said we should leave you in that city, but me, I thought that we should just . . .'

She paused again.

'. . . tell you everything. No, no. Look at what happened to the other one, she said. The other one knew, and see how she ended up, down in the water, arm in arm with the Bucca. Thinks that just because I get distracted, she knows best. She always was a smart-arse. Always acts like she has all the brains. It's not true though.'

She wasn't making any sense. 'Tell me what? Tell me everything about what?'

'She said the other one had a terrible mother and that I was better than that. It's different with you. That's nice though, isn't it? That I brought you up better. Never hid from you, no. Never told you things I shouldn't. You had a nice time, didn't you? Your friend didn't, but you did. I always thought that was nice of her to say, that I was a good mother.'

'You were a good mother, you are. But what were you going to tell me, Mum? You said you wanted to tell me something?'

'I've always been smart; you know that, don't you? Just in a different way. The older I get the more I can see, and now every evening I come out here,' she waved her hands towards the sky, 'and look out over the fields, just for a little bit of peace,' she turned to me then, finally, and gripped my knee, whispering theatrically, 'The memorial is all pretend!' And then she laughed.

It couldn't be. It wasn't. I dropped my cigarette on the floor and grabbed my mother's face, turning her gently towards me, so I could look into her eyes. I needed her to stay still. She was still laughing, wriggling under my touch.

'What do you mean?' I asked, speaking as slowly as I could. Her eyes were dull. I couldn't tell if she'd skipped her meds or taken too many.

'There's no memorial. Not even one. They couldn't celebrate the life of their girl after what they did to her. But you had to come, you see? Ignore Ysella. She thinks she's the smart one, they both did, but I know more, I know more than any of them,'

'What did they do to her? Who?'

'They tried to keep her. That's what they did. Tried to keep her.'

It didn't make sense, but at least she was answering me. I spoke again, cautiously. 'And who do you know more than?'

'Mam. Mam and Ysella. Trying to tell me what to do ever since you—' her head snapped around as a door shut inside. I tried to pull her back to me.

'Mum.'

She smacked my hand off her arm. 'Shhh. Be quiet.'

'Mum, come on.'

'No.' She stayed staring at the door.

I got up from the step and moved in front of her, crouching by her knees.

'It's only Ysella, it's fine.' I squeezed her shoulder, my hand sliding against the clamminess of her skin. She waited for a beat and then, when no more sounds were forthcoming, she finally turned back to me.

'Don't tell her you went to Dozmary.'

'Why not?'

'Mam took you there once. For the water. She wanted to put you in. Dip, dip, dip the baby. Fix you right up,' she said, wiping her sweating hands on my scalp as she spoke, as if she were trying to baptise me herself.

'What were you saying about the memorial, Mum? Why would it be pretend?' I asked, trying to steer her back. But it was too late, she was stuck. She kept stroking my head, mumbling about dipping the baby. I placed my hand over hers, following her as she traced the lines of my skull.

When we lived in the cottage, she had one of those ceramic phrenology skulls. The skull split into sections, with personality traits related to the shape of the head. She'd picked it up from the market, and it sat in the middle of the coffee table in the living room. There was nothing to it – it was cheap and hollow and the silk-screening was off, so the labels were too large for the sections of the skull they were attributed to. 'Self-destruction' and 'Combativeness' crossed over each other at the front. 'Assuredness' was missing an s. Most of the time, the head would be placed on its side and my mother would ash into it. Occasionally, she would get me to sit in front of her so she could read my skull, assigning meaning herself when she didn't like what it told her.

She was my mother, and I had always felt like I should know how to help her, but instead, I had been pushing against the tide of her illness my whole life. The greatest pain of all was how this thing within her would sit just below the surface, waiting for the right moment to burst through and take over. There could be weeks and months when my mother seemed steady. And then, the breaks occurred. Moments like this one, where she regressed, I was reminded that there was no happy outcome for my mother's wellness. What scared me the most, as she rubbed her hands along the ridges of my ears, tapped the roof of my skull and massaged my temples, was the thought of all this *sickness* bubbling up within her. I'd never been told her exact diagnosis – I'd read about residual schizophrenia, post-partum psychosis, PTSD, but no one thing quite explained it. I often wondered how much of her was within me. This thing that sat before me, this woman, on her haunches, this creature squeezing my face: was this my future? Or was she my root? Was she the answer to why I did not feel at home in this skin, in this world?

She pinched my ear then, brought me back into focus. I hadn't been paying her attention.

'Sorry, Mum,' I said, cupping her hand and moving it with mine, like Ysella had taught me to do as a child. We went to the bridge of my nose. 'Individuality, here,' and then the space behind my ears, 'Destructiveness, here.'

She giggled. It was the quickest way to calm her down.

The door opened just as I was guiding her to the spot where hope lives. She startled, and then grimaced at Ysella, who towered over us both in her long skirt. Ysella gave me an apologetic look, just quickly, and then turned to my mother with a gentle smile on her face.

'You look like a pair of monkeys down there. C'mon, best we get you in now it's getting dark,' she said, taking my mother's hand and guiding her inside.

'Is it true?' I asked Ysella.

'What?' She held the door open for me, but I shook my head. I wanted to stay sat in the dirt for a little while longer.

'The memorial. Is it real?'

Ysella looked at my mother, hanging off her arm, and at me, fingers scratching at the ground, and made a grunt of disgust.

'Christ. Now is not the time. Look at the state of your mother,' she shook her head and went inside, leaving me to scoop up little pieces of mud and rub them against my gums.

That evening, I charged my phone and found a text from Chris.

Asked Selena about the eel thing you mentioned. Obviously she doesn't know much about you Cornish folk and your weird ways but she said it sounds like a ward. Looked it up and think she's right. It's like putting a protective seal around your house to stop any dark spirits getting in. Spooky.

v.

In the weeks after the camping trip, Claud's skin broke. It started with the skin on her elbow. It was raw, and when she scratched it, it began to bloom with seeds of blood. Her eczema was flaring up, the way it did whenever she was stressed.

She'd just moved into a bedsit of her own in town. Me and Chris helped her move. He drove us both to Bodmin, his car full of bin bags of clothes. He knew things still weren't right between us, and I could feel his awkwardness in the way he drove, too fast, wanting us out of his car as quickly as possible. He was angry with me especially. He was friends with Claud, and he cared about her deeply, but he couldn't understand why I allowed her to treat me the way she did, especially after the camping trip. Every time he asked me about it, whenever we were alone, I wanted to wave my hands in the air, gesture to my whole being. Claud was me. I wasn't a full person without her. We were tied. I could let her go, just a bit, lengthen the string enough for me to move away in September, but I couldn't cut her off completely. I was all she really had, or at least I wanted to be. There were others, people she'd share her bed with, but I should have been the one that mattered. And the only way to be that was to keep showing up.

Chris left to pick up his mum from work and me and Claud dragged everything up the stairs to her flat. We gave up on unpacking quite quickly when we realised there wasn't enough furniture to hold her things. I folded her clothes in piles in the corner of her bedroom as she sat on her mattress. She looked small. The pieces of her bed frame leant against the wall.

'Do you want me to put that up next?' I asked.

She shook her head. 'Let's leave it. It'll give me something to do tomorrow.'

'OK.' I watched as she scratched at her neck. It looked angry.

'Will you lie down with me?' she asked. I crawled onto the mattress and lay next to her, so close I could count her eyelashes. We swallowed more words than we gave each other in those days. We breathed them into each other's mouths, lying face to face, not a single part of us touching.

We stayed that way for a while, maybe an hour. At times I thought she'd fallen asleep, but then she would begin to pick at her elbow or roll her trouser leg up so she could scratch the back of her knee. The room had grown dark around us.

In the low light of evening, Claud said, 'I hate my body'.

She'd lost a lot of weight over the last year. Ever since we'd first kissed, she seemed to be getting smaller and smaller. I knew how to look after Claud, but I didn't know how to get her to look after herself.

I was jealous of her skeleton; it got to hold her up. I told her so.

She laughed. 'You're so dramatic.' She meant it kindly.

'I know. But it's true.' I shifted slightly, touched her wrist. Broke the space between us, 'And you should look after yourself. Have you eaten today?'

She shook her head.

'I'm worried.' I closed my eyes as I said it.

'You don't need to worry,' she replied, draping her long hair over her bare chest, 'it's just a little hollow for you to rest your head. I've made a nest for you, right there. I'm like a tree.'

'No,' I said, 'not a tree. A huldra.'

'A what?' she asked, smiling. She was always excited when she thought she was going to learn something new. She was a creature, wild hair and flushed chest. I reached out and touched her there, and it was scaled. One of her arms was wrapped around my waist.

She was ready to slip into the sea; I wanted her to take me with her.

'A huldra is a spirit in the body of a naked woman, with a hollow back.' Empty, empty. 'So, see, you're like a huldra, but backwards. Instead of a hollow back, you've got a hollow front.'

'Like magic,' she grinned.

She wasn't taking my worry seriously. 'You need to look after yourself,' I said. It came out like an order. I tried to catch the words and shove them back into my mouth, but they'd already fallen all around us. 'You don't look healthy. I mean, I don't think you're healthy.'

'I just told you I'm not happy with myself and now you're telling me I look bad?'

'No, no that's not what I meant. You look great, you always do.'

'What do you mean then, Merryn? What's the problem?' She took her hand from my waist.

'There isn't one. I just want you to look after yourself.'

'For fuck's sake.' She pulled herself up, so she was sitting. 'You need to stop telling me what to do.'

I scrambled to my knees, knelt in front of her. The mattress made me lose my balance and I saw the quirk of a smile on her face before she covered it up. She was mad, and she wasn't mad, at once. I could save this moment.

'You're right,' I said. She scowled at me, and I tried not to smile. 'I shouldn't tell you what to do.'

She nodded. 'You shouldn't'.

'I very much should not.' I reached out and stroked the soft-sore skin on her elbow. Her face stayed impassive, but she pushed her arm into my touch. 'And I'm sorry.'

'For being bossy.'

'Right. For being bossy.'

'And annoying.'

'That too. Are we good?'

'Keep stroking me and we will be.'

'I can do that.'

She moved so that she was sat between my legs, and tipped her head towards her chest, offering the back of her neck to me.

'Here please,' she said, from underneath her hair. I ran my fingers back and forth across her neck.

After a few minutes, I asked, 'What do you want to do tonight, lil' huldra?' She made a non-committal noise in response.

'I do have one idea.' I said.

'Are you going to try and tell me to do something?'

'Kind of.' She tensed. I squeezed her shoulders in apology. 'In a fun way, though. D'you have any porridge? Or oats?'

She ducked away from my touch and looked over her shoulder at me. 'I don't want to eat any porridge.'

'We're not going to eat it. It's for a bath. An oat bath, for your skin, it stops the itching.'

I ran her a bath in her tiny windowless bathroom and together we poured two pint glasses of oatmeal into the water. It wasn't the right way to do it, but it was better than nothing. She stripped off and stepped in, holding my arm for balance. I barely ever saw her completely undressed. It had always been me, offering myself to her in all my vulnerability. She was white edged and shiny, scars from her eczema splattered like wax on the hidden pieces of her skin. The inside of her thighs. Below her armpit, skating across the top of her ribs. A fresh pink patch ran down the valley between her breasts, a shiver on her sternum. The rest of her tanned a dry-grass yellow, but these secret bits glittered with tissue.

FOLKLORE

The farmhouse wants to remind those that live in it that their time is only fleeting. It has stood long before them, and it will continue to stand long after they fall. It groans with the weight of its age. Listen carefully now – can you hear it? Can you hear the shudder of the pipes and the scream of the floorboards as they are pressed on?

Poor house. We pity the house, in all its youthful old age. It is young, see, impermanent. No more everlasting than those that grow and fold within its walls. It is still new on this land; our grounds were carved out by weather and burned for centuries before any bricks were laid.

It is not hard to find something older walking on the moors – a kitchen wall in a pound, a stone circle made from menhirs, Her, or Bucca-Widn, guarding the lake.

The way-markers still stood, those boundary stones carrying the initials of land-owning men, the men who wanted to capture the land. Forgotten everywhere except on juts of granite poking out of grassy banks.

The visitors often walk across our lands with reverence. They remember, even when they don't. They whisper in church and hold their breath before stepping underground. It's the reason they falter on thresholds of old buildings but burst through the doors of skyscrapers as if they already own them.

DAY PYMP

i.

As the days of my visit dragged on, I had little hope that I would return to the city before the nights grew longer. My aunt had put my mother to bed last night, dosing her up with an emergency medication that left her sleeping until lunchtime. Later, when I was in bed, I heard the door of the farmhouse slam shut, but running to the window showed me nothing.

I got up and reached under the bed for my bag, but when I looked, the bag was gone. I searched my room, and then downstairs, starting by the front door. I kicked wellies and heaved foul-smelling wax jackets across the porch, in a desperate search for it, assuming I'd dumped it when I came in, without thinking. My phone was in the front pocket. I wanted to call someone else, anyone else, to see if they had heard about the memorial. It couldn't be done spontaneously; it took planning. Maybe I had never been invited at all and nobody wanted to tell me that, but I needed to leave in two days time if I was going to make it back in time to start my summer job. And if, by some miracle, the memorial was within the next two days, I needed to try on the black dress I'd brought down with me, maybe iron it. I wasn't sure if you were supposed to wear black to a memorial, or just a funeral.

If Claud were going with me, I would wear a suit. It would be bearable, going with her. She would be inappropriately loud and friendly, and her light would distract everyone from my shadow.

Claud would probably wear a dress too, something cut short and black, and then no one would be surprised to see me in trousers and a shirt.

With Claud in a dress, we'd make sense to them. With my newly shaved head, they might not even recognise me. They'd see me and Claud as a couple. As long as we mirrored a straight relationship, it wouldn't take long for the heterosexuals in attendance to forget we were both women. I wanted people to see us together, to show that what we had wasn't some sordid little affair: it was a partnership. But if Claud was here to come with me, there'd be no need for a memorial at all.

Ever since reading the story of 'The Baker and the Bread', I had felt imbalanced in the house, as if my sneaking around and reading the notebook were marked on me for all to see, and now my bag was missing. The two things felt connected, as if I was being punished for my intrusion. I wanted to know what Claud had to do with the Pedri, once and for all. I had woken up with the determination to find out, to put an end to whatever this was, but then I had been blindsided. My bag had been removed from my room in the night, squirreled away. It was not just the bag itself that worried me, but what it represented: my escape. My phone, my wallet, everything I needed to leave here was in that bag. And somehow, during my sleep, someone – something – had come into my bedroom, crawled under my bed and taken it.

I cleared the floor in the porch completely and found nothing.

Downstairs, the house was warm. Boiling, in fact, for the morning, the heat toying with the smell of fish. Without wanting to, I touched the nearest windowsill. It felt like flesh, thick with grease and guts. Ysella's ritual seemed to take place daily. Each afternoon she made her mash, sealing the house up with it. It knitted everything together, clamping the windows shut like scar tissue. The heat was attracting flies. It wouldn't be long until they laid eggs in the old fish and soon enough, the eel would be alive again, grafted onto the walls.

I took the stairs two at a time, noticing the fur of damp on the walls, the flakes of paint piled at the sides of each step. It got hotter as I rose, but the walls were danker still.

The smell of damp, the fish, blocked my throat. I could taste it on the back of my teeth. I stopped part way to catch my breath – my stomach roiling with the smell, my whole self too queasy to run upstairs in one go. The hallway was in a worse state than I was. Books with broken spines lay upended, as if they had been catapulted out of rooms. Only the rug protected bare feet from rough wooden floorboards, but that had been kicked to the side, dejected. I leant against the radiator to rest and then recoiled quickly, as the heat of it hit the backs of my thighs.

They were trying to burn the damp out of the house, with the radiator on full heat. It made little sense – the clumps of paint on the walls, wet to the touch, the house shedding its skin. Things hadn't been this bad when I arrived. They weren't even that bad when I went downstairs earlier. How had I not noticed it before? I was so focused on the bag when I left my room the first time, I missed everything around me. How could something crumble so quickly?

She must've heard me curse at the radiator, as my aunt called out, 'In here, Merryn'.

I followed Ysella's voice, stepping into her bedroom. She was sat on the edge of the wrought-iron bed, legs planted apart, back straight. She looked statuesque, unsurprised by the state of me, my feet bare and my cheeks coloured. Between her legs on the floor was my mother, sat forward facing towards the wall, knees drawn to her chest, fingers roaming the floorboards. A clump of her hair was in Ysella's fist. Scissors were on the bed.

To the left of them, large, black, open – my bag. I started towards it, but then the troubled looks on their faces pulled me up short.

'What? That's my bag – you took my bag,' I said, pointing towards it lamely. I couldn't place why it felt like I was invading their privacy, rather than them intruding on mine. Ysella rolled her eyes at me.

'I'm cutting your mam's hair. We borrowed some things, as you said. We're done now.'

She held the bag out for me, and I took it from her. I walked out of the room, nodding, smiling. Calming myself.

'Will you be down for lunch?' Ysella called after me.

'No,' I shouted back, balancing on the top stair, 'no thank you.'

I ran along the hallway, away from the image of the two of them, and shut myself in my room, bag held against my chest. I no longer trusted the lock on my bedroom door, so I pulled a chest full of linens in front of it and perched on the bed. I had my bag back; I had a partial explanation for the loss, and yet I still felt anxious in a way I couldn't explain. I picked at a scab on my knee, grounding myself.

I tipped the contents of my bag onto the bed, checking that everything was still there. Wallet, phone, Ysella's notebook – *had she seen it?* – some socks, my hairbrush. The brush caught my eye – I didn't remember packing it. Why would I when I had nothing to brush? I assumed I had left it in the bottom of my bag, thrown in there out of habit and then forgotten about, but it looked different, new.

I turned it over in my hands, rubbing my thumb against the cheap plastic handle. It took me a moment to realise why it seemed changed: it was clean. Someone had been through it and pulled away the dead hair that matted around the bristles.

ii.

The rush of the morning, the stench of the house and the un-wavering heat had left my head pounding. I waited until the sounds of lunchtime – the popping of the toaster, the clattering of plates in the sink – were done, before I took myself downstairs, in search of some water. My mother and aunt were both in the kitchen, seemingly well and at peace with each other.

When they saw how I was moving, they began to fret around me. My aunt directed me to a chair, pulling open my mouth to check my tonsils, testing the temperature of my forehead with the back of her palm.

I said I was tired, but my mother wouldn't let it go, and instead of letting me sleep, she sat and watched as I drank a pint of her homemade golden milk – a mix of turmeric, pepper, cinnamon, and ginger root, heated through full-fat cow's milk. I watched her throat bob along as I swallowed, a kind of harmonising with me as I drank.

She told me it would help the inflammation, that it was her mother's recipe, and that I needed to finish it all, even when it came back up. And it did, over and again, sweetening my mouth a second, sickly time. She simply placed a hand over my mouth and told me to swallow, her chewed-down fingers pinching my jaw.

Ysella worked in the kitchen behind us, face hidden behind cupboard doors, tongue caught. She tore at an eel with her hands, hooking her nails beneath the loose flap of yellow skin she had cut. The pliers had been long abandoned now; the skin no longer removed in one pure piece. Instead, she peeled it back like wall-paper, chunks of meat sticking to the pieces she tore.

I drained my milk and eyed the sediment that gritted the bottom of the glass as Ysella picked up her bowl and moved towards a window.

'That looks like it's been pulled out of someone's throat. Why are you doing this again?' I asked, unsuccessfully resisting the temptation to poke the white marbled meat as she passed me. It was softer than I imagined it to be, like grabbing a fleshy hip, which somehow made it worse. Ysella cradled her bowl protectively.

'It's research, for work. Perhaps you ought to go and see your doctor in the city if you're so ill.'

'Work, for your story stuff, you mean?' I asked, sounding more dismissive than I felt. I was tired, and my patience for her deflection was waning.

She said nothing, so I spoke into her silence, eager to fill in the awkward gap.

'Sorry, not your story, your research. That's cool. Bit weird, isn't it?' I paused. There was slime on my fingers from where I'd poked Ysella's bowl. I knew I needed to be more direct. 'Is that what this Pedri stuff is about, has it got something to do with the eels?'

Ysella froze, bowl in hand, her back stiffened. And then my mother laughed, forcefully, her attempt to block the conversation coming a beat too slow. It was a shrill and uncomfortable noise, and in that moment, I knew it had not been a good idea to bring this up.

Before Ysella could respond to me herself, my mother began to talk and didn't stop.

'That's a funny word, isn't it? Peddy. Seems foreign. Shall we all eat dinner together later if you're feeling better, Sprig? Should be nice, shouldn't it? I better make you another cup of something warm before you're off up to bed, you are looking peaky. Isn't she looking peaky, Ye? Don't you think?'

She darted around me in a complicated two-step, magicking some loose herbal tea from a shelf and a strainer from the floor behind a Bag for Life full of empty juice cartons.

Across the other side of the room, Ysella had broken from her freeze frame and was slopping her mixture onto the windowsills again. It spread as thick as oil paint, with only trace amounts of blood catching on the glass.

I watched as Mum poured the tea, my stomach turning with the thickening of the water as the limescale settled near the top of the cup. I grabbed my mug out of her grasp too quickly, spilling hot water down the side and leaving a trail across the floor as I ran back upstairs.

I heard my mother's voice trailing behind me, her voice hitching with panic as she said to Ysella, 'I told you not to do it whilst she was in the room, for God's sake'.

I knew then that this was something. I had been fearful, before, that my obsession with the Pedri was a misplaced symptom of my grief, a way to avoid thinking about Claud, and everything that happened in the time before I left for the city. But now I knew I was right, it *was* something. The Pedri was worth knowing, and worth hiding.

When I got back to my room, I was sweating. I walked to the mirror, contorting my body into different positions, trying to see myself as Claud would have. The damp had left my skin puckered and clammy, sticky to the touch. The hair under my arms was growing out. The first time it had ever done so, after being shaved away ever since it first dared to grow. My legs, also covered in a fine sheen of hair, shiny now from the damp. Looking in the mirror then, my head shaved, droplets of sweat still running down my forehead, I felt more sea creature than woman – a kraken, a merrow. My thighs stuck together, and I saw myself, tail and gills, snarling teeth, dragging people down with me into the deep.

My head began to throb and swim, and the quick pain made me feel foolish, stood naked and feverish looking at myself, so I crawled back into bed. Ever since that first time, my migraines tasted like sloe berries. I closed my eyes and willed the taste away.

I opened my eyes and saw the window shattered. My migraine had darkened the edges of my vision and I saw an aura fall into the room. I pressed my fingers against my eyelids, willing the dark splotches to go away, but when I opened them, it was still there, a large dark slug of shadow, dragging itself across the floor. As if it had hauled itself in through the cracks. A living thing.

I tried to scream out to Ysella, but my voice was hoarse, my sight still pulsing from the migraine. The darkness moved across the room, sucking up everything it touched until it was all consumed. It couldn't be. I tried to shake the sight away, but the pain in my head was dull and smothering, and I couldn't hold on.

I felt boneless, a wisp with no substance, as if the dark sky were matter, holding me down. Still it reached for me, closer again. I needed to push myself up, get off the bed, but my feet only hooked into the mattress, the pain in my ankle from the night outside locking me in place.

The darkness closed over my foot, casting it in shadow, before I could finally move. When I could, I slammed my body back in panic, let my skull smack into the wall.

I woke to pain. A mouth so dry, my gums felt as if they were cracking. It was still daylight, just. Something had lifted. My headache was easing. When I looked to the window to see the damage, it was unbroken, solid. Not even a crack.

People and places and brains can trick you. Ysella once told me about Plato's allegory of the cave. How the people trapped inside, faces turned to the wall, thought the shadows projected onto the walls were real, when actually, the real objects were blocking the light that shone from behind them. He reasoned that when one of the prisoners broke free, he'd be overwhelmed by the sight of the real world. If the shadows were fake, what was blocking the light in my room? What if the real world was worse than the projected one?

FOLKLORE

You would be mistaken if you believed all the horrors of the world belonged to Her. She is powerful, but She is not the only one older than time, disappointed with the way the world moves on. There are many names for creatures like Her.

There are houses in Leicester that are kept small, with windows no larger than cat-flaps. The people in these houses live with little light, so that Black Annis, which is the name they give their horror, won't reach inside and snatch them.

In South Africa, a man is placing bricks into four neat piles, each as high as his hip. He is not making a wall; he is a making a stand. Upon the pile of bricks, he puts his child's bed, so that his boy can sleep far above the ground. The horror in their house is the Tokoloshe, and it will steal their breath as they sleep if they are not watchful.

Fish and lard are spread across windows and doorways in Cornwall, England.

Children are held back from water in Savonlinna, Finland. Skogsrå is in the woods in Sweden. Baba Yaga is in the Russian forest. Bunyip haunts the Australian billabongs.

There are three women in a house and none of them is telling the truth.

A man is cutting down a hedge.

A woodland is razed to the ground.

These horrors bring death and birth and loss and hierarchy, and all of it will end in ruin. She has been watching.

iii.

There wasn't much of Claud left near the end. She was still herself, just in slithers. You'd have to pull back her eyelids and shine a torch back there to glimpse a bit of what she had been before. Sometimes I thought it was me, or us, that had made her like that. The deeper the two of us got, the less sure of herself she seemed. It was as if, in loving me, she'd carved out chunks of her own self until she was pockmarked with uncertainty.

She kept getting boyfriends, which I could just about cope with, even though the thought of their sausage-like fingers inside her made me want to scrub myself raw, but it was the only thing that seemed to keep her grounded. I think it was the attention – the way in which they shone their light on her made her feel whole. She said that to me once. 'You take my light,' she said. It was a month after the camping trip, and though things were still strained, she'd started to accept the fact that I would be leaving at the end of summer. She hadn't forgiven me, but she'd let me back in, and I was pathetically grateful.

We were at her flat watching something pointless on the TV. She'd been swimming before I came round, and she'd seemed agitated all morning. I was there, posted up on her sofa, this sticky fake leather thing that came with the flat, all hard angles and no cushions, and she was fiddling round with the HDMI cable from her laptop to her TV, trying to connect it so we could watch Netflix. The cable wouldn't work – the picture came through on the telly, but the sound was still coming out of the tiny laptop speakers – so she got frustrated and slammed her laptop closed.

'Fuck that,' she said, getting up from the floor and stretching,

'I've got a dead leg now. I'll make us a brew and then you can just tell me a story.'

She walked to the kitchen, barefoot on her carpet speckled with grime, and I thought about how thin she looked, still, all these years after she first told me she wanted to disappear. I wanted to put her in my mouth. I wanted to twirl her hair around a fork like spaghetti and swallow it whole, until it wrapped around the inside of my stomach and made a nest there.

I'd nip at her shoulder when we were in bed together, nibble on her toes and suck on her fingers, and she'd laugh, say she wanted to shrink herself so she could sit in my stomach without giving me indigestion. That's what it was about, carrying each other. I suppose if we'd been somewhere else, or some other people, we could've said these things a different way, or shown them a different way. Maybe there would've been a ring, or dinners with the parents, hands held on busy streets or even a picture taken together and plastered up on Facebook. As it was, the world we had was a small one, and we were pressed together so tightly that we had no choice but to absorb each other, all of it.

She came back from the kitchen carrying two brews in stained JD Sports mugs. She put the mugs on the floor by our feet, milky tea spilling on the carpet. Her hair was still wet. I arrived just after she got home, so she hadn't showered since her swim in the lake, just scrubbed at herself with a towel. She smelled damp.

'Can I borrow a Rizla? I asked.

'Take it to the window,' she said, passing me a gossamer-thin paper.

When the window was cranked and my cigarette was lit, she asked me again to tell her a story. All she wanted then was stories. Anything to take her out of that flat. She was sat cross legged on the sofa, hair scraped back from her face in a way that should've looked harsh. All I could see was her skull. She held the mug close to her chest, dipping a finger into the tea every now and then, checking to see how hot it was but never drinking it.

'Did I tell you the one about the giant?'

She shook her head. Blew on her tea, all for show – that drink was going nowhere.

'All right, well, Ysella used to tell me it. This was when I was young-young, when we lived in the village, and I'd stay at the farm when Mum was on one. There's this giant, the giant of Carn Galva, and he lived on some cliffs near the sea, right at the top. At the bottom of the cliffs was the village, all these little houses and horses and villagers, going about their business, peaceful. So, the giant sat at the very top of his cliff, watching the villagers and feeling lonely, because he had no one. Obviously, the villagers were scared of him, and the other giants didn't like him because he wasn't big enough, or scary enough. So, he spent all his time on his own. And then one day, there was a flood in the village, and the giant leant down and scooped up all the villagers, and he took them to safety. After that, they liked him a little more, and he even made friends with one of them, this human boy called Choon.'

'Choon?'

'Yeah, I know. Choon. Anyway, they hung out, and they'd play this game called quoits, which is where you throw these hoops—'

'I know it.'

'Right, so they throw the hoops over the sticks or whatever. And the giant was obviously better than Choon because he was bigger than him – not as big as the other giants, but bigger than Choon, at least. So they practised, all the time. And one day, Choon finally beat him.'

'Go Choon.'

'Go Choon. Except, the giant was so excited when Choon won – he was so proud of him – that he picked him up and gave him a hug. He really squeezed him. And because he was a giant and Choon was just a boy, he squeezed him so tight that he crushed his head. There's a story in Greek mythology that's basically the same, but I can't remember their names, the guys in that one. The Gods. But yeah. That's that.'

Claud screwed up her face. 'So, what's the point?'

'You don't get it?'

A pause.

'He loved him so much that he crushed him.'

'You think you can love someone so much that you crush them?'

'I could probably love you that much.'

'I don't think that's how it works. When Davey says he loves me' (Davey was her newest boyfriend at the time), 'it's like he's giving me something.'

'Right.'

I took another Rizla from her packet, without asking this time. As I pinched out the baccy, I imagined I was pinching up and down the goose flesh of her arm. Not to hurt her – never to hurt her – just to show her how it feels.

'Like, it makes me feel happy and full. It's weighty. Shiny.'

'Sounds pretty fucking crushing to me.'

'Shut up.'

We sat in silence as I tried to light my fag. The lighter didn't work – the flint must've gone, because there was plenty of gas – and I dashed it against the wall. Claud sighed then, louder than she needed to. This happened whenever we spent time together, then. She talked about loving all these other people. As if there was enough of her to share, as if her love was an untapped well that kept going and going. Suddenly, I felt like I was being held hostage in her shitty little flat, just a bit part in her shitty little life, and I wanted to scream. I knew if I did, I'd end up tearing my own throat out. Instead, I walked into the kitchen and lit my fag off her toaster, holding the lever down until the element inside glowed orange. The heat of it flushed my cheeks.

I walked back into the living room and sat on the window-sill, leaning my back against the warm pane. It was late afternoon, and the sun was lighting up all the dust that was gathering in the air. We'd been like this ever since that night on the moors. You'd think she'd feel like she owed me, and that's why it was awkward sometimes. But it wasn't. It was like she knew that she could do anything to me, and I'd keep sitting at her feet, chewing on her ankles until she disappeared, and neither of us would ever do anything to help each other.

'It doesn't feel like that when you say you love me,' she said.

I pulled the cigarette from my mouth slowly, exhaling through my nose. It burnt but I didn't want to open my mouth – there were too many words building up there already, waiting to come out. We didn't talk about these things.

'When you say you love me, you aren't giving me anything. You're taking.'

'The fuck, Claud?' So much for keeping my mouth shut. She's up then, her cold cup of tea dumped on the floor, arms wrapped around herself like she's got the shakes and she's trying to hold herself still.

'You take from me, that's all you do.'

'That's bullshit. I give you everything. Everything I have is yours.'

'No,' she stuck her lip out, and she immediately looked like the eleven-year-old I first met. It makes me angrier than it should.

'Yes. All my free time, my energy, whenever you call, I'm here, whenever you're upset, I'm here. All my attention. Even my fucking coat,' I wave at it, dumped in the corner like an animal that's crawled away to die.

'No. You take. You take my light. Every time you say you love me, something dies.'

'You can't say that.'

'It's true! I die! It's like – you sicken me, OK? I didn't want to say it, but it's true. I'm *disgusted* around you. It just feels wrong, all of it is wrong and it makes my skin crawl. Every time you've been here, it's like I need to go and scrub you off in the bath afterwards.'

She stopped, just for a moment, and looked me in the eye to see if I was going to argue back, but I was shattered, split into a thousand tiny pieces and I could not put myself back together again to respond.

She carried on. 'And you know what? I do. I go into the bath after you leave and I scrub myself raw. The way my skin is, all this eczema, the bleeding and the cracks and the sheer fucking pain I'm in every day? It's you. I'm allergic to you being in my life and it's killing me, so you just need to leave.' She took a breath. 'Leave. Please.'

I try to hold myself together for some time after that, but it feels precarious. If Claud is allergic to me, then I am allergic to my own skin. Knowing the way I make her feel makes me want to peel myself apart, bury everything that I am. I want to disappear. I don't want to be a part of the world if I make it painful for her. But I couldn't take myself away, because I knew she would need me again. I knew she would ask me back, even if I – somehow – made her sicker. And I was right; she did still need me. Perhaps a stronger person than me would've kept their distance, allowed Claud to heal, realised that our relationship wasn't right, but I was not strong. So, we saw each other again, we slept together again, I continued to tell her stories and she continued to show me texts from her boyfriends.

Something had changed though. I saw the way we pulled from each other. How empty she looked, whenever I stepped back to watch her. How hungry I felt when we were apart, ravenous. I felt the urge to be with her like an itch, like a hundred tiny bugs were burrowing just beneath my skin.

I sat in the garden at Trewarnen, just before I was due to leave for uni, and I dug. I brushed aside the first layer of dirt, the compacted dry stuff, the dust, and dug into the softer layer below. I scooped fistfuls of dirt into my mouth, rubbed it against my gums and pressed it against the roof of my mouth. It was wetter, richer than the rest. I swallowed and felt the iron in my throat, felt the age of it as it settled in me. It was the only thing that stopped the itching, the only thing that cleared my head of her.

My aunt caught me out there. It was the first time she'd ever seen me do it, and the shock on her face let me know that my mother never told her, that she kept my secret for all those years, even though everyone blamed her.

Ysella grabbed me by the wrist and dragged me into the house, cursing me out. That night she locked all the doors, moved the keys somewhere I couldn't find them. I thought it was the dirt she was mad about, but then I heard her talking to my mother, late when they thought I was asleep. It was the digging. She didn't want me to dig.

FOLKLORE

There is always a part of a house that knows those that live in it, better than the people know their home. Trewarnen, this farmhouse, has held the lives and deaths of the Tregellas family. It has served as gatekeeper and acolyte.

The house has warned them, but they will not hear.

We could tell them if they would just place an ear to the ground. If they ran fingers through our tangled bones and pushed deep against our loaming fells. We, like the farmhouse, have seen them grow and birth and leave, we've seen new generations and oh, we've seen much more. We've seen the house as it was raised from stone, the homestead that stood before it razed to the ground. We've seen their visitors, the friendly and the not. We've seen those that lurk, what surrounds at night. Times have passed; we've watched in something like panic as events unfold, but what are we to do? We are witness, alone. All parts of us.

We can only be. In spring, we grow, summer, we soak. Autumn, we bare and in winter we wait. We have witnessed much more.

We have witnessed the visitor they wished for, She who they do not understand, and we have witnessed the protections they placed upon the farmhouse when She arrived.

DAY HWEGH

i.

The next morning, my mother took me out of the house whilst Ysella was running errands. She said we needed to speak privately.

We walked to the next village over, to talk in a café. The floors, walls, ceilings and tables were all the same shade of nicotine-stained yellow. Everything was made of wipe-down material, with lino tables and PVC-covered seats, all carrying a smudgy layer of grime over their surfaces. The back wall functioned as a menu, covered in laminated A4 pictures of food, with prices written on top with a marker.

Full English WITH beans & coffee £3.99!

Mum inched her way towards the stack of veneer trays, ready to join the queue for hot drinks. I shook my head no, before finding the cleanest booth.

After five minutes, she sat down opposite me. But not before spending an excruciating amount of time attempting to place the tray with its single cup of coffee on the table. She lowered the tray down; the coffee swilled in the brown cup; she pulled the tray back up, cuddling it at chest height. Then she stepped to the side, slowly lowering the tray before changing her mind and retrieving it.

I wondered if she was in danger of throwing the whole thing onto the floor and was only just restraining herself. Eventually, I held my hands out and took the tray from her, placing it on the table and then pushing the whole thing towards her. She smiled at me and then frowned down at the cup.

I watched as she licked her little finger and ran it up the side of the mug, wiping a spilled drip away. It wasn't often, if ever, that we found ourselves sitting across from each other. With nowhere else to look, I was forced to face her in a way that felt too intimate.

Mum took a sip of her coffee, and I looked at her, closer. Her lips were chapped and flaky white skin gathered at the corners of her mouth, brittle. She wiped her mouth with her scarf, and I watched as some of the flakiness disappeared, taken into the folds of her scarf.

I forced myself to speak, needing distraction. 'Go on then.'

She looked blank. 'What?'

'You wanted to talk. Is this about Ysella? The thing that's got her smearing shit on the windows?'

'Shit?' she asked, still blank.

I swallowed the urge to shake her. Speaking slowly, I said, 'Not actual shit. Fish guts, eel bits, whatever it is. You know what I mean.'

She nodded. 'Ah, those. No need for it at all, really,' she said, and then stopped. I watched as she unwrapped the biscuit that came with her coffee, struggling with the plastic wrapper before putting it to her teeth and pulling.

She freed the biscuit and then held it in both hands, breaking it in half. The snap she was waiting for didn't come, and she placed the biscuit back on the saucer and frowned at it. I chewed on my knuckle, waiting for the silence to be over. If I interrupted, she'd lose her train of thought and it'd take too long to get her back on topic. The plastic wrapper of the biscuit must've caught the sore skin around her mouth, a small bubble of blood was forming below her lip. I motioned with my hand, but she simply blinked and said, 'Don't make them like they used to.'

I widened my eyes, not following.

'Biscuits. In the little wrappers. Used to be much better.'

I shook my head, but she ignored me.

'Those things, they're wards. Fish and lard on the window, it's a ward. Keeps the house safe. Couldn't get hold of any fish though, could she? Jimmy, you know Jimmy, don't you? Builder Jimmy? He offered some lovely iron window locks. Proper strong. Great big bars that go twice across. Couldn't get them in the house. Ysella wasn't happy about that.'

I thought of the wide farmhouse door. 'You couldn't get them in?'

She carried on, 'Well, I said salt, if she insisted on having something. Can't see why we can't do it the old way. That's what our mum used to do, but no, Ysella knows better. Never mind that she's completely bloody lost, trying this way and that, neighbours stopping her in the street. Always having to act like her books know more than her own blood—'

'Mum—' I said, interrupting.

'I tell you, I've never met a woman so inclined to—'

'Mum.'

'—such ridiculous things. Always prodding and poking where she 'ent wanted'

'Mum!' I said, snapping. She finally looked up from her coffee, face impassive, as if it were the first time I'd spoken.

'Yes, Sprig?' she replied.

'I just. I want to know – why is Ysella putting these ward things up? She said it was just research, but now she's doing it every day. And what do you mean neighbours?'

She shook her head. 'No, no, not research. Protection.'

She pulled a sachet of sugar from the pot on the table and slowly poured it onto the tray, circling her coffee cup.

'What?'

She pointed at the sugar. 'The house, the land, you know.'

'Why?'

'Oh Sprig. It really doesn't matter; it won't mean anything. She says she's trying to keep you safe.'

'But why?' I repeated. She shrugged her shoulders and slowly pushed the tray away, no longer looking at me. The sugar circle shifted, breaking the loop.

'You're safe enough. Remember the hedge around the back field? What's left of it?' she asked.

'Where the cows were?' The far field was more of a rolling hill. At the top, the barn, a failed conversion project, left to rot long before I was born.

At the bottom, the cow shed. I remembered the final time I'd seen the cows, the last ones to succumb to the disease: the buckling of their legs, the scream in Esolyn's voice to call for help, even though she held the phone in her hand. The stone hedge ran around the outside of the field, but most of it had been ripped up years before. I couldn't remember a time when it marked a real boundary. Instead, all that was left were rocky outcrops, bursting from the ground like teeth.

'Mmm. My mother built that hedge. Chose the stones herself.'

I had never seen my grandmother build a wall, but I had seen her wrist deep in the soil of the garden, fishing for potatoes and carrots, pulling up burdock root. I had memories of her ducking into the fireplace in Trewarnen, hidden at the waist by the chimney as she hacked at something caught with a broom. She didn't fear labour. I read her only through her hands when I was a child. Hands that would scrub and pinch and dig and fix. An image of her digging a trench around the field and hauling huge grounding stones into place came to me. She was exactly the kind of woman to build a wall around her land.

'What happened to it?'

'My father,' she took a sip of her coffee, held the rim of the mug against her teeth for a beat too long. We didn't talk about fathers in this family. Whether it was mine or theirs, my mother and Ysella had always endeavoured to keep the names of the men they claimed had abandoned us out of their mouths. I stared at the split circle of sugar on the tray until she began to speak again.

'My father sold the land. Without telling my mother. Some people – strangers – came, took the barn. We were only young.'

'Took the barn? Like moved in? I thought no one else had lived at Trewarnen?'

She picked at the edge of the table. 'They never came in the house. Your gran wouldn't let them. They were in the barn, just for a while. They started to take down the hedge. And then they left.'

'The family?'

'The strangers. My father. My mother couldn't forgive him. All that hard work, ruined for some emmets.'

'The barn? Esolyn didn't do the work on that did she?'

'No, Sprig. The hedge, the old stone hedge my mother built. She put it there to keep Her in, and then they let Her out.'

'She built a hedge to keep herself in?'

'Her. To keep Her in. Your grandmother never gave Her a name, not to us anyway, but she always spoke of it like it was a woman. She. Her. Never it. Esolyn trapped Her in there, and then they tore it all down.'

'I don't understand. I think you're getting confused.' She frowned. I tried a different tact, 'Look, what's happening with the memorial? I was supposed to be going home in two days. Has it been rearranged? Or was it never real?'

'Why wouldn't it be real?' She tilts her head.

'Because of what you said? Yesterday?'

'Oh Sprig. I'm not sure I remember that. You'll have to ask your aunt.' She looked at the clock on the wall and nodded at the time. 'She'll be waiting,' she said. 'Let's go.' With that, she climbed out of the booth and moved for the exit, and I was left chasing after her.

ii.

When we got back to Trewarnen, I found I couldn't be in the house. I crossed the threshold with my mother, and whilst she sat at the table and shed her shoes, I stayed in the doorway. I tried to move forward, but my bones clicked in contention. I could feel my body closing in on itself as I urged it further forward. I tried to shake it off, this anxiety, clenching and unclenching my fists, slowing my breathing so I would calm. It wouldn't work. The house was too small, the rooms too tight. The ceilings of the kitchen draped low, lower than that morning. I would surely have to crawl if I were to join my mother, drag myself across the floor on my belly or press myself against the wall. The house wanted me out, I could tell.

I stepped backward, out onto the yard, and my lungs unravelled. I gulped, heaved in air, fresh air, open space. Immediately, I felt better. I looked up at Trewarnen, the darkened upper windows and the greenish stone. I needed some space.

I walked around the outskirts of the farm, limbs loosening the further I moved from the house. I had never appreciated how unhinged I felt within the walls of Trewarnen, but my reactions had started to become more visceral on this visit home.

I kept my eyes trained to the ground in search of any shivers of eel skin. I wasn't quite sure what my mother had been trying to tell me in the café. Ysella was trying to protect me – from what? My grandmother had built a wall, and when they tried to take it down – what?

I had thought that I could use this trip to purge myself. I would take in the healing air of the country, face my grief head on. I would leave here better than I arrived. But my time spent at the house was pulling me apart, as if my edges were all loose and I was ready to fray and spill and split into the fibres of the old rugs lining the floors.

I found myself near the hedge, what was left of it. Patches lay like ruins, as if it had been there for centuries. I ran a hand along one of the stones that Esolyn had laid in place. I thought coming here would make me feel connected to her, but I felt an emptiness. This hedge didn't represent family, or home, or belonging. It was hardly even a hedge now, with gaps metres wide. All I felt was a desire to pull it down. I grabbed hold of a loose piece of stone and tugged – I wanted it gone; I wanted it broken – but nothing happened. I pulled at it again, my fingers scraping against the granite. The stone didn't move. Then, ahead, on the horizon, a light. I gripped the wall, body suddenly stiff with the memory of the night on the moors. Not the light, coming for me again. I looked around me, desperate for a witness, unsure of what I'd do if I found one. The light moved closer, towards the direction of the house. Roaming down the moors. With the movement, I let go of the wall, relieved. It was not the light I'd seen before. These were colder white lights – headlights. Just a car, then.

Not for the first time on this trip, I felt like an imposter. Like Trewarnen was no longer my home. The night on the moors had unsettled me – to be so easily lost and confused in a place I swore I knew was embarrassing. Humiliating to think I had spent the past year in the city speaking of the moors as if I had a claim to them – painting myself as some kind of wild woman to the people I met. I let them all think I was one with nature. And yet here, now, I was incapable, a stranger in my own life.

There are things you want to leave behind when you leave a place like this. Out with the rural ideals, the small village politics. Out with the judgements, the inherent trappings of traditionalism. There are also things that need to be kept, the things that tether you to a place, reminding you that you are a person with makings and a history, not just a rootless ghost.

To the people in the city, I was the girl of bare feet and dungarees, foraged fruits and calloused hands. I could build a table and bake a pie. I was cottages and tumbling hills and soft winds. They heard countryside and they saw wholesome. I began to believe the things I said. I was telling people I could cook, whilst I melted cheese on toast in the microwave, the bread still soggy.

I told them I sewed, whilst my hemlines frayed and gathered mud. I explore, I said, searching for something different on the unlicensed TV in a communal living room.

There was a weight to the word Cornwall that ensured they believed me too. A mystical quality. An othering. I was home, and I had been avoiding that weight. I had hidden myself in the more familiar aspects. My room, my own company. Each decision showed me I was not the person I thought I was.

When I had finished my loop of the farm, finding no eel skin, I began my trudge back to the house. I was exhausted, bone and body tired. I needed rest. From a distance, it had looked as if Trewarnen was glowing. Oh, if that glow were fire. If it had burnt to the ground in the time I had been gone – a silly little walk to a silly little wall and all my fears availed – it would be bittersweet. All of that history, rid.

With each step closer, I felt the weight bearing down on me once more. It was only when the house was in full view that I accepted that it was still standing. Standing, with the windows glaring bright.

The yard was covered in cars. Muddy ones and Range Rovers and family cars. More cars than I'd ever seen here. And the noise from within the house – the noise was building. As I approached, I could hear that it was filled with voices. People, actual people, more than ever before.

*

Villagers and local farmers had gathered in the kitchen. I squeezed myself into the room, sidling along the wall, ducking my head in the hope that no one would recognise me. The room was so full, the pressure I had imagined earlier was real now, there was barely space to move. I had always thought of our family as forgotten, isolated people, but now the villagers were packed into our kitchen, every inch filled with a body.

I held my breath, trapping my air, unwilling to share in a room of so little. My mother was fraying in the centre of the room, cupping her hands around extended palms, grasping rather than shaking hands.

She had a habit of zeroing her gaze in on me no matter where I was, and it took only moments before I felt her eyes on mine. She jerked her head towards the living room door, eyebrows raised. The twist of her neck told me 'Leave, leave', but I let the bodies swarm around me until I was pressed against the pot rack on the back wall, a cast-iron skillet branding a curve on my shoulder. I couldn't hear a word she said: the din of the room was too full, the waves heavy with voices. With the twist of her neck and the drop of her jaw, she was a dishcloth, wrung out.

I watched silently as she decided not to make a scene – whatever was happening, she was more concerned that I go unnoticed than she was about keeping the meeting a secret from me.

I felt a hand on my shoulder and turned to see Joan stood beside me, strange without her tabard and cigarette. She had a large coat in one arm, and her forehead was visibly sweating.

'It's too bloody warm in here, maid,' she said, 'I don't know how you're coping with all these windows shut.'

I shrugged. It had only been a couple of days since I was at the pub with Chris, but the sudden influx of people in Trewarnen was leaving me dizzy. Joan was right though, it was warm. Far too warm. The crush of people was only making it worse. I felt unsteady on my feet. I leant my head back against the wall and closed my eyes, trying to centre myself in the wash of dizziness which had overcome me.

'Here, it's not my place, but,' Joan dropped her voice, 'I'd say this house ain't doing you any good. Not everyone agrees with me, but I don't think you should be stuck up in here. I think it'd be better if you just let it all go.'

'What are you talking about?'

'Don't you know yet?'

'Know what?' I asked, but Joan didn't answer, because the room had turned silent. The bodies parted as Ysella moved forward, taking her seat at the head of the table. With that, the villagers settled – many dropped to the floor, the only noises the protest of knees and the animal crunch of cracked knuckles. I turned out my palms, ran them against the wall. The wetness remained still, I felt the damp push back against my skin, meeting and yielding.

Ysella inclined her head to the oldest man in the room. Cap in hand, he took her gesture like a gift, turning his free palm upward as he spoke.

'We're worried, from what we've been told. Mary, well, Mary isn't well enough in herself to come tonight. She's had some,' he looked around the room, his eyes trailing up to the ceiling, looking to catch the word. He lands on it somewhere above the kitchen counter. 'Fright. She's had some fright. And she wasn't sure if I should be coming out and all, but I said it's got to be done. So here we are, then.'

'I understand, Vince, if I could—'

'This isn't our problem to fix, Ysella, it's yours,' said a younger man, interrupting Ysella's response. He walked from the back of the room towards the table, stopping to shake a hand as he did so. I knew him, I knew I did, but I couldn't place him for looking. His face was plain, his demeanour nondescript, but his voice – it was low, dripping. Angry. I knew his voice. There were never many strangers in these parts, though I'd often been made to feel like one.

'We've been out on the moors searching because you asked us to. I've been leaving gifts at that damn pool because you said to.

Joan's been keeping you stocked up with enough lard to grease this whole place down. I don't mind helping you, you know that, but to hear word that she's been here, that you brought her back after what happened with the other one, when we've all been following your rules—'

'This is not about my niece, Tony.' Ysella interrupted sharply. 'And I wasn't the one to bring her back.' She looked meaningfully at Mum, who was staring at the Toby jugs hanging from the ceiling, pretending she couldn't hear my aunt, avoiding her gaze. I felt my stomach drop. They were talking about me.

Tony carried on. 'Everyone's losing their cattle, it's like they're being picked off. It doesn't rightly make sense, I know, but your own mam always said there was something not right.'

'She didn't say that.'

'Near enough did!' he said, looking around as one or two others nodded in agreement. 'I don't know what's been going on at this farm but whatever it is, it's leeching out across the whole damn moor!'

I pushed myself forward from the wall, wiping my hands on my jeans.

'What's going on?' I asked. I had wanted my voice to sound strong, defiant, but instead it cracked. Tony laughed when I spoke, Ysella flinched, and I realised then that she had not known I was in the room either.

'Ah well, there she is. The prodigal daughter. Is this an ambush, Ysella?' Tony said, turning to my aunt. 'I came here the other day, and you said – you insisted, actually – that she was going back upcountry.'

Before she could respond, he turned back to me. 'Haven't you worked it out yet?'

It came to me now. His voice; it was the same voice I'd heard reverberating through the walls on my third day home. I'd thought that it was the house talking, or a dream following me as I woke. But it had been him. Tony.

'Worked what out?' I asked, shrinking as he rolled his eyes at me.

'Try asking your mam.'

'Mum?'

Ysella held her hand up to Mum and shook her head her head at me. 'No.' she said. She looked at Tony. 'That's enough, Tony. I understand you're upset, but you're not to bring Merryn into this. None of this is her fault.'

'She is the problem. Jesus. To come to your house and find that she's still here, that you've not sent her back up to the city,' he shook his head and rounded on me again. 'We saw what happened with her and Paul Bennalick. Ain't no way that was nothing.'

Ysella looked at me sharply then. In the confusion after my night on the moor, and the fever that followed, I'd forgotten to mention the near assault in the pub.

'Ha!' Tony said. 'Guess you didn't know then? Your girl there said summit that set Bennalick right off. Now, I don't know what was said. And a fairer man than me might give the girl the benefit of the doubt, but after what happened with the other one, Claudia, and this on the moors – well. Seems like you're right caught up in something.'

'What? What's this got to do with Claud?' I asked.

'Nothing,' Mum said.

'What's on the moors?' I persisted.

'Nothing!'

Tony laughed bitterly as my mother worked her nails with her teeth. 'We don't know what happened with Claudia, that's the truth. But we don't want to see whatever it was again.'

I saw Ysella's eyes narrow before she straightened her face again. Claudia. She'd never been a Claudia to me. Always Claud, with a clip of the tongue at the end. Hearing her named incorrectly forced me to whisper it right, to put her real name back in the room.

'I'll thank you not to bring this kind of behaviour into my house, Tony.'

'Behaviour! You think we're the ones acting wrong? With all that's going on with you?' Tony asked. When Ysella didn't bite, he sighed, rubbed his palm across his shining forehead. 'Look, I don't know what to believe. S'not my fight. I'm speaking for them,' he gestured at the older people behind him. 'Mary found a cow half torn apart, said she felt something following her on the walk home. You telling me you don't know what it is?'

'If we keep going over the same points, I'll have to ask you to leave,' Ysella said.

'No,' a woman spoke. Her grey hair was pinned up with a large tortoiseshell clip. I recognised her from the village. Izzy. 'You brought this here and we need to know how to get rid of it.'

'It's been a difficult summer, that's all. The weather so unrelenting. When there's no rain for this long everyone feels a little off, and the cattle are sensitive to the rise in temperature too, you know that.'

'You can't explain that girl's death with a difficult summer.'

'The girl—'

'Claud,' I said.

She was being spoken about like she didn't matter, like she was me, like these people had thought nothing of her. But that wasn't true. She had been important.

Ysella nodded at me, just slightly, and started again. 'I wasn't referring to Claud's passing. These complaints you have now, these little issues you've brought into my house, they're nothing but acts of nature.'

'You told us yourself! Those are your stories that have kept us up at night, off the moors,' Izzy said.

'But that's just it, don't you see? They're stories. Lessons learnt from the old times. They're not brick and mortar. Maybe I got carried away.'

'If they're no more than stories, how come Jack has seen you dragging buckets out Alternun way each night? You've been warding this house, Ysella. It stinks. What we don't know is why you're doing it now. How real is this?' Izzy asked.

Ysella pinched the bridge of her nose between her fingers. She'd never looked so much like my mother.

'That, well. They aren't really wards. It's research.'

'Oh, we know the research, Ysella. That . . . thing you read about, the theory you have, that's what you're trying to protect against, isn't it?'

'That was just a story, I told you.'

'A story you're scared of. A story that you've made a little bit real, by letting Lowen bring her daughter back. You've exposed us to something, something you're too scared to name.'

No longer facing Izzy directly, Ysella had turned, just gently to the left, towards the stairs. Ready to leave, I realised. Unwilling to speak. Resolved to keep her knowledge her own. Sweat gathered at her hairline.

'Am I right, Ysella?' Izzy waited and then asked again. 'There's some truth in it, isn't there?'

Silence from my aunt, and then talk all around the room. Ysella's refusal to answer had set them off again. The people in the room mumbled amongst themselves, the dissent starting quietly, elevating quickly. I stood in the middle of it, my arms hanging by my sides. I felt Claud wrap her fingers around my wrist, slide them down my palm. Incy Wincy Spider.

The people spoke as one, words burying questions burying accusations. I felt her there with me, steadying me in the wilderness. I saw her nudge my shoulder with her forehead, smelled her earthen hair. Claud. Oh, God. On and on the room roared, voices carried under tables and across ceiling beams.

A man pushed past me and I stumbled, dropping the memory of Claud. I tried to scramble after it, after her. My knees were on cold stone and my hands were reaching under the table, beyond the muddied feet, on and on I reached. The voices were quieter now, wavering instead of booming, some of them saying my name. They could keep it. Someone touched my elbow, tried to pull me up – to take me away – but I clawed back. It was their fault.

If she had not felt so ashamed. If I had not been her shame. When she felt judged by the world for her choices and her love, my comfort couldn't soothe her.

I would have given so much to have her in that room with me.

I took my palm to the floor with a smack. I wanted to get past it, past the kitchen, beyond the foundations. Down, beyond the house, to the fertile soil. Someplace closer to her. My nails were on the stone and it was weeping, it was wet, and I was nearer, I was closer to her, and as I pushed my ear against the floor, as the room was shouting again and my aunt was stroking my hair, asking me to get up now, up now, I could hear her, I could hear Claud, and she was inviting me in, I swear it.

*

It was my mother who got rid of them all, eventually. She cleared her way through the crowd and opened the door, herding them like the flies from the nest. The exertion hit her as the last few visitors left, and she leant her head against the wall, lips moving with silent curses. If I were to place my ear before her mouth, I would hear her threaten blights on their land. Vultures, all.

With all the neighbours gone, someone wrapped my fingers in white cloth and placed me in my bed. I barricaded the door and took my pillow and duvet over to the window. Downstairs, I heard the raised voices of Mum and Ysella, the slamming of doors.

FOLKLORE

There is a tree upon the edge of our land that has lived for 1000 years. The Darley oak is protected by the people. It has been visited by kings and queens; it stood throughout the plague, its portrait has been exhibited, its saplings conserved, its stature commemorated.

The pool, Dozmary, that She nests beside is 11,700 years old. There is no plaque. No royal visits or protected nature. There is no fence, no markers or signs to conserve it. A single drop of saltwater keeps the lake alive.

It is here that the people bring their burdens. They walk to the pool and ask the water for Her help. Over the years, they have called the Pedri many different names. It changes by generation. Whatever they call her, it always means rot, or decay, or corruption.

She knows this means the people have come to fear Her. They no longer know Her, but She doesn't care for familiarity.

She cares only for the glints of cruelty behind the requests, their little inhumanities — that is where the light gets in.

The people still bring gifts, apologies and symbols of desperation. They clog the surface of the pool, blocking the light and contaminating the water, so She has set her own protection: Bucca Widn. Bucca Widn mans the pool. He clears it, cleanses it, gives back the gifts She does not want, collects others.

PART TWO

KNYVAN
Cornish, *noun*: lamentation, mourning

Although Claud's behaviour had been taunting, in the moments when she came back to me – the real Claud – she was unable to comprehend the things she had done. Time and again we would end up together in my bed at Trewarnen, Claud in my arms, and she would make a suggestion.

'Let's wipe it all off,' she would say, walking her fingers across my stomach.

The things I said were never me. That was what she said the most: the things I said were never me.

It was the summer before I left. Claud was living in her bedsit; I was preparing to move. Things between us were strained, but we had reached a truce of sorts.

We were sitting under one of Ysella's apple trees, smoking. Claud was wearing a summer dress, her hair braided across her forehead like a milkmaid. There it was, that unassuming innocence that made people want to protect her. She was still with Davey. He worked on a dairy farm and was so boring that Claud was paying me more attention than she had all summer. He had bought her flowers, baby's-breath, and chocolates, which she had brought round for me to taste. Cherry liqueurs, the cheap kind. Eating them was like biting into batteries.

Davey didn't know that me and Claud had been sleeping together during their relationship. He called our sleepovers 'girls' nights'. Claud took pleasure in the deception, I'm sure. Once he bought her some underwear – pink and frilly, ordered online – and she made me wear it. When I suggested it would be better if I didn't, if she wore it instead, she stared at me blankly until I did as I was told.

I learnt to cope with it, and although I felt bad for Davey, I didn't feel guilty enough to put a stop to it. Regardless of how he would have felt if he found out, I felt worse for myself – all I had wanted since I was fourteen was to love Claud openly, but she still wasn't ready. She never would be. The longer she tamped down her feelings, the worse she became.

I ate Davey's chocolates as me and Claud spoke loosely about relationships – what each of us wanted from life. All my answers pointed to her, but when she spoke of her own desires, she stressed her need for a clean slate. She didn't want to be known, she said, she wanted to exist outside of context. It was then that I mentioned it. I told her about a thing I'd read about called 'transference'. It usually happened in therapy, and normally accidentally, but I needed to stop her from giving up. I said that we could take all of the difficult moments in our past and move them onto someone else. You take all of your negative or positive emotions about a person, and you redirect them to someone else.

She picked up one of the apples from the ground, a rotten one with a soft brown bruise, and looked at it as I spoke. 'And I can move anything I want?' she asked.

I nodded.

'Onto anyone I want?'

I nodded once more.

'In that case,' she said, taking her cigarette from her mouth, 'all the things I did to you belong to you. Congratulations.'

She put her cigarette out in the bruise of the apple and dropped both on the ground before turning to me and smiling.

'Now that's sorted, shall we go to your room?'

Later, as she slept, I buried the apple.

ii.

Just before I left Cornwall, Claud came round to Trewarnen when Ysella and Mum were both out.

I opened the door to find her wet and red-cheeked, her hair pulled into two dripping plaits. She was wearing my coat buttoned up to her chin, and in her hand she held a small plastic bag of cans.

'I can't believe you're leaving,' she said, as she stepped inside and hugged me. The cans hit me in the ribs as she threw her arms around me, but I pushed my face into her shoulder and hugged her back. Her hair smelled of silt.

'Have you been pond dipping?' I asked, voice muffled into her neck.

She laughed and squeezed me tighter before stepping back. 'I've been swimming, Mermaid. You oughta try it sometime, you know.'

'In the dark, outside? I'm all right.'

'Honestly,' she pushed the bag into my hands and then started to squeeze the water from her hair, 'nothing makes me feel more alive. Stressed, sad, angry, whatever – the water fixes it. It's the best place to be.'

I raised my eyebrows and looked down at my bare feet, which were now covered in her second-hand droplets of dirty water. 'At least my feet aren't stressed now.'

'See?' she said, squeezing my shoulder. 'It's working already.'

Upstairs, we sat together on my bed, drinking and talking about her swim. As she spoke, she waved her hands around, spilling drops of beer onto the crocheted blanket on the bed. I stroked my fingers across the edge of the wet patch.

'So, I was at Dozmary, right? I've been there a billion times before, never had a problem. Great swim. And I'm not far from getting out, in fact I'm heading back to the shore when something grabs my leg.'

'Seriously?'

She nodded dramatically before taking a swig of her beer. 'Just grabs it. Like, wraps around my foot and pulls. I start kicking – kicking more – because it's just a bit of pondweed, right? So, I'm trying to untangle myself, because it's late, and it's cold. But then, get this, something grabs my other leg.'

'Jesus.'

'Yeah. Both my legs are being pulled then, and I start to panic a bit, because pondweed doesn't work like that. But it's Dozmary, there's nothing up there—'

'Apart from the eels.'

'The eels?'

'Mmhmm. My gran told me when I was a kid. They drained the pool once, in the 1800s, to try and see what was living in there. And they just found masses and masses of eels. No other fish. Nothing else much living at all. Just a swarm of eels, all knotting together at the bottom.'

I stopped speaking when I noticed Claud looked pale. She had pulled her knees up to her chest. There was a red mark around her ankle, like something had really grabbed her.

'That's *horrible*,' she said, quietly.

Crap. 'I'm sorry, I didn't mean to scare you. They're just fish. Weird-looking fish, but fish all the same.'

'Eels are the weirdest-looking fish,' she hugged her knees, and then smiled, just a bit. 'I can't believe I've been swimming in Dozmary for years and you never bothered to tell me it was infested,'

'Infested might be a strong word—'

'Literally riddled with slimy freaks.'

'Riddled is probably an overstatement too.'

She knocked me with her shoulder. 'Excuse me, I think I can

overstate as much as I want when I was just about drowned by a horde of eels.'

'You're so overdramatic.' I put my arm around her and pulled her closer. For a moment, she rested her head on my shoulder, and I held myself very still. This kind of physical intimacy had been harder to initiate since I told her I was leaving. For a moment, neither of us spoke. 'What do you actually think it was that grabbed you, then?' I asked.

'It was probably just some piece of rubbish that someone dumped in the pool. Like a bit of wire or whatever. You know what it's like on the moor when it starts to get dark, all logic flies out the window.' She scootched away from me then and grabbed two more cans from the bag. Maybe she wasn't ready for us to be close again. 'Beer?'

I nodded and she handed me one.

'So,' she said, 'reckon you're going to fall in love in Manchester? Meet your soulmate at university?'

'Don't be stupid.'

'Hey, it could happen. There are so many more people up there. You could find the person you're meant to be with.'

'Claud—'

She shook her head. 'Don't.'

'You know that's not why I'm leaving. I don't want anyone else; I'm not going to meet anyone better—'

She scoffed. I could see her guard going up. 'I never said better. Good luck trying to find anyone better than me.' She laughed but it sounded hollow. She motioned towards her wet frizz of hair, 'Everyone knows I'm the ultimate catch.'

'That's true.' I reached out for her hand, but she pulled it away, rubbed at the smudged mascara under her eyes.

'It'd be pretty sad if you spent three years on your own though.'

'I won't be on my own. But I'm not going to fall in love with anyone either. Besides, I'll still come back. I'll have you, and Chris.'

She jumped on the mention of Chris's name then, asking if I'd hooked up with him recently. I rolled my eyes. She looked at me and laughed, raising her can in the air like a toast.

'I still can't believe you ever hooked up with him, Mermaid. So weird.'

I wanted to tell her it was her fault. That, really, he was only there to bridge the gap between me and her. That at least he wanted everyone to know we were together. At least I wasn't a secret hidden under the bed.

Instead, I said, 'No, what's weird is you having a boyfriend and still being here.'

Claud laughed more then, showing her pointy little teeth. I thought about pushing her off the bed, out of the room all the way down the stairs. I wondered if her body would find an empty patch of floor to crack on, or if she'd spill over the lost shoes and laundry basket at the bottom of the floor, broken into a million little pieces. I waited for her to stop, knowing that she was just deflecting. She couldn't handle my leaving, her vulnerability, so she was trying to be cruel. I wouldn't let it work. I drank my beer down as quickly as I could.

Once she stopped laughing, I apologised. She grinned at my desperate look and then reached out and placed her hand on my cheek, tilting my head up.

She leant over and kissed me. With my eyes closed, I pictured the Claud from before, the Claud that bit her nails and would call me immediately after school just to talk about the journey home. I didn't fully know this new Claud, the men she dated or the way she lived when I wasn't around. I didn't know what would happen when I left, or how to stop her from being a stranger.

She pulled away messily from the kiss and mumbled *it's OK,* and then, *you taste like flowers.*

I laid back on the bed and she copied me, resting her head on my chest. I waited a moment. When I was sure she wasn't going to be spooked, I stroked my fingers across her back, drawing figures of eight.

'When are you leaving?' she asked.

'Tomorrow.'

'Will you text me?'

'If I do, will you text back?'

'Sure. Will you come back?'

'Yes. You know you can still come with me, right?'

'I know.'

'Will you?'

'No.'

'I wish you would.'

'I know you do. But I've got to stay here. All of that,' she waved her hand in the air, 'stuff that you'll do up there, that's not my life. My life is here. I can't leave.'

I understood what she meant. Preparing to leave had felt like splitting my soul in half. But I knew I had to go.

'Do you think you'll be OK without me?'

She tapped her fingers against my collarbone. 'Does it matter?' I stilled her with my hand.

'Of course, it matters. It matters more than anything else.'

'Then why are you leaving?'

'My course starts next week, I've gotta go and get everything sorted—'

'No, I mean why are you leaving me?'

'You know why.'

'I don't. I don't know anything.'

'I love you; you know that.'

'I know that.'

'And that's why I've got to leave.'

Claud didn't answer; her breathing slowed. I thought she might be falling asleep. I became aware then of the delicate balance of the night. Felt the heat radiating from Claud's body, the rough texture of the edge of the bed against the back of my thighs. If I'd spoken, the sky might've fallen in on us, great waves of stars and dark clouds and overnight planes pummelling down at once.

If it all fell, then I would be pinned there forever, in my bedroom at Trewarnen. Never leave, never change from who I was in that very moment. My life, everything I was, would be made up of nothing more than everyone around me. I would be Chris and Claud and Mum and Ysella and Rob's wet mouth, and I would never be anyone else.

'We can't stay like this,' I said. Claud was silent and I knew that she was listening. Somehow, she had mastered what I never could: she could hear my thoughts. 'If we could, if we could keep going without it hurting so much, I would. I just, I need to make a choice for myself here. It doesn't mean I don't love you; you know that. You could scoop me out and eat me up and I wouldn't care.'

'Scoop you out like a huldra.'

'Exactly.'

'You don't think we're meant to last then?' she didn't look at me as she asked.

'I think maybe we're too much.'

When she lifted her head from my chest, her eyes were wet. I wiped at her mascara with clumsy fingers, trying to keep them butterfly-light. She looked so breakable; I didn't want to crush her under the weight of my worry.

'We're not too much,' I tried again, 'we're not. You know what I really think?'

She nodded.

'I think we're meant to last. I think we're the two people in the world who are meant to last forever, far longer than anyone else. I think we're meant for something more.'

She pulled herself up completely, so she was sitting cross-legged on my bed, and rubbed at her eyes. 'You're more right than you know.'

'You think so?'

'We are – I don't know how to explain it. There's something more to us. More than you realise. It's bigger than us.'

She looked tired, then. Older. 'What do you mean, more than I realise?' I asked.

'You'll get there, don't worry.'

I waited for her to say more, but nothing came. For a moment, it was like we were fifteen again, sat by her bedroom window, quiet only because we'd said so much that our voices were hoarse.

FOLKLORE

1969. The very first of the women from Trewarnen, the great mother, comes to the pool. After each birth she comes, tramping across the moors with a new thing in her arms, wanting blessed water to fix each soul.

There She sits, some six miles away, trapped beyond a hedge.

The great mother trusts in the power of the pool. Alone in the world, there was no one to stop her believing such things. Each child had been born a mouse, mewling and sheathed in vernix.

Her youngest had been born in the farmhouse: straight onto the flagstones of the kitchen floor. The white flakes had covered all but the newborn's eyes, which refused to open. She came to Dozmary in the arms of her mother, still slippery, greasy, like a blind kitten.

The eels, near-blind themselves, nipped at Bucca Widn's feet. They had no young, so they had no death, no age.

Unaware of what lay beneath, the people still came to the pool, year on year, generation after generation. They took to the pool for their births and their deaths, in their famines and feasts. They came in their fear.

iii.

Later that same night, we slept together for the last time. We had
been watching a movie, not quite touching in my single bed,
when she whispered in my ear that she was absolutely starving and
there was no way she'd make it through the night without a piece
of toast.

When I came back to the room, Claud ignored the toast I
offered and grabbed me, pulling me towards the bed. I stumbled
slightly, rolling my shoulder as she yanked me down. Her grasp too
tight around my wrist. She smiled at me, raising an eyebrow when
I lost my footing. Her grip burnt against my skin. Her urgency
registered in the pit of my stomach. I held my breath until she
kissed me, exhaling as she grabbed my face. I would not embarrass
myself by smiling. I still had the plate of toast in one hand, which
I was trying to keep balanced as we kissed, not wanting butter and
crumbs to ruin the moment.

When she finally noticed, she laughed and took the plate from
me, setting it at the foot of the bed. 'You're so weird,' she said, and
I glowed under the fondness of her words.

My T-shirt and joggers came off easily, but Claud was still
fully dressed, in jeans that she couldn't take off lying down. She
stood up and I knelt in front of her, naked, and started to undo
them for her. My fingers fumbled on the zip. What had been fun
moments before suddenly felt off. It should've been reverential.
But something about the pose – me hunched, crouched on my
heels, clawing at her jeans, my body pale and pimpled – made me
feel like a woodlouse trying to scramble up a wall. I was the bug,
and she turned then, became ballast, cold, marbled.

When was the last time our relationship had felt equal? Or fluid? When had she moved with me, rather than against me? I shook the thought away. There was only so much more of her I could have before I left, and who knew what would happen then. Maybe she wouldn't let me back in. I needed to enjoy her for what she was.

I bit my tongue, but then she grabbed hold of my head, forced my face into the pit of her stomach, so I kissed her there instead. The zip of her jeans caught on her underwear, and it seemed like a sign that this was the time, so I started to peel her pants off too, ready to finally touch her again – but then Claud was laughing and shaking her head, and she moved me back onto the bed, her hand strong against my shoulder.

She was on top of me, jeans off, but her underwear pulled back up, and I was lying naked, and I still hadn't touched her, not really. I knew the men she slept with were allowed to touch her, knew that it was just me, my hands and my mouth, that Claud didn't want in that way. The thought of it made my mouth taste like bile and I wanted to jump off the bed, to wedge myself into the space between the wardrobe and the door to ride it out, but instead I tried to focus as Claud pushed my legs apart and bit my hip.

Claud wouldn't let me touch her, but she wanted to touch me. And that was OK. At least, it was just about enough. I didn't know if I minded, but I knew I liked the way Claud's long blonde hair spilled over onto my stomach when she went down on me. It reminded me of being at the beach. Claud was the sea, and I was buried in the sand.

In the morning, she was no longer the sea, instead she was nothing more than a curved shoulder and a jutting spine in my bed, sleeping on her side. I contemplated rolling closer, dropping a kiss on her shoulder blade and an arm around her waist, like I would've in the past. But it wasn't the past, so I didn't.

I left her in my bed without waking her or saying goodbye. I didn't shower, I just pulled off my T-shirt and pressed it against my skin, trying to soak up the heat that was radiating off me. I looked at the top in my hands, straightened it out, and realised it wasn't mine. It belonged to Chris: the four pillars of Black Flag stamped on the front. I held it to my nose and sniffed, wanting to be sure, the way we did with our school jumpers after P.E. There it was, the warm smell of Chris woven into the cotton, mixed with my sweat. But that wasn't all. I pushed my face further into the T-shirt and breathed in again. Layered there, a newer scent – soil. I crumpled up the top and quickly pushed it to the bottom of my bag.

Outside, Chris was parked at the end of the driveway, far enough from the house that only the trees noticed his arrival. I took off with my bags before my mother and aunt were awake, drinking a full carton of orange juice on my way out to try and fight the tiredness that would leach out the little joy I had left.

He was sat with the window of his Fiat down, smoking a fag with one hand, gripping the gear stick with the other. I'd barely sat down when he started to gun it up the road, away from the house.

'What the hell?' I asked, shoving an empty Fanta bottle off the seat so I could do my belt up.

'What? I'm getting you outta here, just like you asked.'

'You're taking me to the train station, Chris. It's not a fuck-ing getaway.' I unwound the window so I could smoke the fag I'd rolled earlier that morning, when I sat on the front step waiting for the day to get light. It was only once I'd lit up that I realised Chris wasn't laughing. He wasn't doing much at all, apart from sweating and gripping the steering wheel tightly. 'What?' I asked. He shook his head. 'Why are you being so dramatic?'

'Are you serious, Merryn?'

'Why are you being arsey? I got like, no sleep last night, my head's pounding. Can we just go to the station?'

'And then what? When are you coming back?'

'Soon enough. For Christmas, probably.' I stuck my head out the window. We were on the dual carriageway now, off the moors technically, but still cutting right through them. Four lanes of traffic splintered through rolling hills. Like a chasm in the pastoral landscape, it always felt wrong, this road. The wind and fumes pressed against my cheeks as I held my face out towards the road – something about it helped clear my head, but I could still hear Chris, droning on in the car.

'Do you even hear yourself? Merryn?'

I let go of my cigarette then, impossible to smoke with that much wind resistance, and watched it for the split-second that it was still in sight, soaring through the air before it disappeared with all the other forgotten crap people throw out of their cars. We used to count the things we saw at the side of this road, me and Chris, when he'd pick me up for college. A badger, a trainer, a pheasant, a strip of tyre, a sideways campervan, once, a dog that ran off before we could catch it.

I turned around so I was fully in the car and looked at him. 'What are you on about?'

'I don't get it.' He looked at me then, cut me off before I could speak, 'No, truly Merryn. I don't get it. How are you acting so relaxed after last night?'

I thought back to the text I'd sent him the evening before – *Can you take me to the station tomorrow please? As early as possible, you're a lifesaver* – I hadn't told him anything about Claud being round.

He laughed then. Not in a pleasant way. It sounded like fear. 'Am I your aunt? The phone call, Mer. It was insane.'

'I didn't call you.' I knew I didn't call him. I spent the night with Claud, then I lay in bed next to her and watched her sleep. I knew that because I wouldn't let myself do anything else. I just stayed awake.

'I came to Trewarnen.'

'No.' He didn't. I would've remembered. And even if I didn't, Claud would've said something about it this morning. But she was still asleep when I left. She didn't have a chance to tell me anything.

'I pulled up and you were out in your garden, it was insane.'

'This isn't funny, Chris. I had a bad enough night as it was without you taking the piss—'

He talks over me then, 'You were in the garden, and you were pulling up the dirt with your hands, just scratching and scratching.'

'Stop it.'

'I had no idea what you were doing. It's like you were feral, clawing at the ground, and I kept saying your name and you weren't responding. I was in bed when you called. I missed it, so I rang you back. You sounded like shit. On the phone, you just kept saying that it was crushing you, and you had to go back. You said you were in the house, but that you had to leave so I asked you to wait for me. You kept saying you had to go back, but I don't know where. It took me fifteen minutes to get to yours after you called, and when I arrived you were already outside.'

Each time he opened his mouth, he spoke quicker, and his words came over me in a slurry. I couldn't remember, I couldn't remember speaking to him on the phone, couldn't remember being out of bed. I looked down at my hands, dead in my lap, as Chris carried on speaking. I'd been scared of myself, he was saying, scared of myself and Claud. In my lap, my hands, my nails short, ragged, black underneath, black around my cuticles. I brought a finger to my mouth, pressed it against my teeth. Was it new? The dirt? Had I truly been on my hands and knees when Chris came? Or were my hands always like this?

'You were just in your pants, and your feet were covered in mud, and it was really cold, Mer, so I hope you don't mind, but once you calmed down – you went all quiet and kinda still – I put my T-shirt on you. It wasn't super clean, but you didn't have anything else on and I didn't know what else to do.'

I looked at him. His face was flushed, his hands white on the steering wheel, ten to two, his eyes staring straight ahead. He was *embarrassed*. Ashamed.

'I was naked?'

'Um, yeah.' He clears his throat. 'A bit. You can keep the T-shirt by the way. It's one of my favourites, but you can keep it.'

We drove in silence until Chris took the right turn into the train station, cutting across the traffic without even slowing. I searched myself for words. I felt in each back pocket, reached up my sleeves, checked behind my ears. I bit the bruise inside each cheek. There was only one thing I could find to say, and it didn't seem like enough. It didn't seem right. But I said it anyway, because my train was coming, and I was so close to being free. 'A nightmare. I must've been having a nightmare.'

FOLKLORE

2018. Nineteen years after the first request, one of the Trewarnen women, the mother, approached Her again. Another gift, please.

The woman spoke to the pool, imagining her words travelling through water and reaching a God. The God slumbered deep in the mud behind her. The woman spoke only to the guardian.

Bucca Widn clapped his hands together, causing the water to move around him, his fingers held together with soft tissue. For many years, Bucca Widn has dreamed of helping the people who come to the pool. The longer he is trapped, the more he is changed. As the years move on, Bucca Widn loses a little piece of himself. More eel than boy, he thinks of what the She will do with the woman's new request: 'Bring her daughter home, one last time.'

iv.

When I got to the city and started university, I started to doubt my existence. Away from home, I felt outside of myself. I had been stripped of the context of who and what I was, and I didn't have the grounding to rebuild myself in a new place, with new people. My last conversation with Chris weighed heavily on me. I would sit in lectures and be hit with memories of it like intrusive thoughts, sliding further into my seat, asking the blue carpet to suck me down into its fibres.

I never grasped what happened that night. I had no cause to think Chris was lying, but in order to believe he was telling the truth, I would have had to accept that there was an ungoverned part of myself, a thing that could overtake me without my knowledge. I knew I had nightmares as a child, night terrors, and it had happened before whilst I was sleeping next to Claud. What Chris described sounded worse, less contained. I hadn't had any incidents since I moved to the city, none that I was aware of. I was sleeping much better. But before I could investigate what had happened on that night, I lost Claud, and everything else dropped out from under me.

We stayed in touch for a time after I left, which surprised me. I had spent the last six months of our relationship anticipating that my leaving would be her chance to finally purge herself of me.

Near the end of my time in Cornwall with her, I felt like little more than a barnacle, something old and crusted over on her skin that she could not work off. At one point this relationship had been symbiotic. When I look back now, I fear that she was dully humouring me, the way you might with a seagull clacking at your feet for food. You don't want the thing to starve, but you're waiting for it to leave, to find someone else, so that you can take your chip-greased fingers and run.

Still, humour she did. She texted me a few times a week, texts that I would reply to immediately, before waiting hours for a response. I cried over Claud approximately thirteen times in the first few weeks after I left Cornwall. I cried because I refused to be the one who contacted her first. My absence must've told her something unexpected, because before the fourteenth cry, she rang me.

It was late at night, and she spoke tentatively at first, whispering in a way that I recognised from the nights we spent at sixteen, hidden beneath her bed covers, phones used as torches to illuminate our faces as we spoke of a future that we thought we could own. Now she rang me and spoke stutteringly, slurred, near silent. I strained to hear her over the rustling of the duvet she'd pulled over her head. I caught only odd words, until eventually I swallowed my surprise at her calling and asked her to speak up. 'I miss you; I miss you; I miss you,' she cried, a round-robin of sobs.

I was in my own bed in the city, having lucked my way into a rented room in a shared house. The mattress creaked and the whole room was filled with old wooden furniture, the walls lined with floor-to-ceiling wardrobes I'd been too scared to open fully. I felt like I'd crawled under my aunt's table and stayed there. I lived out of my suitcase, opened on the floor at the end of my bed. Each morning I would throw on my hoody and walk to class, where I would take notes far slower than my lecturers spoke, and seldom raise my hand in seminars. I'd no big plans when leaving Cornwall; I'd just wanted to leave, and university seemed an easy way out.

I had always silenced my gut, let my heart be my loudest organ. Her voice on the phone sounded so young, so uncertain, soft, in a way she hadn't in years, and I couldn't bear to unbalance the brittle fragility she was sharing with me. Instead, I assented to whatever she said, murmuring quiet platitudes, telling her not to cry, but mainly just letting her talk as I lay still, phone to my ear. I stared up at my new ceiling, patched with damp in this strange city, and listened to Claud tell me that she loved me like it was an apology.

*

Claud went, days later. We knew not to go to Dozmary in bad weather, not to go on our own. It's common sense to leave certain parts of the moor alone.

I wasn't there when it happened, but I know what it would've been like to push her. I would've stumbled into it, my hands catching on her shoulders, barely pressing. Just a quick stroke across the wool of her back, right in that hollow place she said she had and, oh – there she would go, dropping over the edge like a pin.

When they dredged her up – that was the word for it, dredging – she was a weight, a stone in their nets. They laid her body down and heard the hollow thud of rock against marshy flesh. She was still wearing her coat, and when they cut it off, they found treasures lost in the lining. A cabinet of curiosities, full of rock and iron and shell, puddled between the polyester and wool. These were not trinkets, but millstones, each one large and cumbersome, unwieldy in their heft. Like a pillowcase full of bricks. She'd killed herself, of that they were certain – though the people in the village called it a self-murder – but they couldn't posit how she had moved herself across the moor with such a weight inside her coat. The whole earth, there in her lining. Mud and clay, sediment and ore, all stitched in place. Her legs would've buckled, they said, once she put that coat on. She stood no chance in the water, anchored down like that.

FOLKLORE

2018. Unseen by the woman, under the water a mudlark boy helps usher the eels into her buckets, pushing spongy fingers deep into frail ground, sending clouds of mud into the water. Pop, pop, pop come the mud flowers, bursting forth with slippering tails. Herded, they glisten together, buckets of sand, shining glass.

The mudlark boy, Bucca Widn, hair of seaweed, conger of skin, belongs by the sea. Like the eels, he finds himself landlocked in Dozmary, unable to return home. He and the eels grow old and full of malcontent. Unable to breed or seed or age, they knot themselves together, never quite dying, never quite ending.

The two women from Trewarnen come for them to fix what they have done. They come for the eels, not for Bucca Widn. Never for Bucca Widn, the secret guardian, who sets himself low into the mud like his elver friends, hidden from view.

They only come for the eels at night, when the sky pulls her sheet across the lake in a motherly gesture of safety, and the eels pop up from the shallows to frolic and flit and twist in the ways that eels do.

Bucca Widn, if he could, might ask them to stop – to spare just this one group of eels – but he does not. For it is his nature to help the fishermen catch the fish in the sea, and here he waits, without sea, without fish, but the nets still come, so help he must.

Bucca Widn corrals the bed of eels into the basket, little hands made of sediment wrangling glass and slime. He waves them goodbye, knowing that when they return, they will be only husk, shell.

V.

There was a lake near the city where I lived. When I heard that Claud was dead, I went there. It was the closest I could get to her. In a city with no wild places, water would do.

I paid £10 to a man stood on the pontoon, though he had no sign, just two plastic rowing boats coated in a fur of algae. He gave me the oars and helped me into a boat, my trainers skidding on the puddle that swelled in the bottom. He tutted at my grey joggers, the twitch in my fingers, and told me the seat was wet and he hadn't a thing to wipe it with. He waved his hand in a frantic motion at the sky, which was a stew of grey and blue dust, roiling with the urge to rain.

'Give us a quid and you can have a poncho,' he said, pulling a folded plastic sheet from the rucksack at his feet.

The wind was pressing into the lake's surface, printing miniature waves that dip and swell. Out on the water, I was sat in my poncho waiting for rain as old boats swung back and forth, bound to weights. Seagulls perched ceremoniously on hulls, watching me with side-eyes. I wanted to ask them where they came from, if they knew how it feels to be untethered. I dragged the boat through the water. It jerked in circles until eventually I spiralled lazily towards the middle of the lake, ignoring the instructions of the man who told me to keep within the perimeter of moored boats. The wind was riled, whipping at the poncho so the plastic hood snapped at my ears. Still, it did not rain. My phone sat in my pocket, switched on in the morning after a night ignored.

The missed calls had come through quickly, late that morning, followed by messages, and a voicemail. Some from Claud, the rest from Chris and my aunt.

The first texts that came through were apologies from Claud. They hit my phone so fast when I turned it on that the name didn't even show on them, just a string of numbers. A drain had opened, and they piled up on the screen quicker than I could open them. Everything was out of order – the apologies before the missed calls. The last text Claud had sent was a grainy photo of Dozmary, the light grey.

The first voice I heard was Chris's. He was the one to tell me she was gone, in a voicemail, full of static and dead air. He didn't say that much, just, have you heard? Do you know? Did she tell you?

The same three questions, repeated. I listened to his message four times, like I didn't know what he was talking about, like I didn't want to admit to myself that I knew. And I did, I had already seen the message with the picture of that stupid lake, and I had already gone online and seen the old photos of Claud that flooded my timeline. So maybe I already knew that this was the end and she had done something wrong, and by our very nature, by our bond, that meant I had too. But I chose to close my eyes, really squeeze them shut tight and listen to Chris's message four times in a row, knowing I wouldn't get the chance to hear her voice ever again, and that whenever I got a voicemail on my phone in the future, I wouldn't be able to listen to it without feeling sick, a curious mix of grief and shame.

After I listened to the voicemail from Chris, I ate the lavender. Straight from the jar. I scooped the dried stalks and flower heads from the jar beside my bed and slammed them against my teeth. They turned to dust, coating my tongue and the roof of my mouth with a fine powder. They tasted like Parma Violets. Bath salts. They tasted old, like home. I coughed perfume for days. There was no time to brew tea, to take it in properly. There were no complementing flavours or scents, no layers of medicine. Mother, forgive me, but I didn't add peppermint to calm the gut or chamomile to raise the spirits. I was just smothered in it. I needed something to keep the evil down, tamp it at the root. My mother would use lavender for protection when I was a child, stringing it up in the doorways of Trewarnen to ward off evil spirits, sprigs in each room. Ysella was so tall, it would tangle into her hair every time she left a room. At night when she read me a story, I'd comb through her hair for the tiny purple buds. It was everywhere. Mum would put it in my bathwater to draw the devil out whenever I was acting wrong. A burning red slap to the back of the knee and then I'd be dunked into the water, soothing.

I took the lavender like a shot, straight in my mouth, straight to the gums so it'd work quicker. I could feel it then. This fear bubbling up in my gut, something threatening to crawl up my throat. If I let it out, it wouldn't ever stop. The lavender tamped it down. The musty taste of it felt like two hands pressing down on my stomach. I suppose sometimes even the ones who run away need to feel their roots.

Claud was gone. My mother had rung me, near hysterical. The first thing she said was a question. 'Did she tell you she was the same as you?'

'Did she? Did she? Did she?' she asked, between sobs.

She cried for Claud before I had a chance to, that's what angered me the most. The line went silent for a moment, nothing recorded apart from my mother's breath.

'What do you mean, she was the same as me?' I asked.

'They found your things,' she said, 'all of your things in her coat. Shells and little figures and pebbles and some big stones, huge ones. She threw herself in with your coat on. And they found a note, left with her shoes.'

I bit my fist. It didn't work. I wanted to swallow it. All of it. My fist, the phone, the voice of my mother. I needed it all gone.

'Why didn't she swim? She always swam. She couldn't drown. It doesn't make sense.'

My mother read me the note over the phone. It was short: *We are taken back.*

'Do you know what that means? Did she tell you?' she asked.

'No. No, I don't. Tell me what you meant, she's the same as me how?'

My mother sighed, 'I knew she was like you, but I thought she would have told you herself. People don't talk about these things. Everything's kept in the family.'

'What?' The floor was rolling underneath me.

'Sometimes I think you weren't meant for this world. You weren't made for it.'

I hung up as my mother said, 'You'll have to forgive me'.

Ran to the bathroom and threw up all the lavender, the only thing that soothed me.

I wanted to speak to her, Claud. I had questions I needed to ask.

Ask about the night in the tent with Rob, when she was there, and she stayed still and quiet. I wanted to ask what that quiet tasted like. If it filled her up like it did me. I wanted to ask if all the phone calls had been lies, if the love she offered was just something to make this worse. What the note meant.

*

The hull of a boat loomed in front of me, and I drifted towards it, half hoping to crash, but instead my rowing boat just stopped, bobbing mournfully next to the bigger, moored boat, unable to pass. It didn't even splash. I checked my phone. The messages stayed the same. I leant over the side of my boat and pressed my hand against the hull of the other, heaved and pushed my boat away, my wrist creaking with force. We spun off, back into open space.

The weight of the air shifted as the rain finally started and I tipped my head back to greet it as it drummed on the boat. The water ragged on, gripping the boat and pushing it forward, pulling it back. It was alive now, a silken beast. There was a boom as the man on the pontoon shouted to me to come back in, but I pulled my oars up and tucked my head down.

I lifted my head back and screamed, purging it all into the rain, the lake, the clouds. The scream did nothing.

The man on the pontoon shouted again. 'It's time', he called. It's time.

Back at the dock I climbed out slowly, my bones heavy from the wet. The man's paper-thin hands hovered beside me as I stepped out. His face was angry, weathered like his boats, but I gave him no response, just pulled the poncho over my head, balled it up in my hands. The sky spat down on us again and he wouldn't take the poncho back when I tried to hand it over.

'You can keep that.'

'I didn't do too badly,' I said, looking out across the lake.

'Aye, not too badly at all.' He looked at me like a father would, maybe. I walked away, cupping my hands to the rain. Bringing it to my mouth to wash the sour taste away, I wondered how many scoops it would take to feel like drowning, or if I was already there.

PART THREE

KLAV DRE GERENSA
Cornish, *idiom*: love-sick

FOLKLORE

1999. A swelling and then a pain and then a birth. Then a scream,
and another, and again.

And there, sure as anything, another dress ruined, two great stains
seeping across the front of it. Always the same. The baby will cry and
Lowen will seep, her body crawling away from her, trying to feed, trying
to please. At times, during the middle of the night, in the still-haven't-
slept times, she will sit on her hands, willing her chapped fingers to stay
beneath her, trying to contain the urge to reach out, stretch and kiss
and lift. It needs to suckle, if not on her nipples, broken and raw, then
on her fingers, the sharper point of her knuckle. A fair trade at first,
to offer ten fingers for the respite of two nipples, but now her fingers
are bled dry instead. The life is gone from them, the constant damp
has made them crack through, like a split in the paintwork. When the
baby sleeps – though it never does, and Lowen can't understand how
such a thing can last for so long without needing to rest, as if powered
by its own screams, renewing energy with the force of its lungs – she
holds her hands out in front of her and flexes her fingers, bending each
one, checking to see what has been taken from her next.

Her nails are gone, filed, clipped, bitten in a flurry. Too long will
hurt the baby, they said. They: her mam, her sister. Women who coddle
the baby and yet leave her, Lowen, to suffer. They never come in the
night when the screaming is at its worst. They are happy, she thinks,
each morning when she moves through the farmhouse like a ghost, baby
swaddled to her chest. Pleased by her exhaustion, her slow disappear-
ance. She sees how they laugh, rolling their too-white eyes, how they
taunt her, asking if 'the little mite slept?' How happy they are when
her answer is no. How they feed her cups of tea when the answer is

no, treating her, congratulating her for her sacrifice. Better the mother folds away into nothing and the baby is cared for.

She hasn't left the house since it came – It. She must stop doing that, she knows, can't say it, can't say It. Can't even say The Baby, because then they all look at her, with their too-awake eyes, the women without babies and they look at her and they say, 'Not the baby, your baby' and she wants to say it back 'your baby your baby your baby' but her voice is muffled, her throat full of muslin cloth and they can't hear a word she says because the baby cries again. Not the baby, her baby. She can't say it, she can't because it's not right, the baby is not hers, she is the baby's, and she doesn't want, she doesn't want—

She can hear her fingers when she moves them. The smallest one, the pinkie finger, the baby finger, ha! The baby finger is the one most damaged. She, Baby, Baby cannot leave the little finger alone, it is her finger, and she chews, and she chews and on some days the baby finger is the only thing that will stop the baby from stealing all the air from the room with her flexing lungs.

Lowen must give it to her, that's what they say, give the little baby whatever she wants, Lowen. And she does, and she does, and she does, and it isn't enough. Baby takes her little finger, and she chews with her gums, so much wet flesh, and it turns Lowen's stomach as it grates on her bones, and soon the finger is useless. Her nail is only membrane now, the cuticle a fly wing, pulled apart and pasted on.

When she bites, great chunks come apart, layers and layers peel off and Lowen must spend an afternoon with her fingers as hooks, pulling pieces of herself from baby's wet mouth. She takes the fragments of nail from baby's mouth, and she places them under her own tongue, willing them to reabsorb, to make her bones strong again, before she melts away. And baby's fingernails are strong now, clawing at her, ripping the dry skin around Lowen's knuckles until her fingers bleed. Lowen wraps her cuts in muslin and hides her hands from her mam and sister in gloves. When her nipples bled and the soft white milk turned pink, they told her to give the baby her hands instead; she does not know what they will ask of her next.

DAY SEYTH

i.

The morning after the villagers flocked to the kitchen of Tre-warnen, it took me an age to move from my bed. With every flex of muscle, I felt as if my limbs were no longer controlled by me, but by an insect: an ant, a flea – a tiny parasite tweaking and twisting my nerve endings until my knee jerked and my foot moved just so. I was in a body that no one knew how to drive.

When I stood, and I did stand, I was unsteady on my feet. I was unsteady on my legs and pelvis and spine and arms also; I couldn't place all the blame on my feet. I pressed a palm against the wall for balance, but also to assert to myself that I really was standing. I really was in my body.

Although the room was warm, the wall felt wet and soft, just like on the day I first arrived. This time I didn't rap my knuckles against it – instead, I began to pull my hand away, but the reflex toppled me, and I ended up with both hands against it instead, sliding slightly. It was hard to tell whether the walls were rotten in a way that they felt damp, or if they were, in fact, just wet. The windows were open, yet I could feel the layer of sweat across my top lip. I could taste the salt of my own skin when my tongue darted out.

It was hot. No, it was boiling. The windows were open and yet there was no air. I heard a banging, and then nothing. It happened twice more. It could have been my head, or it could have been the door.

I pressed my forehead against the soft-wet wall then, like I was starting a fight or going in for a kiss, taking a leap of faith either way. I wanted to breathe in the condensation that was smudging the wall. I could picture it, beyond the paint and the stone, a patch of damp festering in the crawl space. A broken pipe somewhere, rusted with age or just retired now, dripping brown water. The damp patch that was once just a droplet before it grew and got bigger and braver and stretched from floor to ceiling. In the crawl space it takes up the whole view, and now it is pushing its way through. It made it through the stone and the plaster, and it has started to peel the paint and now it has reached me, and the drip from the pipe was kissing me on the forehead.

I rolled from the wall, pushing off with my head, steadying with my arms, until my back was leant against it. It looked like an elaborate dance, but really, I was just trying to make my body cooperate. There was something in it that wasn't mine. Was I wrong or was the body wrong?

I slid back down to the ground, bare feet rubbing against floorboards. I pictured the sweat that had matted my hair mixing with the condensation on the walls. And then it all went black again.

When I next woke, I was coughing; there was something inside me that needed to get out. I could feel it climbing the ridges of my throat, and I scratched, and I pulled, and I tried to heave the thing out of my chest. I was coughing and there were hands pressed on my forehead, and then there was Mum, bringing something warm and wet and bitter to my lips, and I didn't know what it was, but I took it anyway and in a moment the thing in my throat was drowned. I opened my eyes to my mother, pulling my hair from my face and holding a wet flannel against my head. My hand was wrapped around her wrist, squeezing. I let go as soon as I realised, saying sorry, sorry, sorry when I saw the red blooms on her skin, left behind from my nails.

'Shhh, Sprig. It's OK,' she said, pressing the flannel down, 'it's all just bad dreams; it'll be over soon.'

*

I felt something unusual in my sickness. It didn't feel natural. I felt myself rot into the bed. My bones melted into the mattress, spreading their way past springs and foam, knitting us together. I could hear people coming in and out of the room, feel whispers across my cheeks, but I couldn't place any of it.

At one point, I pulled myself out of bed. It was so warm, I could feel the sweat pooling between my breasts, on my hips. I crawled over to the window, desperate for air. When I reached it, it was closed, but I couldn't work out why. It took me three attempts to move the latch from the sash, my hands were trembling so much. When I finally unlocked it, it opened only an inch. When my arms could lift it no more, I pressed my face against the gap and gulped down what air I could reach, feeling the freshness spike in my lungs. When I crawled back into bed, I texted Chris: *I'm really ill. Lots of people came to the house. Something weird is going on, can you come round? Bring painkillers.*

Ysella visited me just once. She sat on the edge of my bed and tried to take my temperature. The thermometer was old and made of glass, and it felt hot against my skin. I clamped my mouth shut, tucking my lips over my teeth like a baby. Ysella tutted and tried to coax my mouth open. I pushed myself back into the bed, trying to meld with the mattress again. She looked like a giant. Her shoulders blocked out the light as she leant over me, babbling something – *too hot, need rest, no antibiotics* – and her head, her head was too large. I tried to stay very still. If I moved, I might shake her. And if I shook her, she might fall. She might crush me. I thought of Choon, smothered with care and squeezed by the giant until his head popped off. I didn't want to lose my head. I didn't want her to put the thermometer in my mouth, I didn't want anything to be pushed into me by her hand, my mother's hand, anyone's but my own.

She shifted her weight towards me – *for God's sake, I'm trying to help, there's nothing else I can do* – and I gripped onto the mattress, nails clawing the sheet. Don't crush me. She put the thermometer away, dropping it into the pocket of her shirt. The end of it poked out of the fabric, a bloodshot eye watching me. She stood up then; the bed swayed, and I groaned. I watched her brush her hands on the front of her jeans, and then walk around the room. She tucked her hair behind her ears, and rolled her shoulders, moving like she was all alone. She folded clothes, piled coat hangers back into the wardrobe, collected wrappers and bags and mugs. All of my things. She picked up my phone and put it in her pocket with the thermometer. Why? Quiet but loud. She looked at me and smiled. Her face was grey, or maybe it was my eyes. Maybe they were going too. I couldn't hear my voice, didn't know if I had thought or spoken or if she had heard my brain instead, but she smiled, smiled so nicely I almost forgot that she had been the giant on my bed.

'I need to call your work,' she said. Her mouth was moving but the words were coming from the walls. I moved my foot along the mattress until my soul was pressed against the wet plaster of the wall. It was vibrating with her voice, 'and tell them that you aren't coming in, that you don't need the job anymore.'

I didn't need the job anymore.

'Best you stay where we can look after you.'

She patted her top pocket and left the room, giving me a wave that seemed to swirl up all of the dust. She had taken my phone before Chris had replied. Would he come? Did he get my message? I heard a noise after she shut the door. A click. Metal, I think. What does metal sound like? A lock. Was it the door or was it the walls? I couldn't be sure. Did it click or did it jangle? It could've been the turn of a lock. Or it could've been the jangling of a bag of coins.

FOLKLORE

Lowen is alone, and Baby is screaming, and she cannot find her. Left her in the bed and now, gone. Please, please. She checks in the bathtub, under the bed, behind the curtains. Taps the walls as she searches. Please, please. Searches the ceiling for footprints and opens all the windows, peering over the edges. Please, please. The screaming stops and Lowen's ears are ringing. There are sounds in the house that have been lost to her since Baby and now she hears them again. An echo through the floors. Please, please.

She places her forehead against a wall; it is the cool-wet to her hot-dry and she breathes long, gulping breaths, breathes and presses her nose against the wall now. Hears the pulse that moves within it, the voice that belongs to the house, speaking to her now. Greets it like an old friend. Please, please. Wants to step into the wall, force her way through plaster and stone until she is there inside it, be-wombed and safe, where no one can find her. She twitches, involuntary, at the thought. Find it. The Baby. She must find the Baby, or they will think she's done away with it.

DAY ETH

i.

There was a knocking against the glass. Or maybe it was a whistling. Or perhaps it wasn't the glass, but the gravel below. There was a noise. It was outside.

I had not seen Ysella since she waved her thermometer at me, but I had heard her in the footsteps that moved across the yard at night. What was she doing outside, alone, after dark? Nothing good. All I heard were footsteps outside and chittering in the chimney spreading across the walls.

I could hear the birds from my room, the ones in the chimney. The birds were jackdaws. It's almost always jackdaws. Once they've started nesting, they never really stop, just keep building new nests on top of the old. Each one thicker and stronger than the last. Always improving. Or they're just creatures of habit. A group of jackdaws is called a chattering. And chatter, chatter, chatter they do. I tried to speak back to them, I wanted to ask them the time, to find out if they'd seen Ysella walking around outside, if I'd been right about her footsteps. I had been falling asleep often, waking with pins and needles in my hands and feet, the chittering of the birds ringing in my ears. There was no clock in the room.

I was woken in the night by noises outside and managed to pull myself up. From the bed I could see out half of the window. In the dark, the night wrapped the pain in my head in velvet. I recognised the low voice as Ysella's. I had been right – I said that out loud, so the jackdaws could hear me. I wanted them to know that I wasn't imagining things. I moved slowly, straining to see, but there was nothing but darkness.

Then, there was another crunch of gravel and the footsteps that woke me doubled-up. Ysella was walking with an echo. I crawled, shuffling my knees and hands across the floor slowly so I didn't fall and spill. I pressed my head against the window. I was so hot. My breath sweated on the glass.

An echo. No, that wasn't right. Ysella couldn't echo. Four steps. Four feet? Was someone out there with Ysella? I wiped at the condensation on the window, trying to peer through into the darkness. It's nighttime, I said to the jackdaws. I knew that it was night. I wasn't confused. A fever, it was just a fever. The room was too hot because I had a temperature. I was confused because I was poorly. The window was locked because – because what? I tried to wriggle the window up further, maybe it was open after all. No. It stayed in place, not even an inch of air.

The noise happened again, and although I whipped my head around to glare at the walls, to the spot in the top right corner of my room that I thought of as the mouth of the jackdaws – they were in the walls, all over, but I needed somewhere to focus on their sound, so I gave them a mouth – I knew that the sound was not coming from inside the house.

It was the slow drag and rip of the gravel which made me grasp hold of the windowsill. Something was being dragged across the yard. Not four steps. Two steps and one drag.

Scraaaaaaaape.

Something heavy.

Hours later, I heard Chris. I heard him, but no one came to get me, no one let him in. I heard his voice at the door, that tell-tale crack that made him sound like a boy. I pulled myself out of bed, gripped the wall to steady myself. My hands slipped against the wetness, the fleshiness of the plaster. I got to the window, pressed my face against the glass. There he was, stood out in the yard. Why wasn't he in the house? I pulled at the sash window, tried to open it further. It lifted an inch, and then stuck, jammed. The window wouldn't go up, not properly, no more than a crack. Not enough for me to stick my head out, to shout to Chris. I crouched down, peered through the small gap. I could hear my aunt then, her voice lower than Chris's.

She must have been on the front step. Chris threw his hands up in the air.

'This doesn't make any sense!' he said.

More murmuring from Ysella. Something angry was in her tone. Something that reminded me of before.

Chris kicked at the gravel, turned back towards his car. I wanted to call out to him, but my tongue stuck to my teeth. I was so thirsty. I pushed my fingers through the sliver of open window, heard rather than felt the scrape of the wood against the hinge of my wrist. I strained my hand into the cold air.

Look Chris, I'm here.

I'm here.

He didn't turn, just unlocked his car and got in quickly, slamming the door.

I'm here.

He drove off, and I heard sounds inside the house. The front door closed, the locks. The chain being hooked on. I heard a whimpering – my mother – and the slam of a hand on a counter-top. And then silence. Nothing but the chittering in the walls again.

As my fever burnt out, I felt something at the bottom of my bed, by my foot. Something sharp, solid. I managed to curl myself around on the bed, stretching an arm just far enough to grip it in the tips of my fingers. When I pulled it towards me, I saw it was a book. There was a piece of paper sticking out of it, with the word *Pedri* scribbled on it in pencil. Embossed on the front is the title: *Folk*. A gift.

I whispered the name and waited for the jackdaws to respond.

My migraine had started to lift, the edges of my eyesight no longer fading out to black. Then, instead of my body being plagued, my mind felt so. I had been alone in the room for days. All I'd heard was the birds. And Chris. Chris who had not been allowed in the house. All I could think of was the Pedri.

I had not yet regained the energy to retrieve the book from where I left it, tangled in my sheets, but my mind was beginning to clear enough to register what had happened. Someone had dropped the book in my room, hidden it so the others wouldn't see. And someone had fixed the window so I couldn't open it fully.

FOLKLORE

Lowen drags herself down the stairs, slipping, sliding, belly-first. Already on the floor because she's sure now that baby will have taken all her bones. Silence in the house, not so warming now, menacing instead. Baby turned big and strong, ready to pull more of her than she can give, and so she moves yellow-bellied, softly, softly, already knows she won't fight it. Take my bones and leave me liquid. Limpid. She will disappear herself into the cracks when baby is done. Please, please.

Then, a gurgle. A noise that is not a scream but a noise that she recognises. Not from baby but from others, the babies that are not hers, the ones she sees on the TV. The ones that laugh and bounce and smell sweet. Sweet-smelling bouncing babies from the TV. Gurgle, then coo. A TV-bouncing sweet-smelling baby somewhere in this room. She skids her way over, beyond the table, past the counter, and there, there it is. Swaddled up all nice in front of the oven. Happy baby, smiling baby. Not her baby, but a different one, a new one. Lowen pushes herself up with her elbows – bones are still there, a surprise. Rests her chin on her hands so she is lying in front of happy baby, smiling baby. Squints her eyes at it, turns her head. Tries to see baby in the eyes of this one in front of her but can't.

'Gurgle, gurgle', she says to happy baby, smiling baby. Tiny hands are clapped.

'Gurgle, gurgle', says happy baby, smiling baby. Lowen gets up, moves herself so she is sitting, back against the hard door of the oven. New baby looks at up at her, blinking eyes, cow lashes. Reaches a tiny fist from the swaddle, waves it in the air. Lowen catches it, gently presses against the back of the fist until the fingers open out. Little nails, baby nails. Not Lowen's nails, big and long and stolen. Lowen takes the tiny hand and puts it in her mouth. Soft and squishy, an overripe plum.

'Chomp,' she says, but her mouth is full, so it comes out like chumpf and new baby laughs.

'Chumpf, chumpf, chumpf,' she says. She doesn't bite, not really. Couldn't bite this new baby, so little and warm and smiley.

She takes the hand from her mouth and holds her breath.

'Please, please,' she says aloud. The walls of the farmhouse hum happily back. She reaches out and picks up new baby, holds her to her chest.

DAY UNNEK

i.

After a few days of sickness, the next day of almost-wellness was nothing but blistering heat and the smog that builds up when one has been left to soak in a bed for too long.

My illness had finally given me a way to sleep well in Trewarnen, and I dropped in and out of reality intermittently throughout the morning. My dreams, when I could remember them, were of red skies and orange sands and slowly slipping into the ground. They felt like relief.

I got up and grabbed *Folk* from the floor beside by my bed, where it had fallen as I slept. There was no dust jacket, just a bare hardcover in a dirty grey, marked with coffee rings, embossed letters in a swirling font: *Folk*. It looked as though it had sat on the table in someone's house for years, a pretentious coaster – probably picked up from a charity shop or a jumble sale. I moved it carefully, touching it with my nails only, pinching it so that my prints wouldn't transfer onto it. It might have been thrown in the box like rubbish, but it looked rare.

Opening it up, I saw the pages were ragged, crisping at the corners. The first page was printed more ornately than the cover with the full title, *Folk: An Investigation* and a detailed illustration. A vase full of drooping blooms: tulips, petals reflexed, fleshy peonies, daffodils, irises and fritillarias – fighting for space from a narrow neck. The lip of the vase was completely obscured with foliage, creeping ivy. It looked like the kind of painting you'd see in a stately home, something Victorian, grand. There was no life in the flowers, the petals wilting, the ivy desperate. A bird's nest with three eggs sat at the base of the vase, on a nest of coins. There was a crack running down one egg, a trail of ants moving towards it.

The spine was too plain, the book itself not obviously ornate enough to warrant display. *Folk* looked dull. I started at the beginning: a solid wall of text.

Folk: An Investigation

The writer of this collection bears no witness to the truth of the stories within, for they have been told by all manner of people, of whom not all could be deemed trustworthy or sound of mind. It is the writer's opinion that many of the storytellers believed their drolls to be fact, as opposed to legend, and that in many areas, this belief has remained withstanding.

At times, the stories that we wreak are more than words. They are recollections. Truth upon truth, layered with human experience until the finished tale sounds more fanciful than anything one may accept. It is the belief of a handful of people that the tale of the Pedri is one such story. The origin is little known. The Pedri has been given many names, though in this account, the storytellers named it in their archaic language of Cornish, christening it Pedri. This Pedri is said to inhabit the natural lands of the region, holding court across nature, bending the will of the people to its gain, until the ground calls it home.

The Pedri has woven its way into many drolls within the local area, due to a bardic aural tradition that allows stories to be told without source or fact. During the writer's research it was found that many claimed to know the Pedri, although when pressed, this was often in the form of a story of an encounter, passed down through generations. Houses are given protection against the Pedri, with some locals attempting to live a life free from greed and desire, so as not to tempt the Pedri to their door.

The Pedri is a creature that enacts a trade. The trade of children from the Pedri comes at great sacrifice to those who enter into the deal. The Pedri was once believed to be the foremother of Cornwall, providing the childless and the lost with a child to continue their bloodline. The new parents would agree to the Pedri's trade without knowledge of the terms, believing the gift of a child to be benevolent. However, though the Pedri gave willingly, it did not give freely. The children that the Pedri provided to the keening families would always find themselves called back to their true mother when they came of age.

Though these borrowed children would die in our known world, the families affected held the belief that they had returned to their natural existence, with the Pedri.

Many of the stories the writer recorded of these children were otherworldly and difficult to source. At times, the stories would align with official records, such as a death, event or recorded birth. Of the families the writer interviewed for the stories, none of the traded children lived beyond the age of twenty-three.

I read with a twitch in my eye. A flickering beneath the lid. By the time I finished, I had convinced myself that there was something alive under there. Something other than myself, creeping its way across the membrane of my cornea, tiny feelers pitter-pattering on the red door of my eyelid. I took two fingers, middle and index, to my closed eye and pressed down, expecting a bump, a squirm, a body under the cloth. I found nothing there, nothing apart from the layers of skin, the small beat of a pulse and the scattering of colour that came from pressing too hard on my own eyeball. I laid back down on the bed, the book open beside me.

The Pedri was not just a figment of my aunt's storytelling, then, but a wider myth, a being that existed in other stories. It unnerved me to find that this piece of folklore I had only read about in scraps was prevalent enough to have a whole book written about it. A book that seemed to suggest the whole thing was real. I read the introduction again, focused on that final sentence. The writer had interviewed families who claimed to have traded with the Pedri, and not one of them had a child that lived well into adulthood. So, according to this book, the Pedri would gift parents with a baby, which they would then raise, until the Pedri called it back home.

I pressed my knuckles against my eyes until my vision swam black. It couldn't be real. It had to be coincidence, or pure fiction, or confirmation bias – whoever wrote the book found grieving families and posited this idea to them, that their children weren't truly dead, just onto their next lives, and that was a comfort to the families, and so they agreed. It was exploitative to present a folk story as truth to people who were mourning. That was the most likely explanation, I knew, but there were things about the Pedri that were bothering me, still.

I was raised on folktales. My mother, my aunt, my grandmother, each of them shared with me the stories that had been passed down to them. Buccas and knockers and giants and mermaids. Jan Tregeagle, Tom Bawcock, Tristram and Iseult. The hurlers and the pipers and the merry maidens. I knew a droll or a song or a poem for every corner of Cornwall. Each strip of coast, pool of water and circle of stones had its history imprinted on it. But until now, until this trip home, I had never before heard of the Pedri. Not even a whisper. There was no mention of her during festivals, on Flora Day, Allentide, May Day, 'Obby 'Oss, St Piran's day, Nickanan Night, Bodmin Riding, Golowan, Guldize or any of the days celebrated in between. The Pedri had been hidden from me. And why would she be kept from me if I had nothing to fear?

In Ysella's notebook, she'd written Claud's name below the Pedri's. And Claud was gone, gone in a suicide that shattered me but didn't surprise me. It felt inevitable that she would go. Perhaps that was the link Ysella was trying to make. Maybe she believed Claud to be one those children from the book. Maybe that's what my mother meant when she rang me in the city after Claud died and asked, 'Did she tell you?'

My mother said more than that on the phone. She wasn't just asking about Claud. She was asking about me, too.

Did she tell you she was the same as you?

I push the thought aside, remembering, instead, a conversation between me, Claud and Chris when we were younger, when I told them about my mother's story of the mylings. Claud said her parents had argued about changelings – I'd ignored it at the time, too focused on the press of her palm against mine to realise what a strange thing that was to say. Claud was otherworldly, she was special. I could see why my aunt might think to draw a conclusion.

But Claud wasn't just part of some story. Claud was real, wasn't she?

*

The thing living under my eyelid did not calm down until I was home alone. I heard my mother and aunt leave the house, stepping together, my aunt's stride forceful, my mother's skittering steps – when did I start to move like her? Was it before, before I left? Or was it new? I've felt myself becoming more like her in the time I've been home, fluttering and small. When they had left, the doors of the Land Rover slammed shut, the screech of the tyres on the gravel gone, the twitch stopped. I ran downstairs to the computer.

I needed to buy a train ticket. Message Chris and ask him to pick me up. Just for some air. For some normalcy.

I needed someone to remind me I was human.

The book had unnerved me. I had come home to try and feel closer to Claud, to try and put her to rest, but instead I was dragging her body from the ground and flaying it. Her memory flaking off, replaced with something much worse.

When I shook the computer mouse, nothing happened. I hit the side of the screen, trying to switch it on. It stared back at me, an empty chasm. The whole thing must've been turned off. I dropped to my knees, peered under the desk to turn it on at the base.

The box was gone. The space where it sat, empty, dust coating the carpet. It was nothing but a screen. A stupid, greying monitor. Not like the new models, where everything is within, this computer was old, ancient, and needed two parts to make a whole. It was there, days before, and now it was gone. No one had told me about the computer breaking – *although why would they, Merryn, when you were so sick?* If it were broken, one of them could've left it there until I was better, to ask me to fix it.

I couldn't switch the computer on, I still didn't have my phone, which meant I had no way of contacting anyone. I decided then that I would walk. I would get dressed and I would walk to Chris's house. I would find him, even if he could not find me.

The summer was heating up day by day. Ysella was right when she said changing weather left everyone feeling a little off. The days were close, the air unmoving. Each day the moors were scorched further, the grass bleached at the tips. Since my fever broke, I had a constant sheen on me, a shivering of sweat that no amount of washing would rid me of. As I hurried to pull my things together so I could leave Trewarnen, I used the cloth of my T-shirt to press against my armpits, tucking it up behind the underwire of my bra.

I wasn't ready to let *Folk* out of my sight, and it didn't feel safe in my hands, so, I used a thin scarf stolen from the cloakroom in the farmhouse to tie the book to me. I held it against my stomach with my left hand, placed wide and bracing, whilst I used my right to pull the scarf behind and around me. I wrapped it around my back and over the book a few times before tying the two ends in a knot and then tucking the loose tips under the other layers. I stood in front of the mirror in my room, with no top on, and twisted with my arms in the air. The bump of the book followed my movements. I jumped up and down, twirled around, even squatted down to the floor, and the scarf barely moved. I grabbed a larger T-shirt, one that had belonged to my aunt, and pulled it on.

Into my bag I shoved what I could from my room – Ysella's notebook, my hoody, my pointless hairbrush. I looked in my wallet. Ten pounds and a tram pass. I put my trainers on – no socks, too hot – and felt the pinch of them against the bruise of my foot. Each time I bent to pick something up, *Folk* tickled my ribs.

I moved through the hallway quickly, slid down the stairs, my feet barely kissing the floor. In the kitchen, the Toby jugs hung from the ceiling, staring down. Esolyn's legacy. Hello, hello, hello, I said. Goodbye, goodbye, goodbye, I nodded to each of them.

I was just about to leave when I felt a drop in my stomach. When did I last eat? My mother had brought me tea, the bitter kind that Ysella made, a soup of leaves and stained water, and a broth, something that tasted like the ghost of a chicken. Liquid, nothing else. When was I last hungry? I ate toast when I arrived – the first day? The second? Some pork scratchings in the pub, picking through them for the hairless ones, I remembered that. I could taste the salt, still. That couldn't be the pork scratching though, that was days – a week? – ago, but I could taste salt in my mouth. I pressed my tongue against my cheek. Sediment. I peeled it away.

There on the counter, large and unguarded, for the first time, stood Ysella's bowl. The one that held the meat and the butter, the bowl that sealed the windows. And in that bowl, a mass of flesh, strands of it. Moving. The eels. Small ones, maybe about fifteen of them, skinned and alive. I didn't know how – I'd seen how Ysella skinned them. A nail straight through the head isn't something to be argued with. But in this bowl, they were undressed and living.

I reached a hand into the bowl. I needed to touch them. I have no word to describe the way they felt other than raw. Grieving. They were limpid, moving drowsily, as if drugged. Entirely skinless. They shouldn't have been. Not when they were alive. But there they were. Pink and unseeing, unhomely, umbilical, something pulled from a person after they've given birth. A scoop of insides, not suitable for the outside world, dumped in a bowl. They were horrifying. Wet yet drying. I could see their bones under their fat, rippling like rows of teeth. A bowl of living gums. They were darling. How they turned themselves over each other, knotting and twirling, heads burrowing into the coves of each other's stomachs. At least, I thought they were heads. Without the skin, I could tell nothing. I guessed only from the parts that rose up in the air as I moved my palm across the top of the bowl. They sniffed towards me. Curious.

My aunt walked in as I was cradling the bowl in my arms. Her bucket dropped on the floor with a dull plop. Anti-climactic. She rushed towards me, took the bowl with a force that practically threw me into the table.

'Oh Jesus, Merryn. You didn't touch that did you?' She shoved the bowl in the fridge, leaning against the door once she'd shut it, like she was caging a wild animal. I suppose she was. Mum came in behind her, skeleton steps to Ysella's thunder, and now she stood by the kitchen counter, somewhere in the middle ground between me and her sister.

'Did you see her touch it, Lowen?' No answer. Ysella turned back to me. 'What're you doing, girl?'

'They were moving, I thought they were still alive, I had to be sure.'

'What're you on? Of course they weren't moving.'

'They were, I put my hand in, and—'

'You put your hand in? For Christ's sake, Merryn, why would you do that?'

'I was trying to help.'

'You aren't helping anyone. Why can't you leave well alone?'

'This is too much.' My mother finally found her voice. Wavering, near silent. But there, just about.

'Don't you start.' Ysella smacked her hand against the fridge door. 'We're in this because of you, don't forget.'

'It isn't my fault.'

'You asked for all of this, Lowen. And you', she turned to me, 'need to go back to your room. You look like death.'

'I was about to go out, I need to meet Chris.'

'You'll do no such thing. You're not well enough. I don't want you out, it's not safe.'

And that was that.

FOLKLORE

1999. The woman, Lowen, took the new baby from the farmhouse and spirited her, quick-fast, across the moors. She flew over spikes of gorse and waded through bouncing marshes, landing safely in the village, in the cottage where together they would live, for eight long years, before the two of them would come home.

The new baby, she named Sprig. A sprig of thyme. A shoot, a twig, a spray.

The sprig and the woman could not root in the cottage house. It would not let them. Oh, how welcoming the farmhouse had been before. What precious gifts it bestowed upon the woman, what chance it had given Sprig. The cottage did not want them. The cottage knew too much already. The buildings in these parts are almost as old as Her, almost as old as us. They have no patience for the fleeting whims of people. And the people, the people of the village, they had no patience for Sprig and the woman either. They did not trust Sprig, who seemed loud and dirty. Sprig, whose words were muddied and whose play seemed scavenging. And the woman, so clearly desperate, so quietly regretful – away from her mother, the great mother, and the rest of her family. The villagers knew that the woman had done something wrong, that the sprig was the wrong thing. And so, they closed her out.

When the villagers closed her out, the cottage copied. With walls made of pumice stone, it had soaked up too many stories in its years. It did not want the loneliness in its stone.

Eight years passed before the woman and the little sprig of thyme left the cottage behind. Trewarnen waited for them. It welcomed their return. And so did She, ever closer to recalling Her trade.

In the night, I walked downstairs, and I was hit with a wall of heat and musk. My mother and Ysella had argued all evening, before leaving again, the front door locked behind them. I had watched them stalk across the moors, Ysella with her bucket, my mother trailing behind.

There was nowhere for me to go, nothing for me to do but roam the house. After switching the lights on, I went straight to a window for fresh air, but it was sealed shut. I placed my hand on the closest radiator: cold. The warmth had to be radiating from somewhere, but I couldn't place it. It felt like body heat, a room packed full of arms and legs and sickly-sweet breath.

I settled for removing my cardigan and dumped *Folk* and Ysella's notebook on the table, pushing old coffee cups and plates out of the way. I was sure that *Folk* must've come from my mother. Ysella had been far too evasive about it all to give me the book.

I pulled my tobacco from my pocket and rolled a cigarette, not bothering to go outside. The stuffiness of the room should absorb the smoke without anyone realising. It took me five clicks of the lighter to get a flame, and by the time it finally sparked, my eyes were watering in frustration.

The question remained: why was Ysella being so secretive about it all? Clearly, the rest of the village already knew something of the story, just as Paul did that evening in the pub. They had arrived at the house in a mob, angry and scared. Ysella thought the Pedri had something to do with Claud, but the villagers seemed more concerned about me. When they all came to Trewarnen, Tony had acted like I was a catalyst for the things that were going on across the moors. Or a conduit. Like my return had kicked everything off again, made everything worse. But if that were true, why did my mother ask me to come home? Why did she make up the memorial and lure me back here? Was that what they had been arguing about? My aunt clearly didn't want me to know anything about the Pedri, she'd tried her best to keep me away from it all. So why have me here at all? Why not just answer my questions as I asked them? If the words themselves scared her, why keep the notebook in the house? I kept coming back to the same thought: she would only keep it hidden from me if she truly believed in it, if she actually thought I was in danger.

Cigarette in hand, I looked at the book in front of me. Maybe the task would be pointless, but the research itself was surely the smart step to take. Attempting to find reason in unreason-able behaviour is something a well person would do. It felt like an impossible task, like I'd find nothing at all, or something much more complicated than I'd started with.

I turned the thin pages of *Folk* with one hand, ignoring any sec-tions that looked too pristine. I was looking for pages that had been scribbled on, folded over, marked in some way, anything to help me make sense of what I was reading. I found what I needed when I reached a section on trades and children. At the top of the page, an illustration, skewed like those at the beginning of the book. A landscape, rolling hills, trees, low-hanging clouds, almost idyllic. And there, coming out of the ground like flowers, babies. Babies everywhere. I read quickly, greedily. Most of the writing was factual, listing out specific cases of the Pedri using its – her – children as an object of trade, offering up babies to desperate families and then recalling them years later, when they were fully grown. The different ways these supposed *spriggans* were returned made me pause. Each death was in connection with the land, this very moor. A gorse fire, a suffocation in a marsh, a landslide, buried alive, frozen. Drowning.

Claud, weighed down in the water at Dozmary pool, not even trying to swim. In the same lake she visited weekly, the same lake

Esolyn used to baptise my mother and aunt. The same lake my aunt didn't want me visiting as a child.

I turned to the next page, to see if there were more illustrations, but instead I found a note, in pencil, written down the side of the margin.

EL – DO NOT LET LOWEN SHARE THIS.

I choked on the smoke in my lungs, coughing onto the page in front of me in shock. Little droplets of spit sprayed across the handwriting. It wasn't Ysella's, looping and neat. It couldn't be my mother's, though I was sure she'd given me the book. This was written by someone else. A steady hand. Were the EL initials?

When my breathing calmed, I went to take another drag from my cigarette and found it had stuttered out, the end gaping black. I must've tapped it against the table too hard, dislodged the little burning cherry of light somewhere onto the floor. I made a quick plea to my lighter, cartwheeling it in my hand a few times to spread the remaining gas through.

There were certain subjects that I never discussed with my mother – she would not speak openly about grief, her illness, my birth, or even her life before I was born. All knowledge I have of their childhood has come to me from Ysella, who is liberal with her recollection of family history. My mother, on the other hand, would only speak to me of the past in warnings and lessons, and even then, they came in code. I've learnt about her through the myling, the night-time whispers, the stories. My mother cannot handle reality – that is what me and my aunt have kept from her, tried to shield her from. She loves to tell stories, to share them with whoever will listen, always has. Which meant whoever wrote the note, demanding that my mother not share it with others, believed that the book – or this section, at least – was true, and that it would be a problem for her to pass that on

I looked at the note again. Ran my fingers over the squat block capitals, felt the way they were indented deep into the paper. It was familiar – and so was the *EL*.

I ran into the kitchen and pulled open every drawer until I found them: an inch of cards, held together with a fraying elastic band. I carried them back to the table and placed them in front of me, breaking the elastic band with my nail. The first few were birthday cards to me from my aunt. Thirteen, Fourteen, Fifteen. A Christmas card from my mother. I moved through them quicker, my hands clumsy with impatience. There had to be older ones in there somewhere. Seeing that *EL*, along with the handwriting, had sparked an idea. After flicking through almost thirty cards, I found them. Two old Christmas cards, creased and cheap with robins on the front.

Inside the first, in the same handwriting, addressed to my mother: *Lo, Nadelik Lowen, Esolyn X*

And below that, for my aunt: *El, Nadelik Lowen, Esolyn X*

The only person brave enough to shorten Ysella's name that way.

*

Ysella found me bent over *Folk* at the kitchen table, where I had been sat for most of the night. Her hand on my arm made me look away from the page – I looked at her fingers, wrapped nervously around my wrist, and saw that I was bleeding. I had been scratching at my arm as I read, raising welts from my wrist to my elbow. When Ysella let me go, a pimple of my blood had burst against her finger, which she put in her mouth to suck clean.

The book had been splayed open in front of me, and it wasn't until she'd dropped my hand that she realised what I'd been reading. Her hand moved from her mouth to her neck. She held herself there, gently, caressing, as she spoke.

'I suppose there's nothing for it now,' she said.

She had caught me. I watched quietly as her voice broke.

'Don't look surprised, I knew your mother would find a way to get that book to you eventually. Just like I knew you had my notebook. This is what Lowen wanted, for you to come back and learn it all. I tried to keep you from coming home, I tried to send you back because I knew this is what would happen. Once you were here and you had that book, I knew I was running out of time. I tried to fight it; Lord knows I did. We did well, didn't we?' she asked, looked down at me. I could smell her need, the reassurance she wanted. It was earthy. I didn't reach out, didn't blink. I wanted to see if she'd cry. Her throat dipped, in and out, quickly. I thought of the eels in the bowl, twisting.

'We did. We did everything – I did everything I could, but God, I'm tired. I've fought and fought for you, but even I can't defeat nature, no matter how hard I try. I hope you can see that, how much I've tried. Do you have anything to say, after what you've read?'

Which bit was she referring to? Her notebook? Claud's name on those pages? Or *Folk* – the one thing that made it all seem real? She looked nervous, holding her throat like that, as if she were balancing her head, scared of losing it.

'Her mother knew, you know? Just like yours. But you were lucky, really. The way Lowen dealt with it. It was much kinder. I know it wouldn't have felt like it, especially when you were small. But better that than what that woman did to her girl. The cruelty of it.' She shook her head. 'Unfathomable. We never wanted to leave you like that, you understand?'

Mothers, everywhere. Whose mother? My grandmother? Or Claud's mother?

'You know, my mam wrote that book. Your grandmother. She wrote it long ago, before I was born, even, and she wanted nothing done with it. Lord knows where the other copies went, but I had to hunt this one down after she was gone. She'd given her only copy to Mrs Rowe, for safe keeping. And then everything happened with Lowen, and Esolyn told me about it all. About the book, and the stories, and what Lowen had done. I didn't want to believe her. You were only a baby. But I saw the change myself. And I held you at a distance, I admit, just when you were a baby. I'll always regret that, because it pushed Lowen away for a while, too. It gave Mam permission to treat you poorly. I should've been warmer, whilst I could. This was never your fault. Your mother asked for it and then we all had to live with it, you too. But our mam, she could never get over it, she was furious. And Lowen, she's always been so stubborn. The fight between them became bigger and bigger, and that's why you went to the cottage in the village. Then Mam was gone, and you and Lowen moved back here, and she never spoke of it. She wouldn't acknowledge that you were anything but hers. I started to think, maybe I could live like that too. And I did, for a while, at least when I was with you. And we got so close, you and I, because I knew you needed greater protection, and because I loved you. That part was simple. It was never your fault, but I couldn't forget what Lowen had done. You were one of the great gifts of our lives, you understand? The greatest. Maybe I'm as spiteful as she is stubborn, but I couldn't help but remind her, whenever I felt she was shirking her responsibilities with you . . . I would remind her that she'd done this, she'd asked for this. Maybe that made her a worse parent to you, for a while. I'm sorry about that. We're both sorry for a lot of it. And now, with the time . . . I thought I could do something to help. I learnt the stories, and I thought I could change the course.'

She sat on the chair opposite me and sighed. She looked so very tired. 'I really thought I could change it. Tell me, can I?'

I put my hand on hers, and I smiled. The one I'd practised. The tiger teeth I gave my mother, sat under this very table as a child who could not spell her own name. I pinched my cheeks, twice, quickly between thumb and forefinger, and pulled my lips back, like I had in front of the mirror only days before.

Ysella crossed herself. One finger fluttering up and down her face and darting along her shoulders. She'd never done that before. I realised she was scared of me.

'Mam was right.' She shook her head slowly, stepped back from the table. 'You can't fight nature. I thought your mother wanted what I did, what's best for you. To keep you safe. But she's been

just as bad, it's like she wants it to happen. I need you to go—'
she waved her hand at the stairs, '—and get in your room. I won't
ask twice.'

I didn't move from my seat. I picked up *Folk* and held it against
my chest. Coddled it. Cradled it. When I looked back at Ysella,
she had sunk. Her skin was too big for her, her cheeks hung lower,
her muscles spilling off her bones. Quieter, she said 'Please. I'm
not trying to be cruel. You need to understand. I didn't want you
to come here because I can't bear for you to leave. Please, just go
to your room.'

I shrugged, then nodded. As I turned to take the stairs, I felt
arms wrap around my waist. Ysella pulled me backwards, forcefully, into an embrace. She held me there, against her chest, tight
enough that I struggled to breathe. I leant my head against her, the
touch of kindness softening me. She dropped a kiss on the crown
of my head and spoke into my scalp: 'Everything that we've done,
we've done with love.'

With that, she let go of me and I went into my bedroom, aware
that she was following me, but not looking back, not until I had
shut the door and sat on the bed.

I heard my door lock from the outside.

FOLKLORE

Ha! Ha! Ha! Ha! You did not think – did you?

Surely not – that there would be a way out, an escape, a twist of fate, for the mothers and the daughters?

Sweet, sweet child. There is only one ending.

DAY PESWARDHEK

i.

It was day fourteen, I think. There was the before and the after. I had split.

I had been in my room since Ysella found me reading *Folk*. I had been keeping quiet. I pressed my ear against the walls to check if I was alone. The jackdaws were louder when my aunt wasn't home. I didn't know what that meant.

In my room, I read *Folk* cover to cover. I studied it in detail, taking a pen to each page that struck me, underlining passages before copying them out into the blank pages of Ysella's notebook. When there were no pages left, I moved my bedside table out of the way, and wrote onto the pale patch of wall that was hidden behind it. It was only a matter of time before the book would be taken from me and hidden away somewhere by my aunt. That, or I would be taken away. If we were separated, I could not be sure that I would see the book again, or that the stories inside would remain the same.

Much had changed in the time I had been home, and all the things I had once believed to be true no longer felt real. The house I had come back to didn't feel familiar at all. There was an oppression in the walls. I was waiting to suffocate under it.

I had believed there were reasonable explanations for everything that would happen in life – people were cruel because of chemistry or upbringing, coincidences existed because of probability, everything had roots in real life. Changeling stories were child abuse. Even the bottomless Dozmary pool was only nine feet deep. There was no such thing as the unexplained, the unbelievable, the unimagined.

But my homecoming, and all that had happened since, had changed that.

I started refusing the cups of tea my aunt had been bringing me. They were making me drowsy. She must have been putting something in them, something to keep me asleep. She didn't want me to leave the room. Without the tea, I was able to understand things more clearly. Although my brain felt sharper, my body was not. I felt sluggish, my bones heavy. I was sleeping less, which was good. I'd almost stopped sleeping altogether. I was beginning to worry that I might be turning – into my mother, or into something inhuman. I heard Ysella and my mother talking about the same thing, discussing how I was changing, when they thought I was asleep. My room would be dark, the curtains drawn, the ottoman in front of the door.

I drew the curtains when I couldn't look outside anymore. Each time I caught sight of the moors, I would lose hours trying to wedge the window open so I could get out, be amongst the land. I wanted to feel the soil. But the window wouldn't move. And I didn't want to break it, not yet.

I'm locked in, why are they locking me in?

Instead, I focus on what they say when they're outside my door.

'This was always going to happen.' That's my mother.

'Then why did you bring her back here?' Ysella.

'Because it's right. Because it is fair.'

'We can fix it.'

'She doesn't need fixing.' My mother. 'She needs letting go.'

When I could no longer bear the soft, slipperiness of the walls, I began to write on the floorboards. I dragged the rug out of the way and wrote underneath that, covering it up at the end of every day so nothing could see it, not even the house. I copied from the book the dates of a series of 'acts of God' that had raged across the moors in the nineteenth century. Starting with the fall of Warleggan's church spire in 1818, the moor was hit repeatedly by tragedy. In 1819, a mansion at Glynnduring was gutted by fire. In 1847, a broken waterspout in Davidstow caused eighteen feet walls of water to run down the River Camel. In the course of each event, a young person was killed, or lost. Taken back by the Pedri. Two lovers died in Lanhydrock House in 1881 and 1882 – one from the fire that took over the house, the other from grief. The Pedri took them both.

In 1890, animals and people were killed, trains were buried, ships were sunk and trees were felled by a week-long blizzard. In the same year, another house on fire, and a church. And then later that year, a drought, blistering, like the one scorching the grass outside my window in that moment. That drought lasted for so long that Dozmary pool ran dry, revealing at its base bone shards, clay pipes, coins and the bloated, lumpen bodies of eels, eyes swollen after a lifetime trapped in the lake.

The stories used to say that the water of Dozmary would swell and drop with the tide, that the whole thing was bottomless – these were the things that my grandmother believed – but it never led to the sea, it was just a trap, a pit where nothing could really survive, apart from the things that had no choice.

Folk was unlike any book I'd ever read. Now I knew that Esolyn wrote it, Ysella found it, and my mother gave it to me, I felt as though it was written for me. It was in this house because I was there. There were stories I'd heard before, stories I remembered from the nights when I was a child, whispered in my ear. It seemed that some of the messages were left for me, the bits that my grandmother underlined. It took me a while to work that out. In the book, there were four sentences that were underlined, three of which Ysella had copied out into her notebook and I'd already looked at. The fourth, the only one Ysella didn't write out, was in the introduction to the book: *The ground calls it home.*

I wrote out these sections, the breaks in the text. I tried them in a few different variations, and it didn't make sense. It was only when I laid them out in the order that I had discovered them that they made a new story, a story that felt like it might be mine.

The Pedri makes a trade
a babi that has changed
You, come of age and are returned
the ground calls it home

ii.

I broke into Ysella's desk on the day – don't ask me which day, all are blended, all are ankoth, unknown – my mother slid a piece of paper and the key to my room under my door with an instruction written on it: *Look in the drawers.*

I knew by then that she'd been right, about a lot of things. The memorial was a trick by my mother, a way to get me home; that was why Chris had not been invited, why they would never give me a date. It was something to bring me back here, an excuse to lock me in. I willed myself to feel angry about it, but I could only think of what had happened to Claud.

The iron of her face. The way her brittle body bent, her small patches of softness, the downy hair that hid behind her ears. All of the little tokens I had given her, the gifts I'd foraged over the years, the pieces she dropped in her pockets, that made her coat jangle whenever she picked it up, they simply got too big. They grew. And then the weight of them took her under. She had a piece of granite from the wall in each pocket. No one but me knew where they had come from.

I stayed silent when the note came through my door, so that my mum might believe I was sleeping. Or gone. I didn't want her to worry anymore. I listened to the sounds of the house and ran my fingers over the indents of her words. I looked at the floor, marked with the fires and losses of the moor, and the wall, where I had hoarded lines from the stories I had read. Whatever I found when I followed my mother's note would surely be the end of it all; it would have to be.

I waited until it was dark, until I heard the front door open and close again, and then I moved with a whisper into Ysella's bedroom. Wary now of all the ways the house had tried to trick me, I waded slowly on tiptoes through the darkness, one finger trailing against the wet walls for stability. The bare wood floor prickled my feet. As I stepped through the doorway into her room, the temperature dropped – she had gone out for the night with her window wide open. I moved to shut it, eager to begin my task, but the crunching of gravel outside distracted me. Dropping to my haunches, I peered over the windowsill into the courtyard. The view from there was much clearer than from my room.

Ysella, scarf pulled high around her neck, ignoring the nighttime heat, pulled a bucket full of something wet and shining behind her. The skins of the eels, no longer writhing. I watched until she disappeared over the stone hedge, into the fields and moorland beyond.

I turned to her desk. It sat unassuming against the back wall, drawers locked. Earlier that day, I had searched amongst the unwashed pans and dishes in the kitchen cupboard for Ysella's tools and stolen a small claw hammer, which I'd snuck upstairs, held against my stomach with the scarf, forcing it into place next to *Folk*. I didn't bother attempting to pick the lock – I wanted Ysella to know that I was no longer waiting for the slivers of information they offered me. I was taking it for myself.

I tried to prise the drawers open, using the claw first, but I wasn't strong enough to pull them out. Instead, I spun the hammer round and swung it into the front of the top drawer. The effect was instant – and the violence of it joyous. The drawers split and screamed as great chunks of wood broke away from the desk.

I thrust my hands into the yawning throat of it and pulled out every last word.

With Ysella safely out of Trewarnen, on the moors, dragging her bucket of eels, I spent the night in her room, reading through her papers. I found diaries, files, photocopies, drawings. An old dictaphone. Treasure.

Treasure, more than just the Pedri. Myself, my mother, our histories, bound up within those drawers.

I had long ago guessed that my father wasn't local – it was the only thing I could imagine casuing the great dislike my grandmother had felt towards me.

In the desk, I found a series of items that proved me right: train tickets to Dawlish and back, and a postcard from my mother addressed to Ysella, with the coastline across the front. I had asked my aunt about my father's identity many times, and she'd always claimed to be ignorant of it. There it was, locked in her desk. A shame to find that he was just a man. Plain and pale, he looked no more like me than my mother did.

There was more to be found, tucked amongst rolls of receipts and old books. My birth certificate, a blank space where my father's name should be, my birth not registered until four months after I was born. Written prescriptions for my mother, dating back twenty years. The anti-psychotics and benzodiazepines appeared just a few months after I was born, proof of the root.

No baby photos, but a photo of me age six or seven, stood in front of the cottage in the village. It looked like summer; I was wearing shorts, stood next to the blue sparks of an agapanthus in flower. My limbs looked too long for my body, like I had too many joints, beetle-like, and I was holding onto a hand. I couldn't see who it belonged to, my mother or Ysella. I held the photograph close to my face in search of a trace of nail polish, or the butt of a cigarette that would prove it was my mother. At that age, she smoked constantly and held me rarely. When I grew older than the child in that photo, when I grew into someone else entirely, the smell of tobacco would always conjure my mother's face, along with the rose water she would dab on her throat after a smoke.

I dropped the picture back onto the remains of the desk. I did not need to mine an old memory in the search for tenderness. My mother had already done me a kindness. She was letting me go.

FOLKLORE

Occasionally, there are people who get close to Her. Those that know to protect the land, keep it safe, are the ones who come the closest to Her. Those that take, take, take, will never see what She is. Instead, they will move across these parts, outsiders with their lumpen boots and heavy steps, climbing in their cars that move like scarabs. They tear down our houses and plough our fields. They do not remember the spaces as they were before they came – why would they? They barely see us now.

When She visits them, they see only the shadow of Her movements. They catch Her in the draughts that eke through their windows, the gorse that snags on their clothing. She takes from them, like they take from us, with no return. Up burn their houses, down go their cattle, distant are their children.

It was the great mother that named Her. She had no name before; we did not need one.

Pedri. Pedriiiii, they say. The darkest, dankest of names.

The great mother danced on the edges of the room, her ankles rolling under the uncertain weight, her hands pressing on her chest as she waited for the moment when the Pedri would take the stage, and when She does – and She always does, the Pedri, She is always the heart of the dance, the story, the myth – it is as a pool of water. She spills from the curtains and soaks into the floor and from there, She spins. The Pedri spins with Her arms outstretched, spraying the walls and the crowd, until She moves so fast, She is nothing but a tower of water, and first, the great mother, and later, her children, must choose to either drown or open the dam themselves.

See what the Pedri has done?

This story began when the man, the stranger father, pulled down the work laid by the hands of the great mother, and released the Pedri. Oh, how She returned! What joyous day when the Pedri was free once more. A new history was writ. The Pedri toyed with the great mother. She blighted her farm, gentle cows burnt to ash and scattered back upon us, and we fed, didn't we? We took those ashes and supped them up, back into our greedy guts. The Pedri took to the great mother's children too. One, She made stern. The other, She broke. Slowly and softly. Such benevolence, to split them with the sweetest of sorrow.

iii.

With my treasures held in my arms, I moved about the house, near silent. There was one more thing I needed to do before the end.

On the stairs, I balanced my bare feet on the walls on either side of the steps and shimmied up the skirting board. I would not be tricked by disappearing steps, not again. In my bedroom, I unwrapped the scarf from my stomach, no longer caring about the musty smell of it, and peeled *Folk* from my skin. With *Folk* in one hand and my treasures in the other, I pressed myself flat on the floor and edged myself under the bed. Once underneath, my arms were pinned under my chest, my hands near my shoulders. I let go of *Folk*, safe in the cave under the bed. From my position I couldn't check the rest of my hoard – Ysella's notebook, the envelope with my hair. They were all down somewhere near my feet. I tried to turn to see them, but the bed frame was so low to the ground that I couldn't lift my head. My chin was pressed against the bare wood floor, my mouth full of dust. I wiggled my toes and felt the soft brush of the lock of hair, still in its hiding spot.

Mercy.

Under the bed, I held my final treasure, the dictaphone, up to my ear and closed my eyes. For a few seconds after I pressed Play, there was nothing but white noise, room tone. Listening closely, I could hear the breathing in my ear.

And then my grandmother's voice, wavering and close to the microphone, 'How many times have I tried to fix this mess? Useless. This whole thing—' there is a pause. The click of a lighter, a drag of breath. On the exhale: '—useless. Even this, this recorder of Ysella's, it's useless. I've done this twice. Twice, because I've written it all down once before. There's a danger to this, to recording, or writing. A risk to admitting that I know the truth. Words make it easier for secrets to spread. It's a disease, this knowledge. If the wrong person hears of it, oh, the temptation for them. Unbearable. It's what happened to Lowen. Once she knew, she couldn't let go of it. Could not resist. I'll curse myself to my last day for that. I was supposed to keep them safe, both of them – all three of them, in the end. Instead, I brought this story to them and look what it has done to Lowen. And the baby, the poor, sweet baby. The first innocent in this. Ysella, too. A life turned bitter.' Another pause, another drag of the cigarette. I picture my grandmother, sat at the table, ashtray on an open newspaper in front of her.

'I feel sorry for myself, too. I shouldn't say that. I don't deserve a repentance, I know. But I didn't want to live my last years in fear. I didn't want my daughters to lose their way. Ysella is asking for answers, something to fix it all. I told her there's only so much that can be done. Lowen, well, Lowen wants it all out in the open. I told her, she's the one who made this decision, so she needs to step back and let me fix it, not make it worse. Getting it out in the open! As if the child, I suppose – yes – the child, as if it could live at all, knowing all of that. Better to go on in ignorance for as long as one can.

'I've not got long left in me, I know that. The times I've lived, the sacrifices I've made, it all weighs heavy. The girls don't understand. They think I've been hard on them, and what's wrong with that? It's their father they should blame, not me. As much use as an ingrown hair, that man. I had her locked up. That thing, God forgive me, I'll use the name: the Pedri.'

There she was. Finally.

'I can't say exactly what she is, I doubt anyone could, but I knew she came of the moor. Walked on it, fed on it. Gave birth and spread death on it. I'd heard the stories when I was a young girl myself. They called her "it" back then, not she. I knew better when

I heard the stories. They were things only a woman could do. To give and take and give again: that was no man, no creature. They were the actions of a mother, caught between the desire to let go and pull back, to raise and then wean. A mother, knowing exactly how to tempt, what to do to bring her children back to her. So, I trapped her. I built that wall, and I trapped her inside when she was hibernating, and that should've been the end of it.

'If everyone else had left well alone, the girls would only know of the Pedri through stories. Oh, I made sure she was in all the stories I told them, of course. Hidden in the background. I was trying to instil a healthy fear in them.

She takes payment from Lutey to buy his mermaid clothes for land, steals the ground from under giants' feet. Trades magic beans with Jack. She tears the choughs from the sky, drills a hole in Jan Tregeagle's limpet shell. She rips spires from churches and steals babies from beds and all the while, she throws coins at the feet of her victims, telling them it is all a gift, and they believe her. All I wanted was for her to be locked away, and for my girls to grow up knowing that there were things more powerful than them out here, that they weren't as invincible as they thought.'

I pressed Pause. I knew those stories, knew them well from my childhood, and oh, how warm I felt then, in that moment of recognition. How quickly the fear left me, until there was nothing but wonder. I needed more. I pressed Play.

'Their father ruined it all. No surprise. Selling off my family land and letting some emmets tear at my wall. That was bad enough, letting her out the way they did. That was already dangerous. And then, well—' There was a long stretch of silence. I chewed on my thumb as I listened to the faraway noises of Esolyn shifting in her chair, swallowing, 'Well. Suppose I told them one too many stories. Suppose I made Lowen too curious too young.

'Maybe I should've kept the whole thing hidden from them, but like I said, I was trying to teach them to be fearful. I didn't think Lowen would ever go that far. I didn't think she'd be tempted like that. She had the baby, the first one, and she struggled. Lord, she struggled. That baby did nothing but scream. Scream and suckle. I thought I was helping when I told her the stories. I didn't expect her to take them literally. I told her how the Pedri had her own children, little animals she gave as gifts to mothers who couldn't cope. As with all her other gifts, these children came at a price. She only gave them for so long until she called them back, back to the land where they belonged. Another lesson, this, one about greed, desire, superiority. She was supposed . . . it was supposed to remind her to be grateful for her child.

In these stories, the women would try to trick her – the Pedri, the real mother – by protecting their children in the ways they knew how. With baptisms and bibles beneath the pillows of their beds, bunches of lavender over hearths and moorland stones around necks. It never worked because they weren't really children. Like her, they had many names. And she always called them home, she took them back. I need another smoke.'

The recording went quiet again for a moment, and then there was a banging in the distance. When Esolyn's voice came back, she was whispering.

'She's here,' a long pause, 'I don't know – I don't know where. Outside, I think. The walls are warm, wet, but the fire isn't lit. I thought if Lowen left Trewarnen, it wouldn't come back. But it's here, she's here, at the farm. The cows aren't right. And I know it: she has been at the cottage too. Ysella told me she can sense it, in the child. Lowen's not well, the child isn't right. The Pedri wants them both back here, so the child is closer to where it came from. I think that's why it won't leave us all alone. If Lowen had just asked, I could've helped. I like to think I would've helped, but maybe – maybe I wouldn't've. I've been so angry. So angry. It's not been an easy life. This isn't the way I wanted it to go.'

On the tape, a banging noise, distant. Under her breath, Esolyn swears. I listen to a few minutes of movement. Her footsteps hitting the slate of the kitchen floor. A door opening and closing

– the fridge? A cupboard? A squelching noise. She was warding. When she comes back to the dictaphone, her voice is no longer whispered.

'That'll keep the bitch out,' she starts, before letting out a long sigh. 'I did what I could to keep my family safe, but I did it on my own. I shouldn't've had to do it alone. Lowen couldn't cope, so she did the only thing she knew how: she asked for a trade. She got the baby she wanted. I mourn that child every day, I want you to know that. That first child, my grandchild, I mourn him every day. I don't know what happened to him. Lowen never said. Her mind was gone, after the trade. The Pedri took him, probably. I don't know. But he was lost, and he's been lost ever since. And I tell you, Lowen might think she got what she wanted, with the child the Pedri gave her, but one day she'll be mourning her every day too. Because it won't last. It can't last. Everything that comes from the ground has to go back down, eventually.'

The tape shut off.

FOLKLORE

What you must know, what you must learn, if you are to learn anything at all, is that the Pedri remains generous.

The Pedri knew the girl would come back to Her; there was no choice. They always did. This girl, though, was special, the first trade the Pedri had ever made with the Tregellas women. The Pedri had watched the Tregellas women for a long time, longer than most. They never asked for more than they had. They were not women driven by vengeance, not like the others that asked for the Pedri's help. The great mother had suffered at the hands of the Pedri for the actions of her husband, but still, she did not bow to fear. The Pedri was, for the first time, impressed.

No, the Tregellas women did not ask for much. So, when the youngest daughter weakened and asked for help, the Pedri gave her the girl.

At the same time, the Pedri found a lonely couple, a poor couple with no fruit, and she bestowed upon them a child too. One that would become a gift for the girl. And the lonely couple called that child Claudia.

The Pedri gave the girls their time together. Longer than She should have, She gave them their time at the surface, before they went below.

Bucca Widn took care of that one, the lovely beast. A siren song, a temptation, closely coaxing for years – how he bides his time, the patient pike! He was always the slowest of soldiers – until the friend was supple enough to slip into his waters, ripe for Bucca to pluck her pockets and hold her down, down, down.

Finally, I had the truth. My grandmother had told me exactly what I needed to do. Everything seemed to be leading me towards it then, the earthy rot of the old wooden floorboards, the spores of the mould that crept up from the skirting. The chittering of the jackdaws in the walls seemed to be in agreement.

I can only describe the knowledge of what must come next as a settling, deep in the bones of me. It was not an awakening, no, quite the opposite of that. It was to be a folding-in of myself.

I had always felt safest tucked away, folded small and tight. I grew taller than I should've as I aged, taller than I wanted to, and it became increasingly harder to fit myself into spaces where I couldn't be seen. Under the table, in the gap between the fridge and the kitchen counter – those places would no longer do. Even whilst I was under the bed, I was thinking of a better place, somewhere no one would think to look for me.

I read over the underlined passages from *Folk* again and again, feeling more connected to the words each time.

The Pedri makes a trade
a babi that has changed
You, come of age and are returned
the ground calls it home

It was frightening to think that those words were the story of my life, that the things my mother, aunt and grandmother had said and written were true. The thought that I truly wasn't meant for this world was at first a sickening one, something that felt heavy in my stomach, but once the awareness settled in, I began to feel calmer. The churning in my stomach and the sweat that clung to my skin were no longer from fear, but anticipation. Preparation.

That was why I had been called to Trewarnen. It was not for my mother, or my aunt, or Claud, not as I knew her anyway. I was home for the ending.

The presence that I felt calling me home had been the Pedri, the movement in my bedroom at night, that weight on my chest. I thought those things had been down to Lowen, but I see now that they weren't, they never could've been. She was never substantial enough to carry such weight. It was my true mother that wanted me back.

*

In the garden, I dug a hole. At first, I used my hands like claws, the dirt packing deep beneath my nails. The soil was dust, and the work was slow. I dragged a spade from the shed, but before that, I sucked the dirt from under my nails. It tasted the same as the dust under the bed. I chose a spot just below the window, near the old rhododendron that my grandmother always hated for blocking her light. My mother and Ysella were inside, on the other side of the glass. Ysella was folded over, snapped at the spine. I could see her sobbing, though I couldn't hear it. I watched, as my mother leant over her, rubbing her back, soothing her like a child. Our eyes caught, my mother's gleaming, searching for something from me. Approval. I nodded at her. It was time for her to look after Ysella, to leave me. Her smile was gentle, but grateful. Now the two of them could be alone together again. As they should be. My mother straightened Ysella up, lifting her.

I tried to break ground with the spade, forcing it hard into the soil by the roots of the shrub, but it was compacted. The spade felt alien, the ground distant when I approached it with a tool. Instead, I sat back down and spat into the soil, wetting it myself. I pushed my thumb into the wet and turned, mixing myself with the land.

The rhododendron shouldn't even be there. In Ysella's drawers I found a series of official letters about it, all addressed to my grandmother – in 1981 it became an offence to plant or otherwise allow *Rhododendron ponticum* to grow in the wild, and the land around Trewarnen, the space that I had been told was our garden, was wild. It didn't belong to us. Esolyn had kept copies of petitions, parish council meeting minutes and clippings of letters written to *Cornish Guardian* newspaper demanding the removal of the rhododendron from public land. I read them all and felt the same message that must've hurt my grandmother: you do not belong here.

And then I remembered what had happened after my grandmother's death – me and my mother snuck back into this house for years and rooted ourselves deep within the foundations, and like woodworm – like the rhododendron above me – we refused to leave without a fight.

And then I left. But whilst I was away, the rhododendron had continued to knot itself tighter to the ground, ensuring a piece of my family – a patch of our stubbornness, our refusal to yield to who we were supposed to be – would always remain here.

I would make like the rhododendron. I would root.

Ysella thought they were losing me, but my mother knew better. She understood what I was about to become, what I had always been. It was why she was willing to let me go.

I continued to churn the soil up with my hands, wetting it any way I knew how. It began with spit, but once my mouth dried crisp, I pulled down my shorts and squatted, accidentally speckling my feet. On my knees, I dug deep, not wide, straight down. The sun set, and my view of the moor disappeared. Inside the house, the lights remained off.

When the hole was deep enough, I peeled off my clothes and folded them neatly on the grass. I pulled the envelope from the pocket of my trousers and took the sprig of my hair from it. I laid it on the ground, to the side of the hole. It was a final gift from my mother, set aside for this purpose, to hold my place. A temporary waymarker, one that she would replace with stone in the days that followed.

I lined my shoes up, just like Claud had. Where she had still water, I had soil. We are taken back, she had said. She had been called home, and now so was I. If I stayed completely still, I could almost feel her voice. The thrum of it, underneath. Just below the surface.

Naked, I sat at the edge of the hole and lowered myself in, feet first. Roots and stones and old buried things scratched against my legs as I pushed down. The soil warmed around me, burning at my touch. The hole was just wider than my hips, but slightly narrower than my shoulders. When the time came to squeeze them through, my hands were already pinned by my thighs. I had no choice but to force my shoulders inwards, towards my chest. I pushed against the hard wall of dirt behind me until I heard – felt – something pop in my bones. A burst of flame from my spine to my chest, and with that I slithered down, deep into the earth.

There, I found myself ever more grounded in place.

FOLKLORE

Together, together, together.

This is how it starts.

One of them went to the water, the other in the ground. Their bodies disappeared, the trappings of flesh and muscle melted away. They were left with the simple things, the greatest things. Hunger, desire and love.

The people duwenhe – grieve – for their lost children. They believe it is over. But not for the girl, Merryn, and the other, Claud.

There is a song that calls them down, in the end, bys vyken. It goes like this:

'I will meet you in the ground, my love, between the roots and the sand and the silt.

I will hold you near and beside, my love, together our bones shall meet.'

Can you see? Now, they are one.

ACKNOWLEDGEMENTS

To my perfect friends, Alex Turton and Hannah Conway, thank you for being constants in my life for so long, even when we're separated by terrible train scheduling. I'm forever inspired and in love with the interesting, kind, hilarious people that you are, and strive to be just as good – thank you for existing.

Thank you to my wonderful agent, Olivia Maidment. Liv, you saw the real story of this book immediately. Your shaping and wisdom made this whole dream a reality, and I'll forever be grateful (and indebted!) for that. There is nothing more important than having a champion beside you in this process, and I couldn't ask for a better one.

Thank you to my parents – for a house full of books, creativity and support. I'm glad I've finally written something that I'll let you read. For my sisters – don't hate me for dedicating this to the youngest one. Lily, this book is for you, because it's your turn to write one next.

To the Bookstagram community, would I have started writing this book without you? I don't think so. Thank you for reigniting my passion for reading, for getting me through lockdown and supporting me through each stage. Special thanks go to those of you who were my earliest readers – Jen Smith-Furmage and Helen Draper and Amy Twigg.

Thank you to all the authors that threw the ladder back down: Tom De Freston, the best writing mentor in the world, whose sheer enthusiasm for this book, even when it was a scrappy draft, made it into what it is. Thank you to Jessie Burton and her generous prize of a London Library membership – winning that membership felt like permission to write. Alan Trotter for the early mentoring support and Charlie Carroll who helped immensely with querying. Thank you to all the other authors who have shown support throughout this journey, including Kiran Millwood-Hargrave, Elizabeth Macneal and Molly Aitken for the early edits and mentoring.

Thank you to the Brighton Write-On group members: Steve Watson, Ericka Waller, Alex Thornbur, Sarah Bonner, Wayne Kelly, Samuel Burr and Helen Trevorrow. The advice and feedback got me through the difficult months, and I'm sorry for hijacking many a Zoom with my dating escapades. You're all brilliant.

Thank you to Patrik Svensson, who doesn't know who I am, but whose book, *The Gospel of the Eels*, sparked an obsession that inspired a tattoo and a storyline.

Because this is my first book, you'll have to humour me as I try to thank everyone I've ever met. To my teachers and lecturers – Mrs Barnes, who took me out of maths so I could write stories. Now I'm bad at maths but still writing stories – I think it was worth it. To all the women who have taught me English (and drama) in some way, thank you for instilling that confidence in me. Special thanks to Pippa Lennie, Meredith Miller, Freya Lockley and Alison Dures.

To the people who have made the North (and the Midlands) feel like home: thank you to my friend Adam Chilton – I'm sorry this book is not about moles in space. I couldn't have got here without you. Thank you to Ellie Welch, for being the best housemate and combining bookshelves. To Sophie Cochran-Powell, one of my favourite things about Manchester. Thank you to Oliver Fielden, for the support throughout.

Thank you to everyone at 4th Estate and Harper Collins – especially editor extraordinaire Katie Bowden. I feel so lucky to have such a great (and gorgeous) team – special thanks to Lola Downes, Eve Hutchings, Naomi Mantin, Jessa Thompson and Ola Galewicz.